1

'You've bewitched me,' Sarah gasped. Jo bit down harder on her nipple, making her yelp, and lifted his head.

'Au contraire,' he said, staring her straight in the eye. His eyes were dark hollows. 'You're the witch.' He licked his lips slowly. 'And a more tempting one than you never walked the earth. Seeing you like that –' his eyes raked over her '– I could almost forgive your choice of dress.'

'You don't like it?' she whispered, her hands running over the folds of material covering her thighs.

'I love it,' he said hoarsely. 'Especially with your bodice pulled open. But I'd like it even more like this . . .'

He pulled her by the hand to the sofa, and gently pushed her to her knees before it. She leant forward obediently, her sensitive tips brushing the velvet upholstery. In the dark, its pale green background and cream flora had turned to silver, with streaks of gold where the tentative candlelight fell over it. She felt him lift up the full skirt, pushing it above her waist, so that the full orbs of her buttocks glowed pale and bare.

'No undergarments?' he murmured in a strangled voice.

The Ten Visions
Olivia Knight

BLACK LACE

Black Lace books contain sexual fantasies.
In real life, always practise safe sex.

First published in 2007 by
Black Lace
Thames Wharf Studios
Rainville Rd
London W6 9HA

A catalogue record for this book is available from the British Library.

www.black-lace-books.com
http://lustbites.blogspot.com/

Typeset by SetSystems Ltd, Saffron Walden, Essex

Printed in the UK by CPI Bookmarque, Croydon, CR0 4TD

The paper used in this book is a natural, recyclable product made
from wood grown in sustainable forests. The manufacturing process
conforms to the regulations of the country of origin.

ISBN 978 0 352 34119 8

1 **Malkuth**

Perhaps once in a lifetime, if you are lucky, you will live in a house with a history. This is not the history that is written in guidebooks and gives rise to blue plaques, and above all not the kind that keeps the house in a perpetual stasis, exactly as it was when Keats or Wordsworth lived in it. It is a private history, composed of anecdotes passed on from owner to owner, of how the man who built it was an architect and designed it for his young bride as a weaver bird knits its intricate nest, and of how she refused to live in it, or of how this fireplace was blocked up for many years by the old woman who suffered from a phobia of birds and went hysterical upon hearing them in the chimney. It may have grown, village-style, with subsequent owners. It may have been subdivided and reunited with itself, or with much smashing of walls have sprawled on into the adjoining property. 10 Newbury Avenue was such a house. It had risen over the centuries to comprise its original Tudor beams in some rooms, the white plaster thick and undulating, then Victorian gables at odd angles in a multi-faceted façade across its roofs, and a stern Georgian addition to the back in red brick. This had now mellowed to crumbling overgrowth through which flaked shards of brick. Wisteria drowned the central gable, gently tugging its filigree apart with insistent, insinuous tendrils. It had been flourishing purple when Sarah first found the house, but now was old green, turned to blackish olive by the night, hanging low and trailing its leaves like spiders over her hair each time she passed beneath it. Back and forth she walked, struggling inwards with each box and shaking the dust off her hands as she strode back towards the car. The autumn night, already coming so soon after the long summer, smelt of chilling plants and the oily bitterness of tarmac and petrol fumes. The house was heady with lilies in the hall and lounge. The corridors and rooms were not yet friendly, although they waxed rich with the lives that had been lived in them. They shifted shape with each journey. Corners and alcoves changed size before one's eyes. Mantelpieces widened to the diameter of a dinner plate then shrank back until they were no more than a narrow, dust-catching ledge. It was an absurd house for a single person, and as the sky sunk from lavender into black Sarah felt more pressingly the size of it.

It was not, extraordinarily, too expensive for a single person. In fact, the rent fitted snugly into the constrained budget of a graduate student. The landlord had, he said, received approximately one thousand answers to his advertisement in the Daily Information. This was in May, with the wisteria throwing scent around the front in great swathes. He had proffered the information as he poured green tea from a tall, Chinese teapot into two matching cups, the occasional leaf escaping to swirl around the pale water.

'Goodness!' said Sarah, taken aback. 'However did you choose between them?'

He looked up at her, one hand holding the teapot back, as if undecided whether to let her in on his secret. He continued pouring, and said – it was not clear if this was what he had hesitated over saying – 'I cut out all the couples and families, to start with.'

He replaced the teapot and, clutching at the armchair's sides with knotted, trembling hands, lowered himself awkwardly.

'You must understand, this is quite a house. It wants someone who'll fit in with its history. Regrettably, such people aren't always rich, and so I had to advertise it for a very silly little sum.'

'Are there any – problems with it?' asked Sarah.

'Problems?' He stared at her sharply. 'Now I don't want some silly girl who'll be frightening herself half to death with the ghosts. That sort of thing won't do at all.'

'I meant damp – wiring – plumbing . . .'

'Oh.' He relaxed a little against the upholstery. 'Well, let's see. The wiring is probably a bit *old*, now, but I'm assured it's quite safe. The cellar is a little damp in the north corner; that's the tree roots, but I don't believe in cutting down trees, so I patch and make do. I don't think it will flood. But keep your vegetables to the south-east if you don't want them sprouting. Incidentally, one of the rooms will be kept locked; I can't keep my paintings and things in the cellar, because of the damp, so I'll move them all to the back room on Mother's side. You'll have the key, of course. It will be your house.'

Sarah's eyebrows had risen slightly at the mention of Mother, as she mentally whisked into existence a woman still more ancient than the old man in front of her, an etched and tiny crone with straggling wisps of brushed white hair.

'I also intend to let it furnished,' he continued. 'I can't be doing putting all my fine old pieces into some storage unit, and the climate in the Mediterranean would ruin them all. No. They belong in the house. Do *you* have furniture?'

'Not much . . .' She was unsure of the best response, now that she knew she passionately wanted this house, and felt it was already her home. Would her lack of belongings show a lack of affection for furniture in general? 'I used to . . .'

'So you sold up, eh?'

'I was in America – it was too expensive to bring it back to England.'

'Ah. Horrible stuff, American furniture, anyway. The trees spring up there overnight; now European wood, especially the Northern European wood, that grows slowly, as wood should.'

Sarah was beginning to feel dizzy, wondering how to reconcile his love of trees with his passion for old wood.

'Anyway, that's just as well. I couldn't abide some cheap tawdry stuff being squashed in with all my old pieces. It will be your house,' he added, again, 'but all the same, it's *its own*, as well, and wants respecting. Now the marble in the hallway you'll have to be careful of when you wash it, Mother broke her hip there in 1978 and I haven't entirely trusted it since. The lobby is the best place to keep cooking apples in the winter, it stays properly cold. The rest of the house has modern heating, but it must never be too high. The bedroom and my studio, that was Mother's bedroom, have fireplaces, and of course this room.'

As the interview, or monologue, continued on the house's various foibles and curiosities, Sarah grew more and more certain that, as he kept repeating, it *would* be hers. She was startled at three o'clock, to hear him say, 'Right, let me see you to the door, I've lots of people to see still. I'll write to you in a week when I'm done with all the interviews and let you know.'

Now, in September, here she sat, in what was already her armchair, learning the dimensions of the walls and studying the piles of boxes before her. She had not seen the landlord again; everything, after the interview, had been conducted in writing. In her hand she held a letter of welcome and detailed instructions on every appliance and room, and in the dim light of the lamp she savoured every word. At the bottom was a post-script: 'I would naturally prefer that you do not hold any parties. That said, it has to be your house, after all.' A party – it could not be a house-warming party, that would be an insult to the house which was warm with life already, but a new-inhabitant party. For so long she had entertained in a tiny shabby London flat or in a New York bedsit. It wouldn't, she hastily added to herself, be a noisy affair, or a drunken one – a sedate, slightly tipsy maybe, drinks party, to meet people. It's only fair, she thought, that I be able to invite people back to my house.

House music echoed down the marble corridor, mixing with the babble and shriek of voices. Four people spun each other around the lounge, in a mixture of club-dancing, rock'n'roll and ballroom. In one kitchen, the overhead light blinded newcomers; in the other, three flickering candles momentarily blacked out their vision. The counters of both were strewn with bottles, plastic cups, packets of Kettle Fries and Pringles and plastic dip-containers dripping their heavy-flavoured gloop onto the tiled counters. The downstairs bathroom was occupied by a crying couple; at least, the girl was crying and the man was leaning on the basin staring moodily at the toilet brush. In the garden, the dim coal of a joint glowed as it floated from person to person around the circle. Coats and handbags were piled high on Sarah's bed, to which women returned sporadically. The Masters Common Room, or MCR as she was learning to call it, had a mailing list, which had turned up an astonishingly high number of early-comers or current students weary of the summer's ghost-town solitude. Once the invitation had been extended – in expectation of perhaps a dozen – she could not decently change her mind. Another twenty replies had been emailed that morning, and Sarah had spent the day hastily foolproofing room after room, lugging the more fragile or ancient-looking ornaments into Mother's old room. The paintings, pots and bottles she had stacked beside the door. They were, in fact, not paintings at all; just thoroughly primed canvases, plaster-white and a little dusty. The foolproofing turned out to be wise. Nobody was uproariously drunk, but the sheer crush of numbers was perilous. Even the corridors were pressed into service as rooms, where people sat in clusters. Sarah herself was on the first landing of the north staircase, hidden by the turn of the banister from the crowds, in the arms of a blond and naughty-eyed medic from Merton College. Wine and astonishment at the advent of this new life mingled in her veins. The party had become an organism to which the house adapted itself; it could do without its hostess for a while.

'You're trouble,' he whispered again, lowering his mouth back to her neck.

'You're the one biting my neck.' As his teeth grazed over her skin, she felt her hands exploring his waist, his ribs, running around his unknown torso, and desire running riot through her. Licence, she thought to herself, and the word hummed erotically in her mind as his fingers sank into the flesh of her buttocks, tugging her against his groin. She stepped up one shallow stair, so that the crotch of her jeans rested just *there*, close against him. He lifted his eyes to hers, and she was reminded again of the joy of English men, after so much time with unstinting American charm. The cagey, sexy, restrained lure of his stare made her, out of embarrassment and pleasure, place her lips against his for the first time. As she started to learn his lips with her tongue, feeling his warm wet flesh dance with hers, she struggled to remember what in the conversation has inspired this sudden lust. Some chance remark, or not so chance – the sort of thing one says to a new acquaintance, before one's sources and history are exposed, when one's knowledge and tastes are just glimpses of an exotic land. Was he the one who had mentioned wine-tasting and used terms of whose exact meaning she was uncertain? No, that was someone else. She had been listening to the other one, and looking at this one's blond hair and wicked eyes. While his friend tried to enchant her with talk, out on the lawn, he had leant back on one arm and used the other to play surreptitiously with her back. His hands were now at the button of her jeans, her body s-shaped as she pressed her groin close to the heat of his hard erection, her torso twisted to give him space at her buttons, her tongue still sliding this way and that against his. A fingertip found its way inside her jeans, straining towards the slippery folds. Her head sank onto his shoulder, as she succumbed to the moment.

'You're far too good at this,' she murmured tritely, in defence against her crumbling limbs.

'Sit down,' he whispered.

She pulled him around the next corner of the staircase, to the top landing some eight steps higher, and sat on the uppermost step. Behind them, the empty corridor lay dark; only the studio and Mother's room were here. Through the connecting door, beneath which a line of light glimmered, the other side of the corridor hummed; two girls were chattering in Sarah's room. His hand constrained by the unforgiving fabric, he forced his finger lower, so that it played just inside the mouth of her pussy, fighting against her jeans to get deeper. They whispered clichéd obscenities into each other's mouths between hungry kisses as she felt her body soar, overtaken with delightful greed. Licence, she thought again, to do this – to be me – .

The stairs creaked, and his hand was whipped away, wrapped around her back, chivalrously hiding her open zip, and he was sitting back saying too casually, 'So anyway...' as a couple climbed past them, nodding briefly.

'It's locked,' said Sarah, as the couple tried the door to Mother's room. They entered the studio, leaving the door just ajar. As his finger found her hungry entrance again, his mouth on hers, she heard the familiar sound of voices quietly rising and falling in complaint, disagreement, weariness. It was the sound of old fights rehearsed. At the foot of the staircase, a girl's voice said, 'Is there anything up there?'

'Is there nowhere we can go?' he whispered against her, forcing his finger till the stitches on her jeans creaked in complaint. Her hands, holding her hips towards him, felt the hard shape of a key in her pocket.

'Yes,' she replied, surprised. 'Come.' She stood, her jeans open at her belly, and let them quietly into Mother's darkened room. It had no light, but only darkness was required anyway. 'All the fragile stuff is over in that corner,' she whispered, but all their attention was on the lowering of her jeans in time with the bending of his knees, and with her head pressed against the door she felt his tongue descend. She floated, drunk on sensation and wine, hearing her own truncated gasps escape unbidden, as his tongue-tip made a discovered country of her labia. As it flickered sporadically over her clitoris, she dug her fingernails into his narrow shoulders, into the muscles, her hips rocking faintly. She reached for her jeans, which lay scrunched around her ankles, to remove them, just as he pushed a finger as deep into her as it could go. With a cry, she felt her knees falter and her balance give, and amongst a clatter of canvases she tumbled to the wooden floor, her body breaking free.

'Now I've got you where I want you!' he laughed, pressing his finger deep back in. Her clumsy hands joined his spare hand, freeing him of his thin trousers, pulling his underwear down so that his cock leapt out, shaking like a branch. Curled, her thighs clutching at his hand, she put her mouth to the smooth, hot skin and heard him groan. She wanted to lap and lick and suck at it, but their lust and haste was growing too fast; she swept a tongue over his balls and he shoved a second finger inside her. The wet walls of her pussy fought against him, as she came, as if trying to push him out, but he dug in harder, pressing high, while she muffled her own shrieks.

'Jesus!' she squealed quietly, and the room grew still. She felt, for a few seconds, a terrible sense of wrongdoing, until he put his fingers in her mouth like a blasphemy and she lost herself in sucking the taste of herself from each knuckle and web of finger, from around the crevices of the short nails.

'I've got to fuck you,' he muttered. She laughed softly, staring at the ceiling in bliss, knowing the sweetness to come. The feeling of being filled – he had no idea. As his cock pressed hard, wresting its way against the undulating velvet walls of her pussy, she arched against him. Her jeans, held tight around her ankles, kept her legs from spreading wide enough to receive him easily and the constraint made her swim in lust. As if in a dream, she rose against him, her legs held, feeling him wrestle to get closer and their kisses deep and enveloping, everything at once familiar and strange. A strange déjà vu encompassed her thoughts. His arms, resting on elbows, pushed her T-shirt away and peeled away the cups of her bra. As his mouth bit down on her nipple, she felt his groin flying furiously against hers, her wails of bliss unrestrained. She came against him, her mind overwhelmed by images. *A small room – a wooden shack, nothing more, with a floor of beaten earth. A ceiling thick with herbs. As they dried, small leaves would drift down, scattering across the floor in a gentle shower of rustling perfumed fragments. A bed draped with dull fabric, layer upon layer − it would weigh down heavily on the sleeper, creating a cocoon of warmth in the chill of winter. Pots, pans, and knives ranged around the edges of the room, unshelved but neatly lined up and well scrubbed. The shack in a slight dip, and the soil outside muddied where it had rained. From the doorway, swans on the river, their wings unfurled to catch the wind, and furiously paddling ducks. Across the river, a meadow and a round mound. Beyond that, trees.*

She sat on her supervisor's armchair in his dim study, trying not to tug at her skirt which, hardly short, in this position left a neat triangular spy hole between her thighs. He spun slowly from side to side on his desk chair, one sharp white finger resting against his little goatee, his nostrils arching contemptuously as he read her proposal, tentatively titled 'Dissent in the Scriptorium'. She tried to retain a sense of professionalism in her awkward position, deliberately stilling her discomfort and relaxing her clasped hands. His eyebrows arched as he scanned down the page, and she fought against the temptation to make verbal additions to his reading. He was much younger than she'd expected − the ponderous tone of his emails, and the formality of him signing each one 'Dr Piedmont', had led her to expect a white-haired, teabag-skinned professor, not an arrogant young man her own age. His books had borne no photograph and gave no bibliographic details beyond his awards, publications, and teaching post. He lowered the pages at last.

'I can't say I agree with your rather ... *Derridean* interpretation of marginalia,' he said unsmilingly. 'You may want to think on that more carefully. We mustn't confuse the present with the past, you know.'

Sarah bristled. With a Masters in Mediaeval History

from Yale, she'd had to explain that to each freshmen's tutorial class, and thought she could safely be considered beyond that sort of undergraduate lapse.

'When I say "in the margins" . . .' she began.

'Yes – quite.' He interrupted her sentence to return his gaze to the stapled sheets. 'The manuscripts you mention here have already been extensively transcribed, I don't think you'll need to be handling the originals at all. In fact, they've been rather thoroughly worked altogether. I'd be very surprised if you managed to make anything new of them. New,' he repeated, chuckling to himself, his eyes still lowered.

If I met you in a bar, thought Sarah viciously, I'd slap that little smirk off your face. She bit her lip and tried to remember what, in his publications, had made her want to work with him. His urbanity on the page suffered badly in translation to the flesh, but his brilliance was without question. A brilliant prat, she thought, and he lifted his eyes to her mockingly.

'I don't expect you to like me,' he said with a cold smile, 'but you will do extremely well if you work under me.' His eyes, black in the dull half-light, met hers steadily.

'I admire your work enormously,' she said stiffly.

'Yes. You can certainly learn from me.' He still had not looked away, but Sarah had sat through too many job interviews to be intimidated by that tactic. Fight fire with fire, she thought grimly, looking back.

'By avoiding a totalising perspective and seeking the dissent in the margins, we may discover a deeper insight into monastic Christianity than has hitherto been available,' he said. With a jolt she realised that, without leaving her eyes, he was quoting the opening paragraph of her proposal. 'You are not being Derridean, then, but actually working with literal marginalia?'

'Yes,' began Sarah, but he interrupted again.

'Precisely. Your metaphor has led you astray. You will glance at the text and pour over the margins, like a dozen tedious people without a tenth of your potential have done before you, and never think how subtly the mediaeval mind may embed its disagreements. Did you even intend to read the central text carefully? Has it even occurred to you to look at the illuminations, or the choice of colours?' She took a breath. 'No,' he continued, 'or you would have mentioned it in your proposal.'

Half an hour later, humiliated, angry, and clutching a long list of manuscript sources taken by dictation from Dr Piedmont (reclining at his ease on his desk chair, ankles folded, reciting them with his eyes on the ceiling), Sarah left the grounds of Christ Church with the rain spattering her ankles. She was due back in two hours, for dinner at High Table. The invitation was given in the same imperious manner as everything else. Dr Piedmont said: 'I've booked a place for you at High Table this evening, seven o'clock. You will need to wear your gown, and dress suitably.' Even catching the bus, she was cutting it fine to get home, get ready, and return looking presentable.

By the time she let herself through her front door into the lobby, she was drenched from the elbows downwards. She bent down to unbuckle her wet shoes, in which her stockinged feet swam, and caught sight of a wine glass underneath the bench on the side. Red, crisped sediments of wine clung to the base in a circle where the last undrunk sip had evaporated. As she lifted it, wincing at the cold stone beneath her wet feet, she remembered the scene in Mother's room, and the clatter of paintings as she'd fallen to the floor. She hadn't picked them up. She still needed to shower, iron her clothes and her gown, do her make-up. She ran down the passageway, calculating ten minutes for this and fifteen for that, and her feet skidded sickeningly. For an instant, she was sliding fast towards the grandfather clock, and then her feet shot from beneath her and she landed hard on her back, screaming in pain, before being momentarily blinded by a small explosion in front of her eyes.

'Sarah?'

She blinked. The medic from the party was kneeling over her.

'Can you see me?'

'Yes – yes, of course,' she said.

'How many fingers am I holding up?'

'Two and a thumb, you can't catch me out with that trick.' She blinked some more, and giggled. A worrying thought occurred to her. 'Why am I on the floor?'

'I think you fell – I heard a scream. I was about to knock – we were supposed to go for a drink, remember?'

She struggled upwards, and a pain shot up her spine. 'Ow, my spine.' The last moments of her flight came back to her. 'I skidded – towards the clock – I didn't want to hit it. I was holding the glass . . .' She suspected something odd about the way she was answering his questions. 'I'm not drunk, you know. It was already empty. It was left from the party.'

He smiled gently. 'I know you're not drunk. I think you might be concussed, though. Can you stand?'

'The bottom of my spine hurts. I think I fell on it.'

He examined her carefully, and once he was sure she had nothing worse than bruising, he helped her to her feet, where she stood swaying.

'What's your name?' Now *that*, she thought, was wily. She'd never known.

He frowned again. 'Timothy. Come, you need to sit down.' As he helped her to the lounge, he glanced back at the passageway behind him. 'That floor's treacherous, you should put some matting down. An older person would've been badly hurt.'

As she sipped the disgustingly sweet tea he insisted she drink, and answered his questions, she remembered her dinner engagement.

'Shit! High Table! I'll be late! Tim – I'm sorry – my supervisor booked, I have to go.'

'I don't think you're in any fit state . . .'

'I can't not go! I need to change. I have to be there! And I haven't ironed my clothes, or my gown.'

'Is it really that important?'

'Yes, it's my supervisor, and he's a wanker. I can't phone and say I'm concussed. I don't even have his number.'

Ten minutes later, watching him iron her clothes, she started giggling again, and he looked at her sharply, concerned. 'It's not a good sign, giggling.'

'No – I'm fine. My head's getting clearer. I was just thinking how funny it was – to shag a random bloke at a party and next thing he's doing your ironing.'

He grinned. 'Don't expect it to last. Here, put these on.' He held out her blouse and skirt, and saw her hesitate. 'Oh come on, I've already seen all the bits that count. Anyway, I'm a doctor. Well – almost.'

He insisted on accompanying her on the bus back to Christ Church, and escorting her as far as the porter's lodge. 'Remember, no drinking,' he said in the doorway. 'And don't go to sleep until at least two. Have a cup of coffee if you need to. Wait –' He pulled a pen from his bag, and scribbled his number on a receipt. 'If you get sleepy, call me, OK? I'll come over and pinch you all night if necessary.'

'OK, OK, don't worry,' said Sarah, laughing.

'I'm serious. It's important. That floor's fucking hard, you could go into a coma if you go to sleep too soon.' He kissed her cheek, and stepped back through the heavy doors into the rain.

Waving, still grinning, she turned back to find Dr Piedmont standing at the other side of the lodge, his arms folded across his black gown. He extended his arm anachronistically. Awkwardly, she took it, glancing back over her shoulder at the empty doorway as they set out across the quadrangle.

'Your boyfriend?'

He was holding her hand pinned tightly between his forearm and chest; she could feel, against her fingers through the fabric, a riper swell of muscle than she had expected.

'No – a friend.' She wanted to explain further, but was nervous that her judgement, if she was concussed, might be poor. The less said this evening the better, she thought to herself. Better to be thought quiet than a fool. As the thought drifted across her head, she wondered suddenly if perhaps that was the key to dissent – silence. But how to measure the silence of a text? The vulgar presumptions of modern literary theory were wholly inadequate in the mediaeval context. Could one make a study of what might normally be discussed in a manuscript and then – no, too heavy-handed. But perhaps she could . . .

'I must warn you, our sommelier sometimes has extraordinary tastes in wine, and is very susceptible to offence. We fellows must suffer some dreadful assaults on our palates.'

'I can't drink,' she said. Feeling him stiffen, she added quickly, 'Medical reasons.'

'Ah. As the lady wishes.' He gave a jerky, mock bow, and a passing group of students glanced at him. 'We must obey the doctor's orders, naturally.' It was going to be an exceptionally tedious evening with this jumped-up little cockerel prancing about like this. She pushed the receipt with Timothy's phone number into her hand-bag. She would definitely phone him later; concussion or no, some decent chat after this evening would be exactly what the doctor ordered. She giggled inanely at her own pun, and began to suspect that he may have been right about the knock on the head after all.

Dr Piedmont was placed on her left at High Table, and as they stood for Latin grace his gown fell open for the first time. He had not, evidently, heeded his own advice about suitable dress – on a woman, the cut of his shirt would have been called a plunging neckline, and on him it was no better. His pale skin, which on his face looked unhealthily white in contrast to his black goatee, glowed in the soft lamps and candlelight of the hall, and his excellent musculature made ochre shadows that slid into charcoal obscurity. Looking sideways, she could see the edge of his aureole, and she felt her skin rush hot, then prickle with cold, and slowly start to burn again. Everyone else, including the avowedly atheist doctor, kept their eyes closed while the Latin words declaimed by the chaplain echoed around the hall. She felt her mouth dry, and quietly swallowed, lifting her eyes to the distant wall as Dr Piedmont's flew open. She kept staring at the portrait beyond him as the grace ended, and sat down without looking at him. She could feel her blood beating in her neck.

'I do like tradition,' he said, pulling his chair in, 'but I find it presumptuous that we are all to worship the same god. Water?'

'Please.' Her throat was dry as she spoke. High Table was crowded; it was the first Hall of the term and the fellows were out in full force. Her arm could not avoid the brush of his. She was maddened that her body was happy to respond to someone so arrogant, flaunting, and irritating. What on earth had made him think it appropriate to wear a shirt like that? She reminded herself that women were not supposed to be aroused by the sight of a man's breast. He could not have known her obscure tastes. The way his words followed too quickly on her unspoken thoughts, however, made her wonder uneasily how much he did know. She ate a piece of her pork skewer, and paused, surprised at the flavour.

'Pomegranate,' he said. 'No wine for Ms Kirkson, thank you, Henri. Mind you don't eat the seeds.'

She raised her eyebrows, too busy chewing to reply.

'We don't want you to go to hell any sooner than necessary,' he chuckled.

She swallowed. 'Hades isn't exactly hell, Dr Piedmont.' If he thought to impress her with mythological references, she wasn't to be impressed. The story of Persephone's downfall was hardly arcane literary knowledge. And what did he mean by any sooner than necessary? 'Anyway, I thought atheists didn't believe in hell.'

'That doesn't stop it from existing. Atheism is the devil's cleverest trick, they say.'

During the main course she was able to escape the conversational twists of her supervisor in favour of the genial fellow on her right, a semi-retired English Literature fellow called Dr Staunton, who expressed polite interest in her thesis topic and remarked that he did calligraphy in his spare time. This was a response to which Sarah was fast becoming accustomed and they were enjoyably discussing the comparative merits of English and German gothic script when Dr Piedmont, leaning across her, interrupted.

'What do you think of Henri's latest, then?'

'Fine, fine, thank you, Matthew,' replied Dr Staunton impassively. 'The trouble with the German script, I find –'

'Poor Sarah's missing out, I think. He hasn't done so badly tonight.'

'I'm sure Ms Kirkson will have plenty of opportunity to drink wine in Oxford. The German script –'

'No, no, she can't drink, doctor's orders. Terrible shame. And in Oxford, too.'

'I –' began Sarah, about to explain that this was not a permanent disability, but Dr Piedmont had turned back to his other neighbour, leaning at an odd angle so that his knees brushed Sarah's. She tried to twist away, her intense dislike for her supervisor having no effect on the thrills running up her body.

She ate the rest of her meal in virtual silence. Interjecting Dr Piedmont's monologue with replies was hardly necessary, and through dessert she listened to his steady prattle about the college's foibles and his own fortitude in the face of them. Despite herself, she sneaked small glances at his smooth, exposed chest as he spoke, fascinated by its faint quiver as he took quick breaths between paragraphs. She thought, as Henri passed by, disturbing the air, that she could even smell his skin – a quick whiff of something like cedar wood, but sharper. Dittany, perhaps? His features bore the curves of arrogance well, like the face of an eighteenth century costume-drama villain, and as absurdly pretentious. 'Scouts,' he half-cried. 'Lord save us from the scouts! Have you suffered their ministrations yet?'

'What – boy scouts?'

'No, no, it's what the cleaning people are called here, they do your rooms. Does your college not have them?'

'Probably.' Sarah shrugged. She was more interested in the arch of his eyebrow than his words, as he bent over his dessert. The dark hairs curved in a sharply elegant line over his smooth brow, and his lowered eyelids gave him the look of a painted angel. 'I live privately.'

He looked up too fast for her to look away. His eyes glittered, reflecting the table's candles, and in them she saw a glimpse of something genuine, a knowledge, perhaps a self-knowledge, that nothing in his current behaviour or his speech suggested. 'Clever, very clever,' he said. She broke his gaze, feeling uncomfortably that he was reading her too closely.

When she left Christ Church, the rain had stopped. Immense clouds, torn and white in the full moon, swept across the dark sky. With her hands deep in her pockets, she set off to walk up the Banbury Road. It was chiming half-past nine as she passed Carfax Tower. If she had to stay awake until two, a walk would do no harm. All her irritation with Dr Piedmont pounded into the pavement as she strode, but grew nonetheless into a steady fury. So he had thought to seduce her with his cheap Latinate shirt, had he? Sought to impress her with his oh-so-infinite knowledge of Oxford? She knew his game, she thought, staring balefully at the spires of Balliol as she stormed past on the far side of the road. She was here to learn dammit, not to fight off advances. She stepped around a man struggling to light a cigarette, his full academic gown whipping in the wind, and on impulse turned back, and asked for one. He looked up. In the orange light of the lamp his skin looked pure gold. She felt a moment of purely feral lust, and then alarm.

'Yes, of course,' he said in a surprised, clipped voice. He pulled a silver box from his pocket and opened it towards her. The small brown sticks inside looked like roughly-rolled cigars, but she took one.

'Do you need a light?' He cupped his hands around the tip of her cigarette; the match flared. Her groin glowed with its own fire as the tobacco caught. Thanking him, she walked on with the lit cigarette, her eyes wide with astonishment at her reaction. When she turned to cross over through the grounds of St Giles's Church, she saw him still standing on the wide pavement, cinnamon-coloured leaves scudding past his ankles, the coal of the cigarette glowing. In the darkness of the graveyard, she sat abruptly on the grass, leaning against a headstone, pulling on the cigarette to recover her composure. Her stomach ached – too much rich food, no doubt, after a few weeks of her own careful cooking. A yew mostly hid her from the road, its leaves silhouetted in feathery clumps by streetlamps. The church stood at the head of the triangle between the Banbury Road and Woodstock Road. Occasionally, a car would sweep past, its headlights combing the gravestones and the church through the branches. The ground was wet, the damp slowly soaking through her coat, but for now she didn't care. The strange cigarette was nearing the end and falling apart in her fingers. As she glanced around her for a place to stub it, she realised she was sitting on the grave itself and not, as she had thought, behind it. She turned, the mud slick beneath her, to read the name, peering in the intermittent light and half-tracing it with her fingers: 'Jonathan Montjoie, 1790–1811, As I Am, So Will Ye Be'. She exhaled on the gravestone, the air clouding with smoke and condensation over the lichenous stone. 'Hello,' she murmured. If she was going to sit on someone's grave, she ought to at least to greet them. 'I wonder if you smoke?'

'I do, actually.'

She screamed, leaping away from the grave, the glowing cigarette butt flying from her fingers.

'I'm awfully sorry, did I startle you? I didn't mean to . . .' The man from the road was standing on the path, behind the gravestone, looking paler than he had under the streetlamps. 'I always walk home this way. I assumed you didn't recognise me, and wanted another cigarette . . .'

Sarah stood, her hand still flung over her heart, feeling her breath heave. 'God, oh my God . . .'

'Not a wise place to blaspheme, Miss – Miss –'

'Sarah,' she said. Her pulse was still racing from the fright.

'I couldn't possibly call you by your first name.' His smile had a gorgeous, self-deprecating charm to it. 'Miss?'

'Ms Kirkson,' she said. Englishmen, she thought. I've been away too long; their manners seem so odd now. She couldn't place his accent, either; she'd prided herself, at eighteen and before she left England, on recognising all the regional accents. 'I'm sorry if I offended you,' she stammered, shaking, 'I don't believe myself.'

He held his finger to his lips. 'Neither do I,' he whispered, 'but still not a wise place to say so.' He smiled again. 'I've frightened the life out of you, I see. May I at least offer you another cigarette?'

'Thanks,' she said gratefully. The walk up Banbury Road didn't seem quite as appealing right now. He sat at the foot of the grave, his gown wrapped around him, and tentatively she resumed her earlier place. The sound of the bells chiming ten o'clock began.

'Five to ten, Oxford time,' he said. 'Do you know, they changed the clocks when the railways started? I don't think they should have, really. The old way was so much better. Time is not something to be dallied with.'

'It's arbitrary, really,' Sarah answered. 'In America, every state has a different time, just about. You get used to switching about. It doesn't make that much difference, after a bit.'

'Ah, but I'm talking about true time,' he insisted. 'Sunrise, sunset, noon. Five minutes can make all the difference, when it matters.'

She inhaled the cigarette smoke, wondering whether

to debate the arbitrariness of clocks with this well-spoken stranger. At least such an inconsequential subject was calming, after the shock of hearing the dead talk.

'It can make the difference between seeing the sunrise or not, between meeting the girl and not. It can be life or death. For instance, when I –' He halted, abruptly.

After a few seconds, she asked, 'When you what?'

'It's of no consequence. It happened a long time ago. It would have happened, anyway. At some stage. And then I wouldn't be sitting here, talking to you.' His face lit up with his captivating smile once more.

'What are you studying?' she asked, after a few more moments' silence.

'*Doctorus Theolosophica*,' he said. 'I graduated sort of – well, *in absentia*, as they say. I finished in time, I just couldn't make it for the ceremony. And you, Miss Kirkson?'

'*Doctorus Historica*,' she answered. Two could talk in Latin, if need be. 'My speciality is religious beliefs in monasteries in the Middle Ages. I look at manuscripts, mostly.'

'Excellent, excellent,' he said enthusiastically. 'We will have lots to talk about. You have no idea how much I could find out for you. That is, if, as I presume, you're looking at monasteries in the immediate areas?'

'Um – well, yes. But it's fine, thank you, I can do my own research.' She stubbed her cigarette out in the mud, ready to leave.

He shook his head slowly, as he lit a fresh cigarette. 'Never turn down an offer of help, Miss Kirkson. Especially from a stranger. Strangers could be anyone, you know.' He handed her the cigarette, and she took it.

'And yet I'm sitting in a graveyard with a stranger, who, as you point out, could be anyone, smoking too many cigarettes. Too many of his cigarettes. And I don't even know your name.'

'Mr –'

She interrupted him. 'Your first name. You can call me Miss Kirkson if you insist, but my name is Sarah, I've been in America for the last eight years, and I can't go around calling people Mr and Mrs.'

He inclined his head, a curiously old-fashioned gesture. 'Call me Jo, then.'

She stuck her hand out, holding his cigarette between her lips, and he hesitated, then shook it. His skin was cool, and exquisitely smooth; she felt a rush of heat through her body. He held onto her hand, staring at her in wonder and awe. 'You can – You have . . .' he whispered.

She tried to pull her hand back, but his fingers clasped it. 'I can what? I have what?'

His eyes were hypnotic. Everything about the situation was foolish, unwise, unsafe, and still she couldn't bring herself to do the sensible thing and withdraw, leave abruptly and politely.

'I talk too much,' he said. 'I always did, and I still do. Whatever I'm thinking comes out of my mouth.'

'I don't mind. More English people should. Go on, what were you going to say?'

He frowned, looking down at his lap. He withdrew his hand slowly from hers, his fingertips brushing every cell of her palm as he did, even their nails catching briefly before her hand hung, released, in the air. 'I can't say.' His face was narrower in profile than she had realised, the cheeks and eyes dark and hollow.

'It's OK, go on.' She touched his shoulder, and his eyelids sank down in restrained bliss.

'I will tell you if we meet again. Or perhaps in a few months. Or perhaps when we meet again you will know.'

She shivered; the damp was creeping through her coat to her skirt. 'I'm cold, I must get home.'

He stood with alacrity. 'Let me walk you home, you don't know whom you might meet, tonight.'

'I don't know you, either,' she said automatically, as she clambered to her feet. 'But if you're going my way, we can walk together for a bit. I'm going up the Banbury Road.'

'Likewise.' He held his left arm out for her, and she laughed softly as she took it. For the second time this evening, she was being squired – but Jo's company was much more pleasant than Dr Piedmont's, and he didn't surreptitiously crush her hand to his chest either. He glanced behind them at the grave as they stepped onto the path, and out into the light of the road once more.

'You must be familiar with Paracelsus?' he asked, as they turned their footsteps northwards.

2 Yesod

All the way home they talked of mediaeval and Renaissance theology, content that their subjects overlapped enough that each knew almost exactly what the other studied. Jo was unexpectedly passionate on the subject of alchemy, although he had never heard of Jung's psychological interpretations of it and was resistant to the ideas. 'It can't be just in oneself, it can't be all a drama of the mind,' he insisted, again and again. 'Even if one doesn't believe in everything the Church teaches, one must admit there is something more – something beyond – or the Great Work is an impossible conceit.'

'But that is the Great Work – the discovery of one's self. The alchemical master and the soror mystica, they are the *anima* and the *animus* of yourself, your own male and female selves – what could be a greater work than discovering the wholeness of your self?'

'No – the other is important, you cannot contain someone else –'

They argued amicably to her doorstep, and as she pulled her keys out, she checked her watch. It was only half-past ten – another three and a half hours awake, if Dr Timothy's orders were to be obeyed.

'I've got to stay up until two,' she found herself saying. 'I hit myself on the head earlier – my – the doctor – well, a friend of mine – said I shouldn't go to sleep until two. Do you want to come in and have a cup of coffee, keep me company for a bit?'

'I'm not sure I can drink coffee,' he said, 'but I would

be honoured to keep you company. I am still intent on convincing you about the truth of alchemy.'

She laughed, and hit the light switch in the hall, drowning them both in its high-wattage illumination. He flinched, his eyes wincing in the brightness, and she snapped it back off. 'That better?' In the light, his skin had glowed unhealthily white.

'Much better. That light's like daylight!'

'Yeah, it's a bit bright. I think Mother was a bit blind, all the bulbs are like, a hundred watts. You don't see the sun much, do you?'

'Not lately,' he said, then added, 'I was – I've been very ill. I'm better now, but ...'

'Peaky,' she interjected. 'You need Pink Pills for Pale People.'

She led him through the gloom to the lounge, where she lit candles and the gas fire, rather than throw the fierce light of the lamps across the room.

'You sure you don't want coffee?' she said over her shoulder, as she headed for the kitchen.

'Perhaps,' he called after her. 'I will see if I can drink any.'

In the kitchen, waiting for the espresso pot to bubble over, she stared at her reflection in the window, her arms folded around her waist. 'What are you doing?' she whispered to the pale ghost in the glass. Her hair, still held neatly back from dinner, and the harsh light of the kitchen, changed the shape of her face; the reflection was almost that of a young man. The aroma of coffee began to fill the kitchen with rich familiarity. 'You're doing what you want to do,' she murmured, smiling. 'Exactly what you want.' The thrill of being in Oxford, after all, and against all likelihood, and in splendid contradiction to the life plans that had grown so tedious around her, was exhilarating. The reflection slowly blew her a kiss, and she lowered her hand from her lips, smiling at herself. The pot spluttered as the last condensed drops spat bubbles from the tip, and she whisked it off the stove. She made his weaker with a little water, adding, after some consideration, a spoonful of honey. She'd collected it herself, from her mother's farm in Ohio, over the summer, and this was the last, precious jar. It was obscurely important that he manage a little coffee.

'Here you are,' she said, setting it on a coaster in front of him. He was sitting upright on the chaise-longue, and she curled up on the other end. 'The best coffee you'll ever get in England; I can personally guarantee every ingredient.'

In the soft light, his skin was reassuringly, and beautifully, golden once more. 'You made it?' he said.

'Completely. Well – I didn't pick the beans. But I did grind them myself, and even the honey I collected.'

He smiled in delight, and lifted the mug as if uncertain it would respond to him. When he took a sip, she could have sworn she saw the warmth of it rush through him. 'You do have a gift,' he said happily.

'So – convince me about Paracelsus,' she said, cradling her own cup and tucking her bare feet underneath her.

'Do you know St Augustine?' he replied, instead. '*Conloqui et conridere et vicissum benevole obsequi, simul leger libros dulciloquos, simul nugari et simul honestari.*' He took another tentative, pleased sip of coffee.

She laughed. 'You've been reading *The Rebel Angels*, haven't you?'

'*Reading* them?' His face transformed into pure alarm.

'The book – Robertson Davies – isn't that where you got the quote? No, I suppose you're studying theology . . .' His quick, inexplicable reactions were making her nervous. She felt as if he needed to be treated with extraordinary tenderness. His hands were trembling, and she lifted the coffee mug from them before it spilt. When he looked up, his dark eyes were full of tears.

'Are you OK?' She touched his cheek gently, and he began to sob.

'I – I can't – I can't say, but it's all so – so . . .'

She pulled him into her arms as he cried, wondering how such a delicate flower could possibly survive the stringency of academic life. His cheek was wet against her neck, and as she stroked his back, he wept harder. She cradled him close to her as she leant back against the curve of the chaise-longue, his face still pressed against her throat, his other hand curling like a child's in her hair. With her spare hand, she hit play on the remote control, letting the soft strains of Allegri's Miserere tiptoe on the edge of the room. He raised his head, nervously. 'It's OK, it's just some music.' She stroked the creases from his brow. 'I thought it might calm you.' He nestled down again. 'Do you want to talk about it?'

'No, I can't.' he said softly. He lay back a little, his head resting in the crook of her arm. 'I don't know what you must think of me. I'm usually quite calm. Deathly calm.' He chuckled, and pulled a handkerchief from his pocket to wipe his face.

'Maybe you keep it all too bottled up, then. But I think you've been overdoing it, maybe? Working too hard. Can I borrow that? My neck's a bit damp from your tears.' He ignored the hand she held out, and wiped her neck carefully himself, looking as though he might need it again himself. He raised himself on one elbow, leaning over her – to reach the other side of her neck, she thought, and then his lips came down over hers. The trembling flower kissed like a man – astonishingly better than most men, and with a confidence that startled her. His lips were still cold from the chilly walk, but as his tongue twined against hers, she felt them catch the warmth from her skin. The sureness of his lips made her weak and hungry with passion. When he withdrew, she was trembling, and his eyes had lost their tears. The look he gave her now was the same as when she had asked him for a cigarette: recognition, but also fascination, and the self-assurance of a man accustomed to women. She felt again the rush of lust she had felt then, doubled by the effects of his kiss.

'What the hell...' she muttered, staring at him, feeling as if all her body were a candle and her groin the flaming wick.

'Neither heaven nor hell can touch us in this house,' he whispered, kissing her softly again with closed lips, back and forth across her slightly parted mouth. She felt her spine arching of its own accord, her nipples blindly seeking his hands. He lowered his mouth to her neck, and she drew her fingernails slowly through his hair. The piercing falsetto of the Miserere rose and fell as the candlelight flickered. She could feel the buttons of her blouse giving way one by one. What do you know that I don't? she enquired of the moulded ceiling. Her usual self was telling her, from a corner of her mind, to stop, to ask him to leave, but she felt no hint of the danger that it was blathering frantically on about. Danger she felt, yes, but only of the soul. She breathed a soft laugh at herself, 'only' of the soul indeed. He had pushed aside her blouse, and was kissing with exquisite slowness towards her breast, slipping his tongue just under the lacy edge of her bra.

'You have such gorgeous underclothes,' he said. 'Fit for a queen.'

'Have you known many queens' underclothes?' she asked mockingly. Already her nipples stood fierce and hard, eager for him.

'A few.' His eyes flashed sexily, and he pulled her blouse off her shoulders, the cuffs still tight around her wrists, so that her hands were trapped. Her eyes flickered with nervousness. 'You know I can do nothing to you that you don't want.' he said. His hand glided so lightly over the mound of her breast that she groaned.

'I know.' she answered, and as she said it, she did. He pulled the lace to one side, slowly, so that it caught on her erect nipple, and exposed the milky whiteness of her skin, the aureole flushed and rosy. His teeth nibbled slowly inwards, and she stretched her hands against the cuffs of her blouse, her fingers stretching for his skin. He looked down at her hands, and bent from the waist to pull a sharp-tipped finger into his mouth. As she felt the succulence of his tongue wrap around her knuckles, prying down to the sensitive web of skin between the digits, she had a sudden flash of what it must feel like, for a man, to be enclosed in the warmth of a woman and fit there tightly. Her hips heaved upwards abruptly, and he caught his balance with one hand on the back of the sofa. 'Is your bed in the east wing or the west wing?' he asked, adding, 'I know this house – it's been here for years.' When she told him, he scooped her in his arms, strong despite the hints of gauntness about him, and carried her down the corridor towards the stairs.

'Careful, the floor.' she murmured, clinging to his neck.

'I know,' he said, walking safely over and ascending the stairs. 'It's slippery when it's wet.' He pushed her door open with his foot, and laid her on the bed in the darkened room. 'The candles are still burning – do you have a candle-snuffer?'

She nodded, and pointed to her dressing-table where it sat, ornamental and unused. 'I usually just blow them out.'

'I prefer a snuffer.' He lifted it, hesitantly, as he had the mug, and left the room. Alone again, she undid her cuffs, pulling off her blouse and unclipping her bra. She couldn't see her reflection in the bay windows as she sat up, just the cherry tree waving its last narrow leaves against the full moon. Why was she doing this, she wondered? He was a complete stranger; until she'd come to Oxford she hadn't slept with anyone until she thought she was in love with them. He was so strange – so odd. That, she reflected as she lay back against the duvet, was partly why. If this seemed like a routine seduction, with some ordinary fellow, she wouldn't be lying here half-naked. But a seduction it most certainly was. He was skilled. She should ask him to leave. She sat up, reaching for her blouse again, as he re-entered the room and shut the door with a click behind him. He sat down, turning to face her, and ran his hand over her face. 'My god, my god, thou hast not forsaken me.' he said.

'I think you should go,' she said, her throat clenched.

He cupped a bare breast in his hand, supporting its weight on his palm. His thumb grazed the aureole, and then retreated.

'I will – if you want. I would disappear without a trace, if you wished it.' His words were honeyed with sincerity; she wondered how many times he had said that, and believed him nonetheless. 'Do you want me to go?'

He knew how, and when, to use his eyes. They held her spellbound, so that she spoke the truth. 'No.'

As her lips formed the words, he pushed her firmly back onto the bed, and took her nipple deep into his mouth, his teeth grazing at it while she cried out. His hand pressed against her hipbone, so that she could not rock upwards. She reached upwards to untie his cravat. He withdrew smiling, swiftly undoing complicated fastenings, and lay down bare-chested beside her, drawing her half-naked body against his so that their skin rubbed smoothly.

'You're cold.' she whispered.

'So warm me,' he said, pulling her on top of him. She lay her stomach against his, her legs along his, her breasts on his chest, nipples kissing nipples, and with her hair falling around their faces kissed him freely and deeply. He moaned and shuddered, running his hands over and over her skin with certain care, and at the apex of their bodies she felt him swelling stiffly. His hands ran beneath her skirt, as if he were moulding her buttocks from clay, and she lifted herself from his kisses to stare into his eyes. His skin glowed, his eyes were shockingly black with bright white moon-specks reflected in them. She touched the curve of his cheek with the back of her fingers as he explored the shape of her bottom. The same bewildering tenderness filled her as before; he was so sure of himself, such a man of the world, and still he looked vulnerable.

'You are so beautiful,' she whispered. 'How did you get so beautiful?'

'Consumption,' he said, a grin chasing away any hint of weakness in his eyes. His finger swept through the stickiness of her labia, his grin growing lupine as she squealed sharply. He brought the wet finger to her mouth. 'Lick it.' She did as he ordered, tasting fresh saltiness and a queer tang on his skin. 'Now kiss me.' He more licked at her tongue than kissed her. 'The finest *fruit de mer* in God's creation,' he said, throwing her onto her back. Pulling her skirt wantonly above her waist, he dipped his finger once more through the outer lips, and licked at it lasciviously, and then again. The third time, he pushed his finger deep inside her and she bucked. 'A merry horse, and ready to ride,' he laughed, and pushed hard again inside.

'Dear God!'

'I told you already,' he smiled, putting his mouth to her breast once more, 'Neither heaven, nor hell – Neither God, nor devil –' His fingers punctuated each phrase, delving deep inside her, '– can touch – us – here.' He pressed harder, and she wailed, feeling her muscles spasm frantically around him as he rubbed far inside her. Her body rose from the bed in a pure parabola of ecstasy as he expertly manoeuvred his hand in her, his teeth fierce on her breast. She screamed high and clear, golden waves of feeling rolling over and over her. He held his hand still, as her muscles rippled around his fingers, and his mouth on her breast was warm, gentle, and motionless. She opened her eyes to look at him, but his gaze was too much, and she sank with shuttered eyelids against the mattress. She felt his hand withdraw, and his weight leave the bed. Her body still shook and ached for more. Please, she thought, please. She opened her eyes slowly, and saw that he stood completely naked by the bed. His body was narrow, firm, shadowed; his hips more slender than she expected. His cock stood strong, swollen, springing upright from the dark tufts of pubic hair. As straight as an arrow, even in the moon-light she could see how the skin strained, stretched to its tautest.

'I want to know you,' he said, with a curious empha-sis on 'know'. 'But – not unless you truly want to.' She took his hand, and kissed the knuckles one by one. He shook with suspense. Sliding her legs off the bed, one on each side of his, she hugged his belly close to her face, the ardent heat of his cock against her cheek. She felt it leap at the touch of her skin, and wrapped her arms tighter around him, one hand holding his buttock. He gathered her hair gently in his fist as she nuzzled across his torso, his every muscle tight with tenuous self-control. Her lips at last found the smooth, hard skin they sought, and parted to take the tip inside her. His arm shook, his fist clutching her hair a little tighter, terrifyingly careful. 'Please.' he whispered. 'May I . . .'

She pushed her mouth lower around him and then,

reluctantly, let him go, and looked up. His eyes, how could she stand to meet them? They were like the eyes of a dying man, threatening to drown her in another world if she looked too deeply, but now that she had met them she couldn't look away. They glowed with passion. But still, he held himself in check. What would his unbridled lust be like, she thought; what would it do to her if he let himself go? She felt a twinge of fear and agonising anticipation inside her. 'I want you to,' she said. 'I want you to do whatever you want. I want to . . .' and the word he had used seemed oddly fitting, because she wanted to know, and so she said, 'I want to know you – completely.'

A gorgeous power seemed to swell through him, relaxing his shoulders and straightening his spine, as he used her hair to drag her steadily back onto the bed. He knelt between her open legs, and nudged the tip of his cock against her clitoris. Her breath came faster, in a mixture of terror and delight, and he pushed slowly, inch by inch, against her, whispering obscenities as he sank deeper. He held himself at arm's length above her, his cock straining to press deeper inside her, sunk to the hilt between her thighs, and she watched his restraint beginning to fray at the edges like a tidal wave on the verge of breaking. Their breaths held, their eyes locked, the moment endured until she thought she would faint with longing to have him crammed so tightly inside her and so still. He began to pull slowly out, and she whimpered, hardly able to bear it that he should with-draw at all, and as slowly as he had pushed in, he left her, until just a hair's-breadth lay inside her still and her eyes were wide with anxiety. He slid in again, smoother, and faster than before, gasping heavily, and then his control shattered. She writhed helplessly as he pounded into her, his hands dug into her shoulders, holding her down as he hammered her into orgasm after orgasm, until it seemed that with every furious stroke she came again, and as he fell on her their hips flew against each other's unabated, his teeth gripping her neck tightly, her tongue slathering hungrily on his neck, his ear, his shoulder, any skin she could reach for the heavy woody taste of him. They rolled, raking their nails through each other's skin, and still he forced his way deep and hard into her, groaning wildly, and rolled her over again so that he could lift her hips, wrap her legs around him. He towered over her, and words spilled randomly from her mouth between howls of bliss, 'I can't – it's more –' making no sense and absolute sense and dissolving into the longest and most primal of possible screams as his cock shuddered violently inside her. She saw visions as he plunged three, final, times inside her, and they were still. She lay, her hips still spread wide beneath him. Her legs, folded around him, held him tightly close. Her arms were wrapped around his back. His fingers clutched her shoulders in a death-grip. She pressed her cheek closer against his, as if their skin could dissolve and let them closer still, and tried to find the words to speak.

She must have fallen into a deep sleep like that, not waking even when he withdrew from her. She woke with the whiteness of dawn filling the room with milky light, to find herself alone in the bed, him gone, his clothes gone, and a note pencilled in exquisite cursive script on the bedside table.

'My beautiful Sarah – Thank you.' No telephone number, no address.

She unlocked the door to Mother's room, embarrassed to see it after the night she'd just spent in another stranger's arms. A much stranger stranger, she chuckled wryly. As she pushed the door, the smile wiped off her face. The canvases lay all over the floor, in a resinous puddle emanating from a large tin on its side. She stared, horrified. She didn't remember the tin falling, or the smell of – was it paint? As she lifted the canvases, her stomach sank further. The pristine, if dusty, canvases were smeared with the stuff, their white surfaces gluey and hazel in swathes. She knelt down, trying to assess the damage. The stuff came off on her finger, oily. She fetched a kitchen roll, biting at her lips anxiously. Would she be able to fix them – maybe they could be reprimed, she'd seen an art shop on Broad Street, or was it High Street? Would the landlord chuck her out? She had to keep the house, she'd never find anywhere as good. It took half the kitchen roll just to clean up the floor, and it seemed to have eaten at the varnish. She rubbed as hard as she could, and it coloured the kitchen paper but wouldn't lift. At any rate, the paintings still needed attention. She took up the worst of them, and began to rub the canvas as she had the floor. Her eyes flicked rapidly over the others as she worked. She glanced down at her hands, and stopped in her tracks. A massive dirty patch had appeared across the top of the canvas; the paper she held was wet and covered with greenish prime and oil, but not black. She rubbed again, checking the paper and the painting. The painting grew darker, but no black showed on the damp paper. She peered closer. A line ran down the length, with a different colour below to above. She wiped more carefully, with a clean piece of paper. The prime was coming off, but not what lay beneath it. With stroke after stroke, the image grew clearer; dark as a Rembrandt, but distinct. The top of a curtain – open at the centre, hanging in thick folds on either side – swirls in the middle – spikes lower down – which became the tips of trees against a clouded sky. A round, dark patch against them, further down – what was that? Oval, textured – a head.

The top of a head, the hair. It wasn't a primed canvas, it was a portrait.

Sarah sat back on her heels. The messy liquid lay right across the canvas; it had been lying face down on the floor. She had to clean it anyway; she wouldn't be able to cover it with prime again until she'd wiped it all off. I have to, anyway, she whispered to it. She may as well find out what lay beneath.

It took her an hour, maddened with curiosity and working as carefully as she could, to lay it completely bare. She left the face for last, as the final treat, so that she had a sixteenth-century portrait of a woman, face still unrevealed, her hands folded in her lap holding a book of some sort, in a high-backed chair against the window of the darkened room. Only the sky held a suggestion of light, or rather of the grey winter quality that is the absence of dark, rather than the presence of any light. The room had no other source of illumination; only a piece of quartz, on the table by the window, caught any of its pallor. She began to wipe the heavily shadowed face, a hint of light here and there just betraying its features. The nose, as she cleaned it, was familiar, but only once she had finished and leant back to squint at it, did she see her own face.

It wasn't like looking at a photo. The hair was coiffed in a peculiar style, and the square cut of the gown changed the face's shape. It was more like looking in the mirror the first time you put on a polo neck after summer, or when you've just had a new haircut. It's a doppelganger, she thought, blinking at it. It looks just like me. It's not so odd, surely. It must be a family ancestor. She just looks like me. He would have noticed some family resemblance in me, by some quirk of fate. That's why he liked me. I looked familiar. It's not such a coincidence. I'm here because by some chance I happen to look like some ancestor, it's not a coincidence at all, just the curious effects of how people think. People like people who look like the same – tribe, or something. Or good genetic material. Similar to their own. Old instincts.

Her thoughts wittered on reassuringly as she examined the painting. Even through the penumbra, the likeness could not be doubted. She peered at the surroundings, moving her head backwards and forwards to find the best position from which to focus. It was like looking into a darkened room, and trying to adjust your eyes to the light, except morning light filled the room and there was nothing more to be seen than what was there. She set it on the mantelpiece and stood several paces back, frowning. It was an extraordinary painting – reminiscent of Da Vinci, but definitely later. It must be priceless. Or if not priceless, as expensive as to be much the same to her. Could he really have been intending to paint over this? Or had he no idea that a much older painting lay underneath? She looked at the other canvases. Any of them might conceal another masterpiece. The muddied squares and rectangles stood ranged beneath the portrait on the mantelpiece, each one catching the bright light in a different shade of bluish-white and pale grey, each flecked or slathered with dirty wetness. Her own face, with the hands folded neatly in the lap, stared imperiously out at her, eyebrows faintly raised, stern and expectant. It could be just the one canvas, or it could be a treasure house of images.

For the rest of the morning, she worked at the canvases, freeing another two smaller, square paintings from their white disguise. One showed a clay jar, the other a pestle and mortar, and around each were arranged different bundles of fresh and dried herbs, all minutely observed. By noon, she was convinced that every canvas in the room was a painting – but she was out of kitchen roll, and she should be in the Bodleian.

In the penumbra of the Duke Humphrey library, breathing the slow quiet smell of vellum and leather, she could almost believe herself in a monastery and heard, in her mind's ear, the rising and falling chant of vespers. She stared at the shelves opposite, each volume preserved from fading and crumbling under the onslaughts of time by the semi-dark, and thought of the pages and pages inside them, the monks who had bent over each letter, day after day. The tolling of the bells marked the time then, too, she thought, filtering in the endless ringing of the Oxford bells. This was the atmosphere she had tried to imagine for her freshers. She had demonstrated calligraphy for them, and encouraged them to try it themselves – she remembered her voice in a neon-lit classroom, 'Can you conceive what written words must have meant, when each page cost as much as a month's salary, and every word was painstakingly drawn?' She knew, even as she had tried to draw them into the fantasy, that it was nothing but tourist-titbits and curious trivia. In her own way, too, she had contrived to enter that world a little more. For a time, she had written all her notes in calligraphy, but however interesting the impracticalities of it were, her lecturers were more interested in the practicalities of deadlines. She developed a habit, instead, of taking notes with a fountain pen, on sheaves of unlined paper, and was hypnotised by the gloss and shine of the black ink as it dried. For a year, she had worn long skirts, until a friend embarrassed her out of it by commenting on how every student dressed vaguely according to period of study. She knew it was childish, this attempt to replicate a bygone time, that it was theoretically corrupt, that it was impossible – but still, furtively, she clung to these fragments of the past. Simulacra of the past, she reminded herself dryly, our imitations of mediaeval times are always replications of something that never existed, we don't know how it felt. But still, in her heart, she felt at home in the old smells and sounds. And why deprive herself? And in a room like this, it was almost possible to step into the dream.

Day by day, she grew more accustomed to the atmosphere and warm dry smells of the Duke Humphrey, and more absorbed in the manuscripts themselves. With guilty pleasure, she returned to her calligraphy. She set up her slanted table in the studio, opposite the portrait, and ruled up a sheet of vellum. October reds gleamed dully in the garden, through the driving rain, as she worked. Greenish-grey light fell on her desk. The steady battering of water against the window panes, the hissing of the wind, the rattling of the sashes, and the rhythmic strokes of Gothic lulled her thoughts. When she first started learning calligraphy, she had imagined it as a meditative exercise, enabling one to ponder the full meaning of each word as it painstakingly emerged from the careful pen nib. In reality, the steady strokes and deliberate little serifs were pure form, removed from any meaning: writing 'God' was a meditation on nothing but geometry, projecting the angle of the pen nib for the perfect thickness, symmetry, and rhythm. While her mind calculated angles and her hand drew pen strokes, her thoughts drifted on their own path. What had become of Jo? She looked out for him in town all the time, and Oxford was small, but he had vanished. She fretted anxiously about her work. God, that awful terror of ignorance – she hadn't met anyone to whom she could confess that fear. Everyone in the history faculty seemed so relentlessly confident, as if life were one long job interview. Dr Piedmont was out of the question. What if it turned out she knew nothing, that all her scribblings were a scratching of the surface and everything she said humiliatingly obvious? And perhaps everything that could be found had already been found – the mediaeval period, dark and long as it was, could hold only so many mysteries – it was true knowledge she was after, not that fashionable running after theoretical viewpoints that were never true or false. That sounded like Dr Piedmont, was she taking after him? But truth mattered, or she wouldn't be drudging through all these manuscripts. These things had really happened and been thought or not happened and not been thought. Dr Piedmont criticised her for being so black and white in her thinking – but it did matter, truth, even if it was all in the past. Perhaps it didn't matter as much as medicine, for instance – good God! She lifted her pen, and stared at her portrait. She hadn't phoned Tim, even to say thank you for ironing her clothes and seeing her safely to dinner. She owed him a drink, at least.

'I got the strangest letter in my pigeonhole today,' she said, setting the drinks on an unsteady table. The White Horse was crowded, the tiny windows steamed up and the air soupy. As she sat down, she felt again that rush of exhilaration and homecoming that Oxford constantly inspired in her. The small, narrow pub, half underground and squashed with bodies, its floor sticky with wet footsteps and beer, felt cosy and familiar. The stuff of books, she thought happily, as she pulled the envelope from her bag. 'I've no idea what it's about – gorgeous envelope, isn't it?' She rubbed it between her fingers, relishing the softness of the linen paper. 'But look.' From within, she removed an invitation, printed on expensive card. 'Even the printing's lovely quality, but I've no idea what it's about. It's for a Halloween party – but I don't know who it's from. And no one else had envelopes like it in their pigeonholes. What's the Phoenix Society?'

Tim grinned. 'Oldest dining society in Oxford,' he said, taking a long sip of his pint. 'More of a drinking society, really. You'd better get in practice.'

She took a gulp of her wine and smiled mockingly back. After the night with Jo, she had remembered Tim as a little dull – his naughty smile forgotten. 'I could drink you under the table!'

'I'll give you a test run tonight if you like,' he said, 'but on Halloween we'll really challenge you.'

Her eyebrows shot up. 'We? You're part of this?'

'Oh, yes. It's a small society – thirteen members, counting our old friend.' He smirked. 'But from time to time we permit the general riff-raff to join our revelry.'

She smiled wryly as she stuffed the invitation back in her bag. 'So as general riff-raff, I guess I have you to thank for the invite.'

'Let's see if you're thanking me afterwards. As I said, it's more of a drinking society. So drink up.'

When Tim wriggled back into the crush of bodies for more drinks, she pulled the invitation out again, stroking the letters with her thumb. *Dress: Formal*. In Oxford, she'd discovered, formal meant formal. She'd need something that could pass as a ball gown ... Even as she totted up the expense in her head, she gave a satisfied grin. This lifestyle was growing on her: three-course dinners three times a week and lentils between times, champagne at every event and no money for a cup of coffee. The squalor of student poverty was already familiar, but this glamour was something entirely new. She drained her glass happily, throwing her head back – and met the eyes of her supervisor.

'Sarah,' he said, rolling her name out slowly, 'what an unexpected surprise.' Uninvited, he sank into Tim's space next to her, and set his glass on the table. 'I was under the impression you didn't drink.'

'Dr Piedmont!' Irrational alarm rang through her at his presence. She glanced towards the bar; Tim was still a row of people away from the bar, his attention fixed on the barman. She wanted to call him back over, but the babble of voices was so loud that only a shout would be heard.

'I thought it was doctor's orders,' he continued smoothly in his mocking voice.

'I was – it was,' she said, hastily. 'I was – on medication.'

'Not anti-depressants, I hope. The mental stability of our students is so lamentably fragile – they're all perpetually on the verge of suicide, or troubled with irrational paranoias.' His last words were so close to the truth that she flinched inwardly.

'Not at all,' she said calmly, 'antibiotics.'

'Of course.' He stretched his arms out, and crossed his legs. She leant forward to move away from him, on the pretext of reaching for her empty glass. 'I think you'll find that one's empty,' he said.

'This one's full,' said Tim, setting down a fresh glass and glancing at her sharply. Sarah was awkwardly aware of her supervisor's sleek good looks and youthfulness. Dr Piedmont showed no sign of relinquishing his seat, and Tim dragged a spare stool over.

'Tim, this is my supervisor, Dr Piedmont.'

'Nice to meet you,' said Tim, though it clearly wasn't; and, 'Delighted,' drawled Dr Piedmont lazily. 'What are you studying, then? I take it you are a student.'

'Medicine,' said Tim stiffly.

'Ah – the good doctor,' and he winked at Sarah. 'It was on your orders then, that our dear Sarah was unable to sample the wines at High Table recently?'

'It's generally advisable not to drink when you're concussed, yes,' said Tim. Sarah winced.

'Concussed, yes, of course, now I remember.' By some trick of the devil the man seemed able to raise just the tip of his eyebrow, so that Sarah alone could see, while his smile stayed unchanged. 'Well next time, my dear,' he said, throwing his smile onto her, 'you simply mustn't miss out – the sommelier has been outdoing himself, exhibiting uncharacteristically good taste.' He drained his pint. 'And now I must get back to my books, and leave you two lovebirds alone.'

Neither Sarah nor Tim said a word until the blurred outline of his figure had passed the windows outside, then they spoke in unison.

'I'm so sorry –'

'What a prat!'

'He was the last person I expected to see . . .'

'How can you bear to study with such an utter, pretentious git?' Tim looked almost angry.

'He's actually bloody good,' said Sarah defensively, 'but – yes, he's a complete prick. And calling me "my dear" like that!'

When the drinking-up bell rang, they were still enumerating his offences, and all spark of naughtiness had been damped down. Sarah caught the bus home alone, and grouchy.

She stood in front of the full-length mirror in her bed-room, and examined herself. Her limbs glowed in the lamplight, smooth and rounded; the flesh of her breasts rose smoothly, held aloft by her push-up bra. After much anxiety, she had left her hair down, and it brushed softly between her shoulder blades as she turned from side to side. Jewellery sparkled beneath her ears and around her wrists. Her eyes, outlined with the same painstaking care she applied to her calligraphy, gleamed and softened into shadows at the corners. The lace tops of her hold-up stockings clasped her thighs, leaving the curling tendrils of hair between her legs exposed. All that remained was the dress, which lay ready on the bed.

She'd gone to the dress hire shop on Magdalen round-about. Formal wear, unlike smart, or casual-smart, or the many other distinctions she was learning, could not be cleverly created with accessories and hairstyles. She wandered past the folds of so many different coloured satins and stiff, netted overlays, pulling out this one and that, growing increasingly despondent under the sales-woman's bright, implacable smile. Every dress cried out prom queen, or pseudo-bride, and if the styles were bad then the prices were worse. They're not even well-made, she thought crossly, fingering another full-skirted ver-sion of the same theme, and the material's horrible and cheap. Cheap – of course it was! Her eyes had lit up.

Stepping carefully into the dress, she put her hands behind her to do up the hooks and eyes, her breasts pushing out in front of her. If only I could see myself like this tonight, she thought happily, it would be worth it. The material had cost her less than half the price of those dreary dresses, and every seam was perfect. As she progressed up her front with the hooks and laces, the dress nestled snugly against her waist, the gleaming black velvet running smoothly over her hips. Hours of careful sewing, in the pale white light of the studio, were rewarded as she closed the final hook and spiralled before the loving golden glass of the mirror. She had struggled as much to find a pattern as she had to find a dress to hire, and had solved the problem by giving up. Instead, she had copied the dress in the portrait. The smoothly fitting sleeves ran to her wrists, where the soft ruffs hid half her hands in drooping black lace from which her fingers emerged elegantly. The neckline, low and square, didn't press her breasts flat and round like those in the portrait, but showed a dark hollow where the two spheres met and sank into shadows. Her skirts swished around her as she stepped backwards and forwards. She shook her hair, and smiled knowingly at her reflection. Her lips curved in a calculated smile. 'Perfect,' she whispered. For a moment, she imagined arriving at the party, and strangers' eyes seeing her, and she blinked in dismay. It was Halloween. All her outfit was lacking to make her a cartoon witch was a broom and a pointy hat.

The moment she reached the gate of St Mary's, her confidence surged again. The man who glanced at the invitation she held out was dressed as anachronistically as she, in brown tails with an elaborate ruff at his throat, and his eyes followed the line of her dress in unmistakable appreciation, lingering at her generous cleavage. Looking into the churchyard, she saw people dressed in every period imaginable.

'Quite a crowd,' she murmured.

He glanced around. 'Hardly,' he said smiling. 'Wait till it gets started.'

The party, to her surprise, was being held in the graveyard itself, not the church as she'd expected. Large braziers cast warmth onto the gathered crowd, and the lampposts around Radcliffe Square lit up the steam rolling from the great barrels of drink. As the clock chimed six, the man from the gate joined twelve other men, all in brown tails and ruffs, behind the drinks tables. They turned to each other – a brief, private prelude to the party – and all but one raised their glasses. 'Our old friend!' they exclaimed, draining their drink. The object of their toast smiled faintly, warmth in his eyes. His silver hair and beard were neatly trimmed, his face ascetic. He had the distant, knowing, but still kindly look of an eminent novelist in a class of would-be writers. While she was gazing at him, Tim appeared by her side with a tray of glasses and a jug from which issued curling tendrils of orange steam.

'Now we'll see what you're really made of,' he smirked.

'What is that made of?'

'Never mind, just be a good girl and take your medicine.' He winked, pushing a glass into her hand.

'It looks like the devil's brew.' She hadn't eaten, and glanced around for the snacks she'd expected to line her stomach. It was only six o'clock, after all.

'We are the hell-fire club,' he said, with as best a mock bow as he could manage. 'I'll just be a moment – let me get rid of these.' He walked into the crowd, pressing glasses into empty hands and pouring the infernal drink into empty glasses. Most of the society's members were wandering around refilling glasses assiduously. She took a large gulp, looked around for someone to talk to, and realised she didn't know a soul.

By the time the clock overhead was chiming eleven, she had spoken to everyone there – including, Tim insisted, some of the bushes – and felt herself to be intimate friends with at least half the crowd. The deep shadows and sudden glares of orange light, as people shifted from group to group and around the drinks table, were blinding her, and the heat was making her dizzy. She moved away from the cluster towards the side of the church, the coolness hitting her skin like a welcome shower of cold water. She stepped through a narrow archway in the bushes, and leant against the cold stone of the church wall on the other side, in peaceful darkness. A sudden giggle echoed nearby, and her eyes swung swiftly to her left. There, scarcely two metres away in the shadow of the buttress, she saw a woman laughing softly, the sound half muffled by her lover's hands which she nibbled and licked as they covered her mouth. Both of them were dressed in the peculiarly old-fashioned style that seemed de rigueur at this party, and with his free hand he was unlacing her bodice, from which her plump breasts were straining. Fascinated, Sarah watched as he freed one breast from the constraining fabric, the nipple a darker smudge against the spotless white mound before his mouth sank around it and hid it from her view. The woman was murmuring, 'Oh, wicked, wicked!' and arching her back to push her nipple further into wickedness. The fabric around her rump bunched as his hands groped eagerly at her bottom. Sarah sank further back into the shadows, careful not to rustle the leaves behind her, but the couple seemed oblivious of anyone but themselves. With both hands kneading her buttocks, he buried his face deeper between her breasts, and nuzzled his way against the bodice, pulling at it with his teeth, and sinking with a lustful sigh into her other breast. Her head was tilted backwards, now, her throat white in the moonlight and her mouth ajar. Her eyelids fluttered in time with her soft gasps. Abruptly, he sank to his knees, leaving her breasts bare to the leaf-spattered lamplight, their tips swollen with arousal and dimpled with the cold night air. Grabbing handfuls of her full skirts, he pushed them above her waist, and pressed his face into the humid warmth awaiting him. She shuddered, moving her legs wider apart for him, and hauling her skirts up completely. She stood almost completely uncovered now, her bodice unlaced and fallen off her shoulders and large breasts, her skirts bunched up to her waist. Sarah watched his fingers sink hungrily into her exposed buttocks, as his tongue slurped between her thighs. She felt herself beginning to tingle, a trembling between her legs made worse by knowing she didn't dare move a muscle. His head turned this way and that as he delved into the woman with his tongue, and her hips shifted sensuously as she opened herself as much as possible. One of his hands snaked up her belly back to the heavy swell of her breasts, and pinched her nipple sharply, making her cry out, a clean sound slicing through the air. Sarah felt her own nipples stiffen in sympathy, and longed to slide a hand beneath her skirts. He was using both hands to hold her lips open now; they glistened in the lamplight falling over his shoulder as he moved back a little, to stare in bliss at her exposed folds. The woman was moaning softly as his fingers massaged the edges of her labia, and the cold air brushed over the wet skin. Slowly moving forwards and extending his tongue, he let the tip of it flutter on her clitoris. Sarah's knees weakened with longing. I shouldn't be watching this, she thought, but she couldn't leave without stepping back into the light. And as she stared at his tongue dancing up and down, she knew she wanted to stay. Silently, she sank down to sit on the ground, her eyes never leaving the couple in front of her. Still holding her wide open, he pressed the tip of his middle finger in; they were so close that Sarah could see how her pussy eagerly clasped it, how her buttocks clenched involuntarily as he sunk it deeper into her, driving up to his knuckles. Her breath dry, Sarah's own hand found its way beneath her skirts, and brushed her inner thigh. She shuddered, her own touch electric; she longed to slip her fingers inside herself, but restrained herself, savouring the torture. He pushed another finger in, and the woman moaned wildly, lost to everything but the feeling of herself speared on his hand. He pushed harder and harder, twisting his hand, letting her feel his fingers massaging deep inside her, his breath ragged. Sarah brushed with one fingertip against her lips, and her mouth flew wide with lust. She could feel them rubbing against each other, clutching and slippery. He pressed his mouth against her clitoris, sucking fiercely, his face hiding his still-thrusting hand. Fumbling, he was unlacing his trousers; Sarah's eyes were fixed greedily on the bulge as her fingertip tantalised just the curls of her down. Wait, she told herself, wait. His cock sprang out, and he rose to his feet again, still pressing into her hard with his fingers. Holding her by the buttocks, he withdrew his hand slowly, causing her to whimper in dismay and open her eyes wide. He held her lips apart, and fixed his eyes on hers; Sarah's hand hovered, waiting, in an agony of suspense. She watched the woman's thighs shake convulsively, wordlessly begging. Her fingers felt the damp heat of the tendrils; for a long moment of terrible yearning, all three of them were motionless, and then he sank slowly forwards. She saw his swollen shaft nudging against her, forcing her wider, as her own finger sank with unbearable slowness into herself. The woman whimpered as he held her closer, pressing her tighter in against him, her body a parabola as it arched to meet his. As Sarah's finger sank to the hilt inside her, she watched as he flung the woman hard against the wall, pulling her legs over his hips and battering wildly into her. Biting her lips, her eyes watering, Sarah felt the pain of orgasm wrack through her, her pussy clasping her finger. Every nerve in her body seemed to meet in that one golden spot, as the woman gave a strangled scream of bliss, and he groaned, deep and guttural, again and again, shaking as he came.

Weak, Sarah leant against the stone, watching them kiss passionately as they pulled each other's clothes back into place. She felt terribly lonely, even as the delight still rippled through her, and as they slipped around the back of the church she found herself mouthing, 'Sorry.' She pressed her cheek against the stone, cold and rough on her skin, thinking wistfully that watching them kiss, at the end, had been more intimate than any of that. Where was the man she would kiss like that, while he laced her clothes up again tenderly?

'There you are! You OK?' Tim's head had appeared through the hedge's archway.

She grimaced. 'Yeah, fine. I just needed some air.' She stood up, brushing her skirt.

On the other side of the hedge, the party had all but subsided. She sat on the stone bench, her legs pulled up to her chest, sipping a last glass of the evil brew. The members of the Phoenix club, all in their identical clothes, were stacking glasses into crates, shaking out sodden tablecloths, carrying barrels away. All the dinginess of a party's end, she thought. Some of them looked terribly young, nineteen or twenty. No doubt they thought themselves manly and worldly wise, she thought spitefully. A few were in their late twenties, maybe thirties. The silver-haired man, sank down next to her on the bench.

'Good party?' he said.

'Fine . . .' She still felt wounded with loneliness inside. She watched Tim turn from dismantling a table, and wave at her. 'We'll go soon, OK?'

'You're going home with him?' asked the old man quietly.

She glanced over at him. His eyes were surprisingly sexy, and she suddenly wondered if the question might have an ulterior motive. She shrugged, and turned back to watch the other twelve trampling back and forth across the lawn. She felt the old man still watching her. When everyone had moved away, she said, 'Probably not. I'll say I'm not feeling well.'

'You could do better than Tim,' he said, nodding thoughtfully.

They sat in silence as the other members gathered around again, each with a glass in hand which one of them refilled.

'Excuse me a moment,' murmured the man, his hand brushing her shoulder gently as he stood. She felt a rush of her earlier arousal, chasing away the sour feeling. Watching him walk towards the circle, she thought, And why not? Older – but clearly not too old – if his eyes are anything to go by. The image of him making love to her, slowly and tenderly, flashed through her head. It was appealing.

'Sarah!' hissed a voice. She sprang around in fright: Jo was crouched behind the bench. 'Please, you have to believe me, run! While no one's looking – trust me, your soul depends on this, keep quiet but run!'

The terror on his face convinced her more than his words. Slipping her high heels off, she glanced at the group. They were raising their glasses in another toast. The old man, his back to her, was nodding appreciatively.

'Run!' hissed Jo. Without another glance, she sprinted across the lawn, through the gate, and with all the speed she possessed across Radcliffe Square, Jo pelting at her side.

3 Hod

He kept her running all the way up Broad Street and St Giles', her legs flying in long strides beneath the ball-gown. At the fork of Banbury and Woodstock, he dragged her headlong across the road, forcing a car to swerve and hoot, and finally he stopped, panting, in the graveyard.

'This will do for now,' he said. 'We can't stay here long, though.'

She stood in her ball-gown, gasping for breath, her stockinged feet wet and the gravel of the path sharp beneath them. Wild shadows scissored across his face against white and gold, car light and lamplight, as he paced anxiously. In the sudden quiet of the graveyard, after the furious dash, with the cars swishing past on wet roads on either side, she felt a bitter sense of anticlimax.

'What's going on, Jo?' She meant the question to sound brave, or at least belligerent, but it came out in a feeble quaver; she hadn't yet caught her breath.

He stopped in front of her, caught her hands in his. 'Sarah, listen to me carefully. Can you get us to your house?'

She stared at him, her chin jutting forwards in bemusement. 'I can – shit, I mean, I can call a cab, what do you mean?'

'I don't mean a cab, a bus, anything like that; can you get us back?'

'What – you mean walking?'

His hands dropped to his sides, his shoulders

slumped. 'No, not walking,' he muttered wearily. He rubbed his face with his hands, then thrust them through his hair in frustration. 'Damnation, Sarah,' he snapped suddenly, 'you do not have the least idea, do you!' As the words were spoken, he slapped his hand over his mouth to trap them in, and his bewildering anxiety redoubled. 'That's it, Jesus, that's it, that's done it. We can't hide here now. Are you ready to run, again?' He said it bitterly, but earnestly.

'Not until you tell me what we're running from.' This time she succeeded in sounding belligerent, but it was too late. He had grabbed her hand, and was already hastening towards the gate.

'I will explain everything, trust me, but for now, know only that whatever your worst and most hideous fear is, that is what you are running from.' The light was weird enough, his eyes were desperate enough, that her most chilling nightmares flickered through her mind – those nightmares that even as an adult, she could not dispel with good sense, and that lingered throughout the day. Those were the waking nightmares, her bedroom visible around her although blurred, in which she was conscious but paralysed, unable to defend herself and prey to ... She flew again alongside him on her already-stinging feet, up the Banbury Road.

'No lights,' he hissed, as he slammed the door behind them. 'Close the curtains – quick – all of them!' His panic infected her as she dashed around the lounge, yanking the heavy velvet over the cold glass. The black lawn outside, thickly fringed with bushes, suddenly seemed ominous, as if a ghostly face might appear on the other side before she had time to shut it out. As she hurried into the corridor, he yelled 'Be careful – don't run in the corridor,' from the dining room. She heard the hiss of the dining room curtain rails as she ran up the stairs, three at a time, to the upstairs rooms.

'What about the studio?' she called down. 'There are no curtains there.'

'Keep the door closed then.'

The dark rooms scared her as they hadn't since childhood; adrenaline was feeding her fear. She finished as quickly as she could, eager to return to the lounge, to company. Jo was leaning with his forearm on the mantelpiece, in the dark, one hand covering his brow. Sarah stood just inside the door, fumbling in the drawer for a candle. Her uncertain fingers found a nightlight, and a box of matches. 'What was all that about, then?' The house was suddenly still, as she struck the match and the wick flickered to life and sank down. 'You've frightened me,' she added nervously.

He turned around; to her surprise, his face relaxed in a smile. 'Don't be frightened – we're safe here. You're safe here. I didn't want anyone to see us.'

She clutched her elbows tightly, her cleavage deepening. His face softened in the low light as he glanced down, and stepping closer he put his cool hands on the curve of her waist, leaning back a little to admire her. She wrenched out of his grasp.

'What's going on, Jo? You've just yanked me all the way across town telling me my worst nightmare is somewhere out there, and now everything's fine?'

'It's fine for now, you're safe now.' He was in front of her again, one hand sliding against the back of her dress, the other tilting her chin up. 'Kiss me again...' His eyes, huge and black, barely visible, seemed once again that strange mixture of anxious need and liquid suavity. Her heart, still pounding from their wild flight, beat faster as his mouth closed on her lower lip. He sucked on it slowly, hungrily, his arm sliding further around her and imprisoning her against his chest. She felt his fingers reach the side of her breast and rub it softly through the fine material.

'Jo, don't,' she said half-heartedly; her lips brushed his as she spoke. 'I want to know what's going on.'

'I'll tell you,' said his lips on hers, 'but let me – ah,' he shuddered, 'kiss you – more . . .'

His hips pressed tighter against hers as he whispered 'more', and the earlier desire she had felt in the grave-yard of St Mary's Church came flaming back to life.

'This is madness, madness, why am I letting you do this – how do I want you so much, it's unholy –' I'll stop in a moment, she told herself, just a moment then I'll push him away and demand an explanation.

His narrow fingers were dancing nimbly down the complicated little fastenings that held her bodice closed over her breasts. The material strained against the remaining hooks as the generous mounds of soft flesh were revealed, heaving a little as her breath came faster. The sleeves falling off her shoulders made her feel more erotically exposed than she'd ever felt simply naked. The hardening tips of her nipples were almost visible now; Jo's eyes were blurred with lust, sharp with fascination, as he watched them emerge. His lips had parted invol-untarily. As he took a nipple into the sharp-edged heat of his mouth, she felt a rush of blind lust and her thighs were suddenly damp against her tingling lips.

'You've bewitched me,' she gasped. He bit down harder on her nipple, making her yelp, and lifted his head.

'Au contraire,' he said, staring her straight in the eye. His eyes were dark hollows. 'You're the witch.' He licked his lips slowly. 'And a more tempting one than you never walked the earth. Seeing you like that –' his eyes raked over her '– I could almost forgive your choice of dress.'

'You don't like it?' she whispered, her hands running over the folds of material covering her thighs.

'I love it,' he said hoarsely. 'Especially with your bodice pulled open. But I'd like it even more like this ...'

He pulled her by the hand to the sofa, and gently pushed her to her knees before it. She leant forward obediently, her sensitive tips brushing the velvet upholstery. In the dark, its pale green background and cream flora had turned to silver, with streaks of gold where the tentative candlelight fell over it. She felt him lift up the full skirt, pushing it above her waist, so that the full orbs of her buttocks glowed pale and bare.

'No undergarments?' he murmured in a strangled voice.

'They didn't seem – appropriate – to the dress,' she said softly. His hand was clasping the taut flesh of her curved bottom.

'I wonder if you're familiar with the works of the Marquis de Sade?' he murmured, and as the words fell from his lips his hand smacked down in a stinging slap. She jerked forwards, squealing. His finger ran swiftly through the slick valley between her lips. 'Are you?' he said in a firmer tone.

'I –' Her reply was cut short by another smack, sharper this time.

'Only a wanton wench,' he said, punctuating his words with expert slaps across her generous cheeks, 'would read that filth ...'

It hurts, she thought. Each time she spasmed forwards, away from the pain, her breasts rubbed harder against the sofa.

'Jo!' she stammered, 'what – are – you – doing?' She panted wildly.

Another spank caught the edges of her pussy and she shrieked. To her horror, she could feel her thighs tightening with pleasure, her bowels hot with glee. His fingers slid between her legs and the blood rushed to her face with shame. He would feel it, she could not hide how this humiliating treatment thrilled her.

'Apparently,' he said dryly, 'I'm making you very happy. Well?' His tone changed abruptly to severity. 'Have you?' The flat of his hand fell hard again on her skin, rippling it, again and again. 'Tell me!'

'Yes!' she howled, 'Yes!' How could it sting so much, and yet, she knew from the clutching contracting glow of her body, bring her closer and closer to the gleaming edge, until she almost wanted it? His free hand took a handful of her breast, kneading it painfully as her voice wailed on, saying 'yes' again and again. She was yearning now, pressing her breast against his hand, the tip like a coal against his palm, lifting her bottom higher to meet the crisp blows he rained on her. She arched, spreading her thighs. Occasionally his fingers flicked smartly between her legs and her cries would fly up in pitch. The more it hurt, the closer her body surged to orgasm, so that at last she was begging him shamelessly to smack her harder. She felt the smooth, blunt tip of his penis between her open legs. With each shudder of pain, her hips jerked backwards, and he was lodged a little deeper inside her, thick and uncompromising against the straining narrow passageway.

'Yes,' he said throatily, 'I know you, I know you.' His nails dug into her breast, his hand grinding hard against it. 'I know you want this.' His palm hit her buttocks harder and harder, skirting the line where the pain became unbearable, and with renewed cries she felt herself falling into a wild spasming orgasm. He thrust hard as she came, forcing his way deep into her, prolonging her frenzy on and on as his hips slammed against her bum. Pinned down on the sofa, helpless under the waves of ecstasy, she yowled like a cat for him with every fierce stroke.

Sitting on the sofa, her hands still trembling around a glass of wine, Sarah watched Jo lacing and unlacing his fingers. The glow of passion still shone in his otherwise pale cheeks, but his brow was reluctantly furrowed.

'If I tell you,' he began; 'No – I will tell you, I must, for your own well-being, but I fear that – Sarah,' he clasped his hands and looked anxiously into her eyes. 'I cannot pretend I have much to offer you, but just to be with you – you can't imagine the joy – the warmth and life of you . . .' He trailed off, gazing at her longingly. The room sparkled now with dozens of small flames. The small, round white and silver sides of nightlights were clustered thickly on the coffee table and all over the mantelpieces, each with its flickering glow. Sarah had insisted that the heavy drapes would not let the least glimmer of light escape, and emptied her whole bag of candles. Flushed with brilliance, her bodice still hanging from her waist, her heavy breasts swaying, and her full skirt swishing, she took pleasure from moving around the room under Jo's eyes, perversely lighting candle after candle.

She stayed silent, waiting for him to speak again. Her wine shone ruby and black through the glass.

'I fear that I might lose you, that you might not understand.'

'I have nothing yet to try to understand,' she said. The mellow satedness that still persisted in her lent softness to her words.

'I know there cannot be – much – between us, less than you may want, but just to see you from time to time, to hold you in my arms!' His voice subsided, and he twisted the stem of his own glass unhappily. 'But who can say what may happen to you if I don't tell you; I haven't any idea what means they use, these days –'

'Jo, just tell me!' she exclaimed. 'What may happen to me, means for what?'

'Means for removing witches,' he said flatly. She stared at him, frozen. 'They had witch-hunts, once. Sarah, you're a witch.'

'I'm not a witch,' she said distantly, bewildered by his strange talk. Her mind echoed the words hysterically, in tones of Monty Python: I'm not a witch, I'm not a witch! They put this nose on me.

'I realised when I first met you – when you turned around and asked me for a cigarette.' He went on as though she hadn't spoken. 'At first I thought you were very unsurprised – accustomed to it all – and then, when I spoke to you again, in the churchyard, I realised you didn't know.'

She shook her head in disbelief. 'This is the twenty-first century. No one believes in witches. They don't exist. Well, some silly little pagan-wannabes do, but they get it all wrong, I've read the manuscripts and they haven't and –'

'What do the manuscripts say, then?'

'Witches joined covens – they were invited in, by female relatives or close friends – and the devil appeared, a local devil usually, and they all drank and danced around widdershins and naked, and sometimes the devil had sex with them. Every evidence suggests he was just a man from a nearby region, in a mask.'

'Evidence taken down in witch trials?' asked Jo, pointedly.

'That's the only written evidence, yes, –'

'And what does your knowledge of Church doctrine, and interrogation methods, and manuscript-making, tell you about these manuscripts?'

'That they're unreliable!' Sarah snapped. 'That it was

confessions taken from tortured prisoners, stupid ordinary women terrified of the Church's power!'

'So the devil really did come and sleep with them?'

'The devil doesn't exist,' began Sarah.

'Then would it surprise you to learn that earlier tonight you sat next to him, drank with him, and considered having sex with him?'

'What?' Sarah stood up, angry, and raised her glass haughtily. 'This is ridiculous,' she said. 'I'd like you to leave.'

'Please don't ask me to go.' he whispered, distressed. 'Even if – afterwards – you will not see me again – at least let me warn you, first.' His face was drawn with sadness, and she sat back down, stiffly.

'I'm supposed to be a witch,' she said coldly. 'And tonight I drank with the devil.'

'I was looking for you all night,' he said. 'Just to see you and perhaps –' he smiled fleetingly, 'make love to you again. I combed Oxford for you, chasing after women with long black hair – and of course they're all wearing silly black wigs!' He chuckled fondly and gave her an intimate glance. 'A man could look for centuries and not find a woman like you. When I finally saw you, in the churchyard on that bench – my blood ran cold. Those foolish young men, thinking hellfire and brimstone is a drinking game, readying the toast that they think is a fine tradition, never guessed that you were talking to their thirteenth member.

'He would have recognised you immediately. You would have been the only person to look at him. The society makes his potions for him; he could bide his time while you drank the lust-stirring concoction. Their recipes are older than they know; they use the sulphur of the alchemists without knowing it – and the alchemists knew well to temper their sulphur with mercury, *mercurius vulgi et non vulgi*. They complete the final step when they dedicate it to him, and all in the name of tradition. Do not forget that lust is of the devil – not all lust, no. The lust that makes people treat each other like tools for a purpose is his. The lust that takes off the personality and replaces it with a tawdry erotic effect, as if a person's soul were a matter of no concern, is his also.'

She thought involuntarily of Tim, and how they had fucked each other on the floor.

'While you drank and strolled from group to group and talked, it would have been taking its effects. No doubt you talked to the roaming souls, as well – oh, yes, on All Souls' Eve, and without knowing what you are, you could hardly have avoided it. A fine inspiration the chairman of the society had that year – to hold the All Souls' party in a graveyard, so conveniently close to the college! In the graveyard, but not in the church itself, mind.

'When I saw you talking to him, your face was already flushed – I could see the glow spreading down your beautiful cleavage. I saw the look he gave you, his look of knowing charm, and you would surely have followed him. They were filling their glasses for the final toast; I knew he would join them to accept his tribute, and so I took the only opportunity I had.'

Sarah had been listening in a blank silence, trying to make sense of this fantastic account. Now she spoke. 'The old man on the bench – you're saying he was a devil?'

'I'm saying he is the Devil. He has devils – smaller devils – as well, like Mephistopheles.'

'And I was talking to ghosts?'

'Roaming souls, yes – ghosts, if you like, but most souls can only return on All Souls' Eve. The ones with – unsettled business – never get to leave.'

'Jo – I don't know what you think, but I don't believe in ghosts.'

'Sarah – my darling,' he took her hand in his again, and held it to his cheek. His skin was cool and smooth on the back of her hand, his cheek bone sharply sloped. 'Tonight you made love with one.'

When Sarah woke, a thin slice of November sunshine was falling between the curtains and across her face. Her mouth tasted stale from drink and her head ached, but her skin still felt smooth and loved. She remembered Jo taking her so fiercely. Her feeling of contentment vanished abruptly, as she remembered the rush across town, the strange conversation that had ensued. He was gone, again. Looking at her desk, she saw a folded note, as before, and walked over to the window, pulling the curtains open to read it. It was penned in the same lovely copperplate, but this time covered several sheets. Standing in the light, she began to read. He repeated what he had said the night before, and pleaded touchingly and elegantly to be permitted to see her again, promising her all the help and protection he could offer and nights of unimaginable new joys. Some of the latter he had described in fair detail, and warm arousal stirred in her at the words. It finished, 'Until I can again sate myself on your ripe curves, I remain, your most devoted friend and lover, Jo. P.S. Please accept these cards as my gift to you.'

She lifted the pack of cards from the deck – a beautiful, old reproduction of the Marseilles tarot deck, with the old French preserved. Sitting down on the bed to look through them, she pulled out *Le Bateleur* and turned it the right way round to examine it. The background of the card had turned to a dusky pink reminiscent of vellum. The stylised figure stood behind a table in crude perspective, on which stood the tools of his trade. The colours were nursery-school bright: yellow and green, red and blue, sky blue and pink. The magician, she thought to herself. The devil would have been more appropriate, given Jo's wild talk.

November that year was unseasonably cold and dry, and Sarah took to walking home the long route, through Port Meadow. If she left the library at half-past five, she was in time to watch the yellowing leaves glow in the thick dull light of the setting sun behind her. She had bought a cheap book on the tarot from the discount bookshop, and according to its instructions was learning the meaning of the cards, using her long walks as meditation. Already, in the mornings, she was trying out a few simple spreads over her coffee. All it was, really, was interpreting the symbolism and connecting up the meanings, according to the meaning of wherever the card sat – and that, essentially, was what she laboured at so carefully in her studies. With the cards, however, she was at liberty to give her fantasy free reign without proving anything. It was probably all nonsense, but it was relaxing and pretty nonsense – and, perhaps, it helped her understand her own mind better. Musing over symbols was bound to do that.

She was studying the swords, at the moment. Her cards had plain daggers on the pip cards, numbers one to ten, but the book showed modern pictures for each one. The swords were supposed to be the 'sphere of the intellect', and by the look of the pictures the intellect had a pretty fierce time. Only two of the number cards seemed to be positive in the slightest, and even that in a meditative, almost melancholy way. Is the life of the mind so unhappy? she wondered, as she crunched the cold sand underfoot along the canal path, towards Port Meadow.

It was the beauty of things – the beauty of illuminations, and illumination – that had wrapped her up in
old manuscripts, to start with. Starved of the old world
beauty of her childhood, in the bright brash newness of
the States, she had flown back to it. And now, she left
Duke Humphrey's eagerly, every evening, where so
many ancient books were and the air was full of the
smell of them, to get to the fresh cold smell of wild
grass, the gold of sunsets, and late blue light, *maria
mater deus* blue. She flicked through the swords suit as
she walked. *It's supposed to be a journey, from 1 to 10 –
it starts out so well, with the fearless big idea, the ace,
and then* ... She ran through the cards in her head,
trying to find a logic for each one that would bring its
different meanings together. The 6 was pleasant, but
lonely: a journey, and intellectual development – maybe
a discovery, but you don't know about that – a cold river
and a shrouded figure. She glanced down at the river's
icy grey, and back up at Round Hill, and stopped
abruptly, shaken by déjà vu. She walked this route every
day, but something felt so strange about the view. Had
she dreamt about it the night before? She stood, lost in
thought, staring at the shape of the hill underneath its
irregular clumps of grass and thistle, the sheaf of cards
loose in her hand. The low light seemed eerie now,
making the landscape into a lost and abandoned world.
She shivered, feeling the wind's chill fingers creeping
under her collar. A head suddenly rose into view from
the bank below her, and falling back, she screamed,
cards fluttering around her. Her sharp, stammering cries
dwindled as the man hurried over, exclaiming, 'I'm so
sorry – are you hurt? – oh, dear, your cards!'

He scrabbled around her, picking up the fallen cards.
His black hair flopped over his collar, unkempt and
curly.

'No really, it's my fault.'

'Let me.' He hauled her to her feet as she stumbled over a tangled explanation of her sudden strange mood.

'I sound like an idiot; I guess you just surprised me.'

'No, I know exactly what you mean; this patch always gives me the creeps. I only come here because of these.' He flourished a small, clear bag of weeds. 'They grow especially well here,' he added.

She glanced at the bag and beyond it to the Round Hill again. Her heart was still thumping; the uneasy feeling lingered on.

'Sorry,' she muttered distractedly. 'That hill's still freaking me out. You must think I'm mad. Weeds,' she said, trying to return to the subject at hand in a sensible manner. 'You – um – weed the meadow?'

His blank look of bemusement was met by an equally blank look from her, as they both considered her words. His eyes seemed electric on hers, even through her haze of nerves.

'You're really shaken, aren't you?' he said, after a few seconds' uncomfortable silence.

'Yes.' She gave a forced little laugh. 'I'll get over it.'

'Let me buy you a drink. The Perch is just over there, you can warm up and calm down a bit. I'm Adrian, by the way.'

'Sarah.'

She followed him through the overgrown path, bushes clustering above their heads like a wild, skeletal bower. Twilight had fallen, and she walked half-blindly through the shadows. They emerged abruptly onto an unmown lawn, beyond which stood the strong stone walls of the pub, yellow and orange light spilling comfortingly from its windows. She felt a rush of relief; this is what it must have been like, once, to walk for miles before seeing a human dwelling place. Then there it is – full of people, lively fireplaces; the little circles of light we make in the darkness of nature. As the door opened and the music spilled out into the night, life seemed to resume its normal pace.

With a whisky each, they sat down and he laid her cards out, dusting the dirt off each one. 'They're a beautiful set,' he said, lifting the Queen to admire it. 'It's the Marseilles deck, isn't it?'

'I believe so. A friend gave them to me – I don't really know much about it.'

'Well, this is pretty much the most classic set you can have. I've got the World Tarot, which has drawings for all the pip cards – it's helpful, but also sort of limiting, sometimes.'

He pushed the cards back over the table to her. 'I shouldn't really handle them, it's your deck.'

'I don't mind.' In the light, he was even more handsome than he'd looked on the path – although beautiful was a more apt word. His features were both delicate and strong at the same time, finely formed. 'The rest of the set is here, if you want to see.'

'I'll show you mine if you'll show me yours,' he said, winking. She flushed. Now that she could see him properly, she wasn't quite sure what to do with her hands. She began to shuffle the swords back into the deck, to cover her embarrassment. Soon, though, as they compared cards, she forgot her awkwardness. He seemed to know the cards so much better than she did; the book's explanations were trite in comparison.

'I'll tell you the story of the Major Arcana, shall I?' he said, after they'd played with the lower cards for a while.

'There's a story?'

'Oh, yes, it's a good one.' His face brightened with enthusiasm.

She fetched a bottle of wine from the bar while he arranged them in order. Settling down for her story, she felt cosy and comfortable as a child.

'Are you sitting comfortably?'

She filled their glasses. 'Now I am.'

'Then I shall begin.'

The story was the Fool's journey through the other twenty-one major cards, and as he talked he made the Fool bounce along the table, acting out snippets with the salt and pepper cellars. She recognised the usual elements of a spiritual journey; she knew enough of the myths and the tales of the saints. The way he told it, though, it stayed vividly alive, richly embroidered with details and characters conjured up out of thin air. He held a particularly touching scene between the salt and the pepper, as the salt finally resolved to leave the pepper behind and follow the Fool across the seas.

'That's heartbreaking!' she exclaimed, as the pepper collapsed weeping over the ashtray. 'The salt belongs with the pepper!'

'It's Helen of Troy all over again,' he said with mock sadness. 'But these two end up much happier.'

And so they did. By the time the story was over, the wine was almost gone, and Sarah had the warm glow of both wine and a happy ending. She looked round the pub in contentment, thinking of the work she hadn't done that evening, and rested her eyes with pleasure on Adrian's face.

'Why are all the thinking cards so gloomy?' she said. 'They all are – almost all the swords, and the Major Arcana ones – and I'm having much more fun here than I would be studying, and I love studying . . .'

'Thinking is gloomy, on its own.'

'It didn't use to feel that way.' She dug her nail into the soft, thick varnish of the table, idly clearing out one of the cracks. 'I liked it more, before. It felt more alive. But now my work's just – oh, I don't know. I don't like my supervisor, much.'

'Who is he?'

'Dr Piedmont, he's at Christ Church –'

'I know,' interrupted Adrian, grimacing. 'He's my college supervisor. I don't blame you, there's no reason to like him. At least you don't have to worry about him giving you the come-on all the time.'

'What?' yelped Sarah in surprise. 'He does that to you, too?'

Adrian raised his eyebrows expressively. 'Maybe he likes it both ways. Or maybe I'm just imagining things, but I could swear he's trying to – to get at me.'

'I wasn't sure if I was imagining it. It's all these things that you wouldn't mind, or even notice, from someone else – he's just a creep.'

'No wonder you're off your work,' said Adrian, sympathetically. 'At least I only have him for pastoral care, and I damn well wouldn't approach him with my problems.'

'Yes.' said Sarah slowly, beginning an excavation of another table crack. 'But it's not just him. It's my own work, too. It just feels a bit – dry, at the moment. All the thinking. That's why I like the tarot cards, they're relaxing, I can just sort of feel my way through them, without backing everything up all the time with footnotes.'

'Thinking needs balancing out,' he said. Without lifting his eyes to hers, he slipped his warm hand around hers, stilling her nervous scratching. His fingers wrapped around, fitting snugly. 'It needs balancing with feeling. Thinking and feeling – they give each other peace.'

She sat in silence, absorbing the warmth of his hand, hearing the words of the cheap pop music that had been playing since they'd walked in. Like a teenager, she felt every pore on his hand pressed quiveringly against hers. Like an established lover, she drew peace and calm from the skin clasped to hers.

Abruptly, he snatched his hand away and lifted his

wine glass. 'The thing about the tarot is,' he began arbitrarily.

'Adrian! I thought you were savaging the meadow tonight! You should've come to the movie, it was great.'

A trustafarian slung her shabby-chic purse onto the table, kissed Adrian loudly on the lips, and sat down. Sarah took in her elaborately thrown-together outfit, and tensed with instant dislike.

'Hi!' exclaimed Adrian enthusiastically, 'What are you doing here? This is Sarah – Sarah, Clara.' He waved his wine glass too enthusiastically with the introductions, and spattered the cards. 'Oh, shit, sorry.'

'Don't worry,' muttered Sarah, drying them with her scarf.

Clara looked down at the tarot pack. 'Oh, God, you're not another occult dabbler, are you?' She laughed briefly. 'I keep telling Adrian what nonsense it is, but he won't listen to me. So – how do you two know each other?'

That was quick. The fur on your back is standing straight up, honey, thought Sarah spitefully.

She matched Clara's bright fake smile as she said casually, 'Oh, we just ran into each other on the river bank and decided to get a drink.'

'I knocked all her cards into the mud,' added Adrian hurriedly, 'and gave her the fright of her life. I was hidden from view, collecting moly,' he showed the bag, as evidence, 'and when I stood up she got a fright. It seemed only gentlemanly to get her a drink to calm her nerves.'

Clara's eyes flicked over to the bottle of wine, almost empty, the wine glasses, and the two empty tumblers.

'You must have been quite shaken up,' she said sweetly to Sarah.

'Well, it's not every day,' Sarah replied blandly.

'Anyway, listen, darling,' she said, turning back to Adrian. 'I spoke to Daddy about the flat this evening, and he said it sounds absolutely fine – it'll be a sound investment, because once we leave it can be rented out to a family or to students, it'll do well for either. He's coming up to Oxford tomorrow to sort out the deal, and wants to take us round his old haunts. You know what he's like, "in my day this", "in my day that".'

Why don't you just piss on him to mark your territory?

'That sounds great,' said Adrian feebly.

'And he said not to worry about your fees, he's happy to make up whatever the scholarship falls short of.'

'Look, we've spoken about that,' said Adrian sharply, and glanced at Sarah. 'But it's not the time to discuss it now. Can I get you a drink?'

'I don't know, can you?'

Adrian stood up, glanced in his wallet, and swore under his breath. 'Actually, I can't,' he said with a wry smile, his charm briefly reasserting itself. 'Sorry.'

'Oh never mind, I'll get it.' Clara flounced off to the bar, her antique satin purse under her arm.

Sarah fixed Adrian with her gaze, and raised her eyebrows. 'Well,' she said quietly. 'It was nice meeting you, but I think I'd better leave you two lovebirds alone.' She stood up, shoving her things in her handbag.

'Sarah – hold on, I'm sorry!' He glanced over his shoulder at the bar, where Clara was tapping her credit card impatiently. 'I had no idea she was going to come here.'

'Whereas *I* had no idea she existed,' replied Sarah sharply, 'which I'm sure you did.' She restrained a pointed reference to Daddy's flat.

'It's really not what it looks like – I had no intention, I mean I didn't mean to – I didn't plan . . .'

'Whatever. It doesn't matter. Bye.' She strode quickly to the door, before the crumpling of her features could be observed, and stormed into the darkness.

* * *

She had walked for about five minutes before she stopped and looked around. *Back in the darkness of nature, outside the small circle of light.* In the moonlight, the quiet road lay dark grey between the black shapes of trees, beneath the pitch black hollows of space. She strained her ears, but heard neither traffic nor people. Less certainly, she walked onwards, feeling as if she had been airlifted to the depths of the countryside. Was she walking towards Oxford or away? Where the hell was she? She couldn't go back into the pub and ask – Adrian and Clara would still be there. The more she studied the deep shadows that lined the road, the more fear danced through her. Was pride, and a silly muddle about a man she'd just met, going to get her killed? She pulled out her mobile and scrolled through the names, looking for someone who could rescue her. She paused at Tim's name – but what would she say? She hadn't spoken to him for three weeks, not since the bizarre drinking party. Perhaps if she retraced her steps, she could skirt around the pub and get back to Port Meadow. She thought of the mound on the far side of the river, and felt a chill of terror run through her again. No. However irrational, she couldn't face that oddly familiar, frightening sight by starlight. That left only forwards, and for all she knew she'd be walking to Banbury. Better to go back to the pub, wait outside, and fall in with another group of people, ask directions and hopefully walk through the dark with them. She turned, feeling her heart thud heavily against her ribs to have the unknown country road lying behind her. I mustn't look round, she thought as she walked, I mustn't run, it'll only make it worse. She couldn't see the pub yet; surely she hadn't walked that far? The narrative of nightmare came to her – a pub in the middle of nowhere, never seen before, appearing just once and then vanishing, leaving her in a strange land, walking a road that could lead anywhere. She almost choked to hear footsteps crunching the gravel ahead of her – then the comfortable slam of an expensive car door, and the quiet purr of the engine starting. The pub came into view, its cosy windows still lit up, and people trickling out the door. Her fear drained away, though her heart still pounded at the sight of Adrian stepping out after Clara. Neither looked happy. Clara was standing with her arms folded, staring at him, while the front yard emptied of cars and people. Sarah watched them through the trees.

'Now can I fucking speak?' she said, as the last couple drove away. 'Now that I won't be causing a scene?' Her voice was spiked with spite.

'Clara,' he said wearily.

'Don't you Clara me! One bloody evening I leave you alone and you rush off to pick up whoever you can find! Any shabby old cow will do, it seems.'

He opened his mouth angrily, but she leapt in before he could speak.

'Oh, yes, leap to the defence of your new-found fuck, it would be so gentlemanly.'

'Look,' he said through gritted teeth. 'I've said I'm sorry. All we did was talk, I swear it.'

'And hold hands.'

'Yes, OK, I took her hand, we were talking about supervisor troubles, it wasn't...'

'Give me your keys.'

'What?'

'I said, give me your keys. I don't give a shit who you sleep with, but it won't be with me.'

'You are not going to chuck me out in the middle of the night,' he said in disbelief.

She stood with her hand peremptorily stretched out. Wordlessly, he fished in his pockets, removed two keys, and dropped them in her palm.

'You can pick up your stuff tomorrow,' she said, marching to the little sports car.

'This is ridiculous. Clara . . .'

She had already slammed the car door. Revving furiously, she spun it round. As it turned the curve, Sarah was outlined in the floodlights and ugly rage crossed Clara's face – she jabbed her fingers in the air, and tyres screaming, roared away.

Into the stillness that followed, Sarah's voice said quietly, 'Adrian?' She stepped into his line of vision. He looked at her blankly.

'I'm sorry – I didn't mean to eavesdrop – I got lost.'

'I guess you heard it all, then.'

'I came back to ask directions – but I didn't want you two to see me.' She walked a little closer.

'I don't understand her. I mean, yes, it looked a bit compromising, but . . .' He shook his head in bewilderment.

'I didn't make things easier, did I?' she said regretfully.

He shrugged. 'No reason why you should've.' He stared at the gravel for a while longer. Sarah waited quietly. A gust of wind caught at her neck, and she shivered.

'Sorry,' he said, shaking himself out of it. 'You need directions, don't you? It's just back through Port Meadow, the way we came, you know.'

'I know.' She watched him, a dark, cultivated figure standing against the old stone. Behind him, the lights were being flicked off one by one. 'I – the thing is – I was scared,' she finished lamely. 'That bit, the one where I met you, with the mound.' She shuddered, 'I couldn't bear the thought of walking past it in the dark. God, I'm pathetic.'

'No, you're not. Like I said, I know what you mean.

How about we walk past together?' He extended his arm, and she slipped her gloved hand onto it. Despite everything, it still felt instantly right there, and she smiled involuntarily as she looked up at him.

'Come on,' he said with a wry chuckle.

They walked without comment past that chance configuration of landscape that gave both of them so much unease, though he covered her fingers with his other hand and squeezed them. Their footsteps fell in time, their strides evenly matched. She watched the ground swing past to their steady march. *We are the trees and the path is the river rushing by.* She wanted to repeat it to him, but silence had fallen comfortably around them, and her mouth stayed closed. Only when they turned towards town did she speak.

'I'm actually heading in the wrong direction – I live up the Banbury Road.'

'I'm sorry,' he said, coming out of his own trance. 'I was automatically walking this way.'

She opened her mouth to ask where he lived, and remembered abruptly that wherever it was, he was unwelcome there.

'Look,' she said instead, quietly. 'I did hear what Clara said – if you need somewhere to stay, I have a spare room.'

He was silent for so long that she wondered if he had heard.

'I was thinking,' he said at last, 'that if I wanted to sort things out with her that would be the worst possible idea.'

Sarah blanched, and began to apologise.

'No – shhh,' he said. 'I was just trying to work out if it actually mattered or not. I mean – I should be a little more heartbroken, shouldn't I?'

'And you're not?'

'Well, it's certainly a bit inconvenient ... oh dear, I

guess that means no.' He laughed ruefully. 'I was thinking of crashing in the common room and hoping the
scouts wouldn't notice, but the offer of a bed is very
tempting.'

'And scaredy-cat over here wouldn't mind being
walked all the way home,' added Sarah. The idea of him
in the house, of falling asleep with his presence nearby,
warmed her.

'If you're sure it's no trouble . . .'

'Of course not. The house is huge, actually.'

Sarah sat in Duke Humphrey's, comparing Rolle's *Incen-
dium* with Misyn's English translation, and trying not
to think of Adrian. 'Allone sothely sal he sytt,' she read,
'with odyr not syngand, ne psalms rede . . .' It seemed to
be advocating something akin to Gnosticism, or even a
Protestant independence of the Church – no, closer to
Gnosticism – 'not ilk man þus suld do' – not for everyone, this life of contemplation.

She had put Adrian, to her mild astonishment, in a
spare room. Not Mother's old room, of course, but the
room opposite it, so that he and she slept like mirror
images in the symmetrical halves of the house. She felt
no trace of awkwardness, making up the bed and pro-
viding him with a baggy T-shirt to sleep in and a towel
for the morning. The idea that they ought to sleep
together, as they had the opportunity, had vanished
during the walk back through the dark shadows of Port
Meadow. Nevertheless, lying in her own bed, she had
felt his warmth and the shape of his body through the
walls, as if her skin were equipped with infrared. She
had wondered whether he might roam in his sleep. Each
creak in the old floorboards had seemed to herald the
tentative opening of her door – a whispered word.

Abruptly, she dragged her mind back to the text at
hand. Where was she? 'not ilk man þus suld do, bot he

to qwhome it is gyffen, & qwhat hym likys lat hym fulfill, for of þe holy goste he is led' What him likes, let him fulfil, for of the holy ghost he is led. He hadn't come corridor-creeping in the night, though she had twitched awake with every familiar squeak and murmur of the house settling down to its sleep. This morning, they had shared an early coffee, exchanged mobile numbers, and he had gone to 'sort something out'. Whether that meant an alternative place to stay or his relationship with Clara she wasn't sure. What him likes, let him fulfil, and he hadn't, so perhaps that meant he didn't like. Yet neither had she, and she most certainly did like. She blamed the house. Despite the party and the scene with the medic in the past, last night it had seemed too formal and proper a setting for random sex – no, that wasn't quite it. The house had seemed relaxed and lovely, and had made a quick shag seem like ugly, soulless fornication. What was it Jo had said about the devil's kind of sex? Then again, he had also said she was a witch.

For the third time that morning, she found herself staring out at the pale blue light and thin sunshine dancing greenly gold on the bare branches outside. She reeled her attention back in, and transfixed her gaze on the pages. This time, she managed slightly better. The rich smell of books, quiet coughs of students, shuffling steps of the librarian, and hissing scratch of her pencil on paper, mingled with her thoughts which at last began to dance through the intricate steps of academic argument. The silvery-grey pencil lead shone under the glow of the table lamp; the tiny hairs at the back of her neck teased her nape in the irregular, warm breeze.

'Sarah.'

She spun her head at the soft whisper. No one was behind her. At the end of the corridor, she could see the librarian quietly talking to someone; no doubt a brief sibilance had caught her attention. She resumed her reading and scratching.

'Sarah.'

She heard it again, hardly a breath but distinctly her name. Her spine stiffened. The librarian and the other student had left her section; no one was in sight. She looked cautiously around her, up at the ceiling, and even – feeling foolish – under the table. Leaning over her books again, she couldn't move her eyes from one word to the next. The hairs on her arm stood upright. She waited.

'Sarah.'

Soft and sourceless though the voice was, it was also familiar. Glancing around her again, she whispered herself. 'Jo?' No reply came. The warm breeze tickled the back of her neck again. Feeling sick, she wondered if she'd ever felt it before. She always sat in the same place, in the library. She always noticed the tiny textures, views, shades of light, and experiences of her studies – they were her sensory mnemonics. It was possible she hadn't noticed a tiny draught. A tiny, warm, localised draught in the middle of February when the air outside was suddenly sharp enough to pinch one's fingers in the morning.

She took her hands off her papers. 'Jo,' she said, her vocal chords hardly stirring, 'if that's you, move the papers on my desk.'

Impenetrable silence seemed to have settled over the library as she stared at the sheets before her. One of them fluttered at the corner. It's the draught, she thought; we all experiment with the supernatural, but most of us give it up when we're still teenagers. The sheet of paper shifted briskly half a foot across the desk, and the pencil rose into the air. With a shriek, Sarah flung her chair backwards, the pencil fell, feet padded

swiftly towards her, and the librarian rounded the corner, wearing an outraged expression.

'Sorry.' Sarah mouthed. The librarian frowned at her,
scowled, gave an especially stern look, and disappeared
behind the shelves again. The pencil still lay on the
floor, near her feet. She stared at it. The hexagonal strip
of wood, striped red and black, was motionless. The
thought of picking it up made her sick. Its fractional
weight threatened to sit heavier than mercury between
her fingers. With her eyes frozen on it, her stomach still
twisted with fright, she wondered how heavy it must
be from – from the other side, was that what one said?

'I'm sorry,' she mouthed, this time to the empty air
around her. 'If – if you are Jo, can you try again?'

Everything around her remained motionless, obeying
the simplest laws of physics in which she believed, plain
Newtonian law. Things don't move unless you make
them. Then again, she reasoned, there were perhaps
other aspects of physics that she didn't know, which
could make pencils move, and lift from the ground,
untouched, which could make them float in clear air,
and shift to an oblique angle, pencil lead pointing
downwards.

Her fear, like a wild-eyed nostril-flaring stallion,
danced while she strained to hold it in check. 'How do I
know you're Jo?' she croaked almost inaudibly.

The pencil drifted to the paper, and began to jerk. In
beautiful old script, appeared the words, 'You know I'm
Jo, because I know you enjoy a sound spanking, my
dear.'

She stared at them, wondering if they would disappear later on, leaving her with only the fear of madness.
Was she writing them herself by some ghastly power of
mind? Only she and Jo knew she liked spanking, and
she wasn't even so sure. She kept her chair pushed well

back against the shelves, with a superstitious dread of the space near the pencil.

'Why can't I see you?'

The pencil moved again, swifter this time. 'How often have you seen me? When last did you see me? When shall you see me again? For both our sakes, think!'

The last word was underscored heavily, the pencil clicked down, and what she could only call a sense of presence vanished. The words, however, remained.

4 **Netzach**

Sarah sat on the steps of the Bodleian, staring out at the King's Arms across the road, smoking a brand new pack of cigarettes. She hardly used the lighter she'd bought, lighting each from the previous one in relentless self-suffocation. When had she seen Jo? Why was it for anyone's sake? Anyway, how could anything harm him if he was a – oh God, she really had slept with a ghost. She'd put that whole stupid night out of mind, attributing it to the overly-intense conversations one has after a bucket of mysterious punch and a superfluous bottle of wine. She felt sick, stubbed out the cigarette on the chilled, pocked stone next to her feet, and immediately lit another. *When had she seen Jo?*

She'd met him when she was walking back from dinner with her supervisor. She'd felt an odd urge for a cigarette, and asked him for one. She'd wanted one because her supervisor's rudeness had upset her. Well, his rudeness and his attractiveness, to be honest, but the attractiveness didn't count because she'd been ovulating. It had been dark – no, not quite dark; she remembered the clouds whipping past the full moon, a ghostly galleon indeed.

She'd seen him the night of the All Souls' party; he'd persuaded her to run away from the party and convinced her that she'd been talking to the devil, just because she'd been horny enough to find an old man sexy. They had dashed home in the bright moonlight. He said she'd been fed a lust potion. She'd counted afterwards, and realised she'd just been ovulating; the lust potion was nonsense.

She'd been ovulating. She ovulated with the full moon. She hadn't wanted sex last night; something in her body had felt calm, quiet, and safe; something in her had said wait. Wait until you're fertile. When was full moon? She dug in her bag for her diary, cigarette clenched awkwardly between her lips.

'Sara, isn't it?' She looked up, and saw the immaculately made-up and immaculately shabby Clara standing in front of her, featuring a Christmas tree's worth of layered baubles around her neck. A black headband completed the faux-twenties look.

'It's Sarah,' she said, pulling the cigarette clumsily from her lips. The filter clung for a millisecond, tugging her mouth into a brief, lopsided pout.

'Ya,' said Clara briskly, flaring her hand. 'Anyway, so glad I ran into you, it saves me a trip to Christ Church. Could you give these to Adrian, please.' From her voluminous beaded bag she pulled a toiletries case. 'His razor and things.'

Sarah stared at her. 'Look,' she said flatly, 'I don't know what Adrian told you, but I'm not particularly expecting to see him and I certainly don't need his razor in my bathroom.'

Clara maintained a sceptical look, still holding the bag out. Sarah's phone began to twitter in her bag. She pulled it out. 'Just give it to him yourself, will you? I've got nothing to do with it.' She turned her head, pressed answer hastily, and purred, 'Hello?' in a fruitless attempt to seem cooler than Clara.

'Adrian!' she yelped. 'Um, hi. Fine, thanks – just taking a break from the Bodleian. Yeah. Oh, right. Yes. Yes, of course you can, no trouble at all.' His voice was as warm as she remembered it, and Clara's eyes were cold steel daggers. She looked down at her cigarette stubs instead, shading her face with her hand. 'Of course

I don't mind. Yes. Oh, how about . . . shit, um, look, can I ring you back? Just give me five minutes.'

She looked up, but Clara had vanished, leaving the toiletries bag on the steps.

At her writing desk, Sarah shuffled the tarot cards endlessly as the day turned the room dark, first with clouds and then with twilight. As the cards skipped from palm to palm, she tried to phrase a proper question in her head, without success. She couldn't work out how they could answer a question like 'Is Jo a ghost?', but what else could she ask? The full moon was ten days away, so perhaps she should just wait to find out. Then again, he might deliberately visit her on that day so she would think he was a ghost. Nonsense, she told herself. Either you briefly went mad and wrote the words yourself, or he is – dead. A roaming spirit. With a penchant for spanking. Did she like it? It had certainly made her come wildly. She felt her inner muscles twitch sharply at the memory, and then relax slowly and sensuously. Spattered streaks of rain appeared on the window, increasing steadily until the front garden was veiled in streaming grey. The car lights of the afternoon school run showed the water dancing on the tar as they approached, and then the car would appear briefly in the gap between the hedges, leaving behind a cloud of mist and shooting splashes. She stared out, lost in thought, the cards resting in her hands. Another car passed, illuminating the dark, angular silhouette of a man, stooped over the front gate. Sarah gasped in fright, her hairs prickling as the figure unlatched the gate – and then, as he bent down to pick up a collection of shopping bags, she recognised him.

'Adrian, you're soaked!' she exclaimed as she opened the door. Water ran in rivulets over his face and down the open neck of his shirt. His thick black hair was plastered on his cheeks as if it had been painted on. His jaw was covered in light stubble. He laughed, and she felt her eyes flare with admiration. She shouldn't be alone in the same house as this man.

'I sort of noticed that,' he said. 'But I come bearing gifts.' He gestured the bulging bags in his hands. 'It's market day, so I thought the least I could do was cook you supper.' He sat down on the bench to pull off his wet shoes and socks. 'This hall's chilly,' he said, wincing as his bare feet touched the stone slabs. 'Good place to keep your cooking apples.'

'I don't have any.'

'Oh yes, you do.' He nudged one of the lumpier carrier bags with his foot. 'They were practically giving them away, I tried to pay twice the price, because I couldn't carry two bags full. But they weren't having it, if it's a quid for two bags then you're having two bags, like it or not.'

'Would you like a shower, to warm up? I'll get you a towel.'

'That sounds like heaven. I could do with a shave, too,' he added wryly. 'I'm really sorry about that, by the way. I wouldn't wish Clara in a strop on my worst enemy.'

The house seemed to mould around Adrian as if he were a part of it. Whistling in the shower, laying groceries out on the kitchen table, chopping vegetables with an apron wrapped around him, he seemed to belong there completely. Sarah sat on the counter, sipping the wine he'd brought and watching him cook. She felt completely relaxed with him, most of the time, but every time he looked in her eyes it seemed to last a second too long, and she had to look down to break it off. When she looked at the nape of his neck, beneath curling fronds of hair, or at his arms emerging from his T-shirt sleeves, she didn't know what to do with her hands.

Sitting opposite him at the dining-room table, she felt shyer still. Candlelight sparkled on the array of cutlery at each place. The tablecloth matched the wine-coloured walls, and she'd even found white linen napkins in the sideboard. The meal he was making seemed to deserve a proper setting, but the soft lighting and music suddenly embarrassed her.

'I hope this isn't too formal,' she said, 'I thought . . .'

'It's perfect. Good food should be enjoyed in proper style. These are some of my favourite dishes, I figured I should make you something I know will turn out alright.'

The food was more than just good; he really did know how to cook. He served her asparagus spears, then a gorgeous creamy risotto with mushrooms and blue cheese, roasted pine nuts sprinkled on top, and finally pears baked in red wine.

'How did you learn to cook so well?' Sarah asked, lifting a glistening spoonful of crimson, spiced pear.

'I just love it,' he said, shrugging. 'And most of it's plants, which are kind of my speciality, anyway.'

'Does the whole botany faculty cook like this? Your faculty parties must be amazing!'

He laughed. 'Nah, it's – well, I mean, I really am a bit obsessed with plants. Not just academically acceptable botany, but all the other stuff as well – the meanings, the old uses, the folklore about them. You can make really amazing food when you try combining the meanings of plants, rather than just thinking in terms of flavour.'

'So what do the pears mean?'

'OK – red wine, cinnamon, nutmeg, vanilla pod, and honey – nutmeg and cinnamon are both stimulating, nutmeg's actually a hallucinogenic, if you take enough of it, but this is just a tiny bit. Chinese women used to use it as an aphrodisiac.'

'Is it one?' She took another small mouthful and rolled it around on her tongue, tasting all the different flavours he'd mentioned.

'It's a stimulant, so yes, most stimulants are. Not rosemary, though, because that also sharpens your thinking.'

'Is that a bad thing?'

He smiled sheepishly. 'Well, there's a time and a place ... What you really want is something warming, calming, and stimulating.'

'Like nutmeg.'

'Yeah, or cinnamon, vanilla, red wine ...'

She raised her eyebrows. 'Quite a dessert, then.' Whether it was the effect of the spices, or just of the regularly refilled wine glass, her veins were starting to tingle with life. She wasn't sure, in the dim light, if he were blushing or not, but his expression suggested he was. 'What about the others then?'

He thought about it for a moment, looking up in concentration, and then sank his face into his hands, hiding a broad, embarrassed smile.

'Oops,' he said, muffled by his fingers, and then looked up. The word aphrodisiac seemed to be curling around the air, floating in serif, as his eyes, dark and shining with reflected candlelight, met hers. She didn't dare look away too abruptly, but holding his gaze was even worse.

'What ...' She stopped, and cleared her throat. 'What's the oops for?'

'The asparagus, the white wine in the risotto, the pine nuts, are all pretty – umm – they're on the same list. I swear it wasn't intentional, I just bought nice things at the market.'

'It's OK.' She laughed a little, and found she was

almost trembling. Plants and cooking had seemed a fairly safe conversation.

'You don't mind?' His tone was hesitant. Was he asking for reassurance about the meal, or something else? She hardly knew him, but she realised suddenly that she didn't mind. His beauty took her breath away, and it still felt familiar, as if she had looked at and adored his face for years. Having an elaborate love-spell served in three courses seemed beautiful, not a cheap ploy.

'I'll make some coffee,' he said. 'Shall we drink it in the lounge?'

He left the room quickly, and her heart sank. He wanted to sober up and get out of the candlelight. She bit her lip, suppressing her disappointment, and forcing herself to think sensible thoughts. She should clear the table, not sit here like a dejected stray. She stood up, and started gathering the dishes. He popped his head back in.

'Would you mind taking the candles through?'

A bright smile lit her face. 'Sure, no problem.'

She could hear him in the kitchen, grinding the beans and lighting the stove. She moved quickly, trying to light all the candles and dim the light before he came in. Glancing around in satisfaction, she flicked the switch. The flames crackled quietly. Music! Quickly, she switched the light on again and flicked through her CDs. Having music already playing was somehow acceptable, but being caught putting it on was too obvious. She pressed play, turned the light off again, and sat down on the sofa. After a few minutes, she felt she was sitting like a patient in a doctor's waiting room, and crossed her legs. That seemed contrived, and she uncrossed them, shifted angle a few times, and settled for tucking her legs underneath her.

'Comfortable?'

He was standing in the doorway, holding two espresso cups, watching her. Her face caught fire with shame, which she hoped it was too dark to see.

'My secret recipe,' he said, handing her a cup.

'Coffee beans and water?' she said, meaning to be flippant but sounding hostile to her own ears.

'Smell it.' He sat down right next to her.

She lifted the cup, and let the fragrant steam drift up her nostrils. It reminded her of mulled wine, in a way. She tried to separate out the smells, and couldn't.

'What's in it?'

He clinked his cup gently against hers, and said, 'That's why it's a secret.'

She took a tentative sip. 'There's chocolate in here!'

'Pure and dark and savoury. The real stuff.'

She let it linger on her tongue, which began to tingle and almost burn. 'It's – it almost stings, it's – spicy! What is it?'

'My grandmother's recipe. "Love" coffee. Seeing as I've already filled you with aphrodisiacs all evening, I thought I may as well be hung for a sheep as a lamb.' He paused, and ran his sentence through his head. 'Bad choice of words. But great coffee.'

'I thought you were regretting it and trying to sober me up,' Sarah heard herself say.

He turned his head towards her, and fire seemed to leap in his eyes.

'Are you mad?' His voice was quiet, and rasped a little over the word 'mad'. They stared at each other, motionless. Dance me to your beauty, sang Leonard Cohen's bass voice in the frozen silence. The lyrics spun on, painfully clear. She searched for something to say, in a tone between hardened flirtation and soppy ramblings, but could find nothing. He looked away first, and drank again. She looked down into the small black well of her own cup.

'I feel like I know you,' he said, staring at the fireplace. 'I know I want you,' – for a searing instant his eyes returned to hers – 'but I also feel like I know you.'

'I know what you mean,' she said, and then floundered for words again. Describing the intense feeling of him belonging in the house would be too much – the hackneyed phrase she'd just said was too little.

He rested his cup on the table, turned around, and took hers from her hand as well. Her hand was shaking; she dropped it to her lap. He drew his fingers slowly down the side of her face, and her lips parted, longing to be touched. The soft pads of his fingertips explored her features, drifting ever closer to her mouth. Their eyes were locked on each other's. One finger lightly skimmed her lower lip, and the already unbearable yearning was tripled. She wanted his finger in her mouth, but already it was trailing along her jaw again. All her being seemed concentrated on that one, small thing, that overwhelming need, to have her lips and moist tongue fastened sensuously around his finger.

At last, his hand found her mouth again, and she tasted his skin luxuriously. As her suckling mouth tugged at his finger, the hot ache in her groin deepened and her breasts cried out for his touch. A groan escaped his lips. She whimpered in reply. His free hand found the edge of her blouse, and traced the deep, narrow V, following the curve of her skin. Her gasp released his other hand. Still drinking from her eyes, he unfastened every button, and then his eyes shifted as he slowly parted the curtain of fabric. The deep swell of cleavage was alive with goose bumps and her nipples stood up hard through her bra. His hands danced in slow motion with the music, touching the tender skin beneath her collar bone and gradually, with feathery touches, finding his way nearer to those two taut epicentres. When he reached the edge of her bra cups, he slipped his arms around her in a smooth-skinned embrace and loosened the clasp behind her back. She gave a small sob as the bra fell slowly down, catching on her nipples. Her breasts had never felt so bare as they did then, with the feeling of fabric sliding off still fresh on her skin. Still, he didn't touch her nipples, but circled them slowly with his fingers, and ran the backs of his nails up her sides.

'I'm not sure we should be doing this,' he muttered huskily.

In reply, she reached for the edges of his T-shirt and pulled it slowly over his head. She watched in fascination as his smooth chest was exposed, his muscles tight and compact, his own nipples crinkled. She bent down, and took one in her mouth, exploring the small hard nub of flesh with her tongue.

'Sarah, please . . .' he whispered, 'I don't want to take advantage – of – uh – the situation . . .'

His words faltered as her lips nuzzled. The smell of his skin made her hungry for more, and she suckled more eagerly, tasting the edge of salt and arousal in his pores. Pushing his hips away from her, she lay along the sofa, her mouth clasped to his breast, her own breasts invitingly close to his face. He blasphemed softly as he pressed his cheeks between their inviting softness. Lifting her mouth a moment, she murmured, as she remembered Jo saying, 'Neither God nor the Devil can touch us here. They have no rule in this house.'

'Who does?' His words were a muffled groan against her firm, yielding skin.

'I do,' she said, sinking her teeth onto his chest, nipping him lightly. He wailed in shock, and then she squealed, as his teeth found her nipples. All carefulness, all gentleness, was forgotten. Savagely, they bit into each other, rubbed their faces over the aching sensitive flesh, and suckled as hungrily and fiercely as babies, remembering long-forgotten rhythms. She needed him; her veins thrummed with longing. The intensity was too much to even tear off his clothes and pull him into her. She had to take everything she could now, give everything she could, as they were. Curled in the foetal position, in mirror images, their mouths were drinking straight from each other's hearts and still it wasn't enough. Her nails dug into the small of his back to pull her along his body, and sink her face into the heat of his crotch. Her hips lay in front of his face, and he groaned deep in his throat. Clutching handfuls of her long skirt, he hauled it above her hips and her cleft lay bare to his view. She scrabbled at his jeans as she felt his mouth close on her full lips. The scent of his groin was intoxicating her. She could see the tight seams straining around the hard protrusion, as she fumbled at the buttons. At last, she ripped them open, pulled his boxers down, and his cock sprang out. His tongue was running over the length of her slit, up and down, again and again. His hips strained towards her mouth. With one movement, she pushed his jeans down his thighs and lowered her mouth onto him. As he felt the succulent warmth engulf him, he slid his tongue inside, to touch her delicate bead. Her clasping lips and busy tongue slithered up and down him, tasting the sweet stickiness at the top and coating his shaft with slippery saliva. He was lapping deftly at her, gliding his tongue between her lips to taste her juice, and returning to the sensitive tip. She kept her thighs close together and relished the slow agony of lust building inside her. Even so, she pressed her hips closer and closer to him, and with each movement took him deeper. She tipped her head, the better to swallow his thick member. Wrapping his arms around her legs, he forced his palms between them and slowly spread her open.

For a few moments, he lay still, his senses overwhelmed. His nostrils and taste buds were full of her juice, his cock strained in the slick grip of her throat, her flowery folds were exposed to his eyes, her intermittent whimpers of bliss sounded in his ears. He lowered his mouth slowly again. His hand fanned, and two fingers probed at the small, moist aperture. As the opening yielded to and clutched at his digits, her mouth released him and she howled in delight. That animal sound sent a new wave of lust rolling over him. Swiftly, he swung astride her and lay pressed against her, feeling her breasts crushed under his hard stomach. With his mouth drawing furiously on the sweetness of her clitoris, he dug into her with his hand, and played her screams of bliss like a violin. Wild with ecstasy, her lips darted all over him. She licked at his balls, tongued his shaft, nibbled his glans, clutched his thighs, and wailed. Her flailing hand found his shaft and grasped it. It felt as firm as a rudder against her palm. While her mouth lapped and sucked at his tip, her fingers slid along the sticky length in a perfect echo of his fingers' rhythm within her. Her thighs spread as far apart as they could, the inner muscles drawn tight. Her hips bucked in time with his.

She could feel the shining ball of gold deep inside her, spreading along her veins like a spider's web. For once, she did nothing to hurry it, just felt it spread and savoured the taste of him wantonly. The pitch of her wails rose. All her body, every vein and muscle and particle of soul, seemed to shimmer in anticipation. Slowly, his fingers withdrew, his mouth lifted. Her mouth and fingers stilled. In silence, he shifted from her. She lay motionless and breathless on the sofa, her thighs still parted, as he stood. Now that the moment was upon her, she felt a thrill of fear that she had never felt before. Her skirt, she realised, was still bunched around her waist. He dragged his jeans off his feet. Bending over her, he pulled her skirt over her head. The intensity of his eyes made her tremble when she met them. Both he and she seemed to be wading through dark gold air in slow motion. The very walls of the room seemed to hum with tension. She watched, frozen and burning, as he knelt between her widespread legs and leant slowly forwards. His mouth touched hers as that blunt, blind tip touched her entrance. In unison, his tongue and his staff nudged at her different lips. She shuddered, feeling the suspended, shimmering frenzy returning. His lips pressed hard against hers as his flesh fought against the straining passageway. He seemed to be dividing her in two, as his thickness pushed gradually and relentlessly inwards. Her pussy felt as if it were screeching with ecstatic need, her breasts heaved against him, his lips had not yet left hers. Her hips bucked against the unyielding rod, unable to wedge it deeper. Kissing her deeply, he clasped her shoulders tenderly in his hands, and with one hard shove sank fully into her. The uncontrollable yelling of her orgasm was caught in that first, long kiss.

When at last she subsided, they were kissing still. Their tongues entwined languorously. Slowly, he withdrew to half his length, and pushed gradually into her. She received him, deep inside her, with a sensuous moan. Again, he pulled away, and unhurriedly sank to the hilt in her again. Her legs closed beneath him, leisurely, enclosing him even more tightly. Their thighs pressed; their arms wrapped around each other. With each motion, all the skin on her body rubbed smoothly along his. A rich ache built inside her as he kept on grinding slowly. Their breath came faster, they began to pant, their hearts beat furiously against each other's breasts, and still he maintained the same, steady pace on top of her. Each time he drove slowly into her, he seemed to fill her more. All her body was glutted with him, every cell crammed and ready to burst with intensity. Her head swam as she drowned in his kisses. The raging passion was unbearable, his barely controlled thrusts dizzied her. His gasping breath was hot on her cheeks. The pounding of his veins echoed in her ears. She felt something deep, far down in the depths of her, awaken, as she approached the excruciating crux, she began to scream as he did, the sounds lost to her passion-deafened senses. Her whole body clenched his as she reached the summit with him, and sank into unconsciousness.

The room was small and built of rough, untreated wood. Daylight hardly penetrated the gloom. A forest of drying herbs hung from the ceiling, brushing her hair as she pulled her thick skirts up to avoid the mud around the doorway. Despite the dimness, she knew the exact shape of each bunch and each of its leaves – the long, trailing leaves, the tiny spear-like ones, the small serrated ones. Stray fragments crumbled into her hair as she passed, imparting their dusty perfume. She shaded her eyes against the brilliant sunrise with one hand, the other dangling by her side, holding the water jug. Warm, southerly wind lifted tendrils of her hair. Far in the distance, squinting in the light, she could see the breast-shaped rise of Round Hill, and silhouetted against it on the far side of the river, the gilded silhouette of her darling. As she watched, two horse riders cantered up the meadow towards him. In horror, she saw the menacing steeds closing on him. She was sick with dread as she sank to her knees, pulling her fingers through the mud. She felt the grainy muck under her fingernails, but didn't look down; her eyes were fixed on him. Round and round her tracing hands moved, stabbing and smoothing at the wet ground, she had to do it faster – she had to move faster – she was muttering under her breath, she mustn't look away, the bile of fear was rising in her throat . . .

A violent fit of choking ended the murmuring litany. As she spluttered, a warm arm gripped her around the waist, a hand patted her back hard. She drew breath at last, through her gagging coughs, and felt the welcome oxygen spread through her veins.

'You're OK!' she exclaimed, falling into his arms in weak relief. Her head lay against his chest, feeling the warm lifeblood flowing through his skin. 'I was so worried – it was so awful . . .'

'You were worried?' said Adrian in disbelief, tilting her head back to look at her. 'I'm OK? You passed out cold!'

Sarah looked around her in confusion at the spacious room, full of soft furnishings and warmth, with its high ceilings. A few candles still glowed.

'I – had the weirdest dream.' She shuddered. 'It's still with me – it felt so important. You were there, you were in terrible danger, these men with horses were coming for you, but the water was between us and I couldn't do it fast enough.'

'Do what fast enough?'

With his arms wrapped safely around her, the dream was evaporating, shreds of it flying away as her full consciousness returned.

'I don't know – it was important, it was so important.' She shook her head to clear it. 'I had mud under my fingernails.' She examined one hand, half-expecting to see the soil still ingrained.

He was silent, his forehead furrowed.

'Sarah,' he said gently, taking her hand. 'Why did you pass out?'

Suddenly, she was tired to her bones. 'I don't know. I was fine. But I'm so weak now. Come to bed with me?'

Arms around each other's waists, they climbed the stairs naked together, and entwined together under the soft, heavy duvet on her bed.

'Shit! It's out of paper!' Sarah was hopping on one leg, trying to put her tights on and print out her thesis chapter simultaneously.

'I'll do that, you get dressed,' said Adrian.

'Thanks!' She began pulling out the contents of her underwear drawer. 'Have you seen my strapless bra?'

'The one you were wearing yesterday? I think it's in the kitchen.'

They grinned at each other, and Sarah bolted downstairs.

'Where's the paper?' Adrian called after her.

'There should be some in my bag,' she yelled back. She found her bra draped over the fruit bowl and fastened it hastily. What next, what next – make-up. She raced to the bathroom, and started slapping foundation on her face. She heard the printer buzz back into life, and resume churning out pages.

As she finished dressing, it spat the last page out and she seized it, looking for the stapler.

'Give it here,' said Adrian, amused. 'Have you got your gown?'

'Oh yeah!' She slammed coat hangers to either side in the cupboard, and flung on the sleeveless black gown. Adrian pushed the stapled, folded chapter into her handbag and handed it to her.

'Dinner with Dr Piedmont. I wish I didn't have to go.'

'It'll be fine.' He kissed her, blotting her lipstick. She

laughed, as his lips came away crimson. 'It's your territory, remember. Now hurry!'

She scuttled down the stairs, slowed down in the corridor, and catapulted out the house.

Her college held a graduates' dinner each term, to which they were expected – although not obliged – to invite their supervisors. Standing beside him in the dining hall, she deeply regretted having done so, especially when she saw how many of the graduates had invited their partners instead. The chaplain finished muttering the brisk Latin grace, and they sat. A moment later, a pretty, petite girl slipped into the empty place opposite. She was wearing several layers of madly coloured stripy tops and skirts, creating a psychedelic effect.

'Hi Sarah,' she said, her small, heart-shaped face lighting up with a grin.

'The hall allows students in after grace, then?' said Dr Piedmont coldly.

'Oh, we're relaxed here,' she said smiling. 'I'm Henrietta.' The slight sing-song in her voice was all that betrayed her Danish origin.

'This is my supervisor, Dr Piedmont,' said Sarah, after a moment's silence. 'Henrietta's doing a PhD in biochemistry.'

'Any specific area?' Dr Piedmont's tone made the question sound hostile.

'Deadly viruses,' said Henrietta happily, tearing apart a bread roll. 'That's why I'm late – not the kind of thing you can hurry!'

'I see.'

The evening passed with ghastly stiffness on Dr Piedmont's side, and increasingly desperate attempts of Sarah's to maintain a friendly, sociable atmosphere. His previous air of malicious charm had vanished and she hardly knew which was worse.

As final grace finished, he remained standing, saying, 'I really must go now, I have rather a lot to do.'

'Well – if you must,' said Sarah, trying hard to look disappointed.

'I was rather expecting a chapter of your thesis.'

'Oh – yes, here it is.' She fished it out of her handbag, and handed it over.

'I'll be in touch at the beginning of Hilary term.' Without a further word, he left.

'God, he is so cold!' said Henrietta. '"I really must go now," as if you have wasted his time!'

'He's a dickhead,' said Sarah shortly. 'Come on, let's get some more port from the MCR. Can I cadge a cigarette?'

As the second dessert swung underway, Henrietta and Sarah settled on a bench outside. The first half an hour was spent dissecting Dr Piedmont's behaviour, and concluding several times over that he was inexcusably rude.

'I could poison him for you,' offered Henrietta, draining her glass and taking Sarah's to refill. 'What will it be – Ebola?'

'Call me a bluff old traditionalist, but I think I'll stick with the port.'

They giggled.

'More port?' Duncan, one of the MCR members, appeared at their bench with an open bottle. 'Timothy was asking after you,' he said, filling Sarah's glass.

'Oh. How – uh – is he?'

Duncan smiled at her embarrassment. 'Out of luck, by the sounds of things. I believe you don't return his calls?'

Sarah thought guiltily of the missed-call messages on her mobile when she'd been in the library. Mostly she didn't return calls until she got home, to save money, but somehow she never got around to phoning Timothy back.

'I told him he should probably take the hint.' He looked questioningly at her.

'Well – I'm sort of seeing someone, so, I guess . . .' She floundered.

'Say no more. She's seeing rather a lot of someone. I'll let him know.' He chuckled. 'You're better off without him these days, anyway, that society he's joined is making him a right prat.'

Sarah grimaced as he walked on, in search of glasses with too much air in them. 'Duncan!' she called after him, 'Be nice!'

'So who's this? Who're you seeing?' demanded Henrietta. 'You never said anything!'

'It's only been a few days. Six to be exact. I only met him last Tuesday. And he had a girlfriend then. He's – um – staying with me, because his girlfriend threw him out. Oh stop it!' Henrietta was giggling like mad, and Sarah couldn't help laughing as well. 'It's not nearly as bad as it sounds. Well, it probably is, but he's – ooh, he's so yummy!'

'So what do the cards say about him?' Henrietta also read tarot. In fact, since starting, Sarah had been mortified to discover how faddish it was in Oxford.

'I haven't actually asked. I've been – well . . .'

'Too busy finding out about him yourself?' Her friend gave an impish smile. 'Go on then, tell me everything.'

'Well, I have been doing tarot readings, except we read for each other, and I thought if I asked, maybe he'd know. He's very good.'

'I'm sure he is.' Henrietta winked.

'What are you two witches cackling about?' said Duncan, passing by again with the depleted bottle. 'Last dregs?'

They held out their glasses to be topped up.

'What's wrong with being a witch?' said Henrietta.

'Nothing, nothing at all, some of my best friends are witches,' he said jokily. 'Although surely you should be sitting over there, with the bats?' He gestured towards the other quad, where an ivy-covered wall was home to a host of the nocturnal creatures.

'Of course, what are we thinking,' she said, standing. 'Come on, Sarah, and don't forget your broom.'

They walked arm in arm to the other quad, to an empty bench beneath the ivy.

'That's better,' said Henrietta. 'No eavesdroppers.'

'Do you believe in witches?' said Sarah slowly. She hadn't spoken about Jo and what he'd said to anyone, not even Henrietta.

'Flying on broomsticks and wearing pointy hats, no,' she said. They sat quietly, enjoying the silent dark of the quad, and the muted sounds of revelry nearby. Occasionally, a serrated silhouette would swoop over from behind them, and disappear back into the rustling leaves. Henrietta was rolling a cigarette thoughtfully. Her dainty pink tongue licked the edge of it to seal it, and the flare of the lighter illuminated both their faces for a moment.

'But other sorts of witches, maybe,' she said seriously. 'There are too many stories.' She waved her cigarette slowly through the air. 'No smoke without a fire, *ja*.'

'But by that theory, you would have to believe so many things,' said Sarah carefully. 'I mean, I agree with you, but what about fairies – and ghosts.' She was trying to think of patently absurd superstitions. In the confines of the mediaeval quad, however, none of it seemed absurd.

Henrietta shrugged. 'Possibly.'

'But you're a scientist!'

'Sarah – I work with things that are invisible, yes?'

'Yes – but they're real . . .'

'We say this now, because we can see them. But before we couldn't see them, and they did terrible things, and we didn't know why. I know how little we still know. There is too much, we can't say it's not real because we can't prove it. Think of the moon. Lunar, lunacy, an old wives' tale. But now we're starting to find out the old wives were right. The moon does affect us.'

They both looked up at the misshapen, waxing moon in the sky, above the battlements and gargoyles of the gothic building. Sarah shivered.

'I think Oxford affects me. Since I've been here, I feel like there's a – almost a tune, like music I can almost hear but not quite. Sometimes I feel a bit mad, almost.'

Henrietta nodded. 'It's possible. Oxford affecting you, not you being mad. But madness is another thing we don't understand much, anyway. And Oxford – lots of people here have started to believe in the occult. The Society of the Golden Dawn started here. Gravity – magnetism – soil, and its chemical make-up – these are things we don't understand, we just have a handful of formulae. And that's just material things.'

They moved a little closer on the bench, as if afraid of the looming walls around them. The darkness seemed to widen, as Sarah thought of all of Oxford lying beneath it, its silhouettes that had lasted unchanged for centuries, the shape of the ground in Port Meadow, the curving lines of roads and rivers and canals that were easily recognisable on the oldest maps. A bell began to chime midnight, and others took up the refrain, tolling out the notes in different chimes across the city.

'The witching hour,' said Sarah, trying to inject a little levity.

'Not yet,' said Henrietta smiling. 'In five minutes.'

They linked arms, to wait, and laced their fingers together. 'What do you think we'll see?' said Sarah.

Henrietta pressed her fingers to her forehead, as if to concentrate her clairvoyant powers. 'I foresee . . . Duncan, bringing port.'

'Amazing!' he exclaimed. 'Budge up, you two. This is the last bottle, so if you give me bench space I'll share it with you.'

Adrian's hands pushed deep into her muscles, up the length of her bare back.

'Mmm . . .' She sighed with pleasure.

'Your shoulders are tight,' he murmured, kneading her with his knuckles.

'I've been doing calligraphy again.' Her words were muffled, half by the pillow and half with sheer laziness. Being massaged was like a perpetuation of that wonderful stage as one falls asleep, just before the blackness descends. 'It smells so nice. What is it?'

'Rose and sandalwood.' His hands pressed and eased the tight knots.

'Whatsat do?'

'Rose is very good for women. It balances your cycle, eases menstrual pains. Sandalwood relaxes you. Both of them lift your mood.'

'Lemme guess,' she slurred, 'they're both aphrodisiacs too?'

He chuckled. 'Rumbled again.'

He had been staying with her for over a week, cooking for her every evening. Whenever she asked about the meaning of any dish, his answer was invariably, among other properties, 'aphrodisiac'.

'I think you're a charlatan,' she said. 'You don't actually know anything about plants. You're probably not even a botanist. You just pretend to be one, to get into my knickers.'

'You're not wearing any,' he reminded her.

'See? It worked, your evil plan.' He ran his hand down

her back and up the slope of her exposed buttocks. As his fingers brushed between them, she gave a little mouse-squeak of pleasure.

'Who needs evil plans when you quiver every time I touch you?'

Her bottom arched towards him slightly.

'Uh-uh,' he admonished, returning his hand to her shoulders. 'This is a proper, healing massage.' He resumed his work on her loosening muscles. 'Anyway, I do too know about plants,' he added, after a few minutes' silence. 'Show me any plant and I'll tell you anything you want to know.'

She lay dumbly in her puddle of bliss as her deep tissue yielded to his knowing fingers, and his words gradually penetrated her mind. She thought of the paintings in Mother's room. After the first portrait, she had found only still lifes, all of them herbs and outmoded kitchen equipment. A feminist argument could possibly be made of the subject matter ... 'Domestic subjects: the still life of the Renaissance Woman'. When had bad puns become the apex of academic argument? The skirting boards of the room were hidden by a hem of paintings. She'd grown used to them, even to the portrait, and had almost ceased to notice them. Adrian might at least know what they were.

'I have some pictures of herbs to show you then,' she said. 'They're quite old, I think. They were all painted over.'

'Where are they?'

'Mother's room. The one I use to do calligraphy in.'

'Your Bluebeard's Chamber?'

'You are allowed in, you know. It's so peaceful in there. Whatever the weather, or the time of day, it seems pale and calm in there. But I don't like it at night, much.'

'You're a little hermit at heart, you know,' he said, as

he began on her lower back. 'You should've been a monk in a scriptorium.'

'I do my best, given the circumstances.' She thought of her painstakingly scribed notes and the long hours in the tolling silence of Duke Humphrey's. His hand cupped her between her legs, and she twinged in delight.

'Not very monastic.'

His free hand kneaded handfuls of her buttocks, while the other remained clasped between her thighs. Outside, foul November weather lashed out at the world, driving sodden leaves before its rough winds and flinging rain down like falling lakes. Inside, pure sweet music and warmth were filling the air. She began to hurt with longing as his hand lay motionless, like a shield on her private parts. Under his tender touch, she felt lithe and beautiful, a Renaissance nymph draped along the edge of an inviting pool.

'I want you,' she whispered.

'Again? Isn't twice a day enough for you?' he teased. His finger explored tentatively, and found her succulent with arousal.

'Only once,' she protested, smiling at the memory of the morning. She had woken up in a sea of lust to find his busy hands stroking her breasts and rubbing her nipples. From dreaming of him entering her, she half woke, and he glided into her. As they bucked against each other, her sleepy thoughts tangled with hallucinations. She saw curtains of glossy green ivy parting, torrents of greenery, weeping willows tickling the river, and she came seeing crimson hydrangeas blooming amongst the emerald leaves.

'Twice,' he said. 'The day starts at midnight.' His finger pried further into her creamy depths, which welcomed and gripped him tightly.

'My God,' he said hoarsely.

'Goddess,' she corrected, her voice husky. He fondled the hot, fleshy passage, feeling his cock stiffen. Lying abandoned to pleasure on the soft cushions, she was a vision of beauty triumphant. He watched the flush rise on her cheek as his fingers lost themselves in her heat. Her full bottom formed a shapely curve, and opened slightly as her legs shifted apart. He withdrew his index finger, covered with milky gloss, and pressed it against the small hole. She gave a rough gasp of shock, but arched her back to meet him. With two fingers sliding in and out her pussy, his index finger pressed against her tight, rubbery anus. It found a way in, at last, up to the first knuckle. She groaned from the back of her throat, and tightened up for a moment. Keeping that finger still, he pumped her pussy gently until she unclenched. He slid it in deeper, up to the second knuckle, and she cried out.

'Yes,' he said fiercely, his cock shaking at the sound.

He dabbed his other hand in the small bowl of massage oil, and smoothed it down the cleft of her bottom. His prying finger coated her tight hole with the fragrant oil, pressing it inside her. As she loosened, he pushed another finger in, spreading and preparing her. His erection raged at the sight. Dipping his hand back in the oil, he smoothed it down his staff, closing his eyes with ecstasy as his fist rubbed up and down. Her thighs had opened for him again. With her knees pressed against the cushions, she presented her bottom invitingly and he wriggled closer. His fingers gave way to the inflamed tip that now pushed in their place. The exquisite tightness flooded him with lust. He paused, trembling, his thumbs digging into her fleshy buttocks, trying to control himself. He longed to dive right inside her, to feel that constricting sheath all around his full length. He nudged deeper in, and she groaned violently, contracting. Breathless and tense, they stayed almost motionless. He shifted lovingly back and forth, giving her time to recover while he spread more of the sweet-smelling oil over them.

'Are you ready?' he whispered.

'Yes,' she said, her voice deep with greed.

He angled himself carefully, gripped her hips, and then drove steadily into her without pause. Both screamed, their voices an octave apart, as his whole cock breached her. His hips pressed hard against her, his soft sack resting against her juicy lips. She arched and writhed against him, impaling herself as hard as she could.

'Yes – please – more – God – harder...' A torrent of guttural words fell from her lips when he began to thrust. Her cries echoed around the room as he sank repeatedly into her, his balls slapping against her pussy with each plunge. She clawed savagely at the cushions, almost crying with joy as he sodomised her.

'Yes, my darling, yes,' he encouraged as she flailed against him. He held still, lodged far in her depths, till her madness had abated a little. 'I want to see you,' he said. They turned slowly, tangling and twisting their limbs, so that she pivoted on him without releasing even one precious inch. When she lay on her back with him still sunk inside, he could see the bright flush of arousal on her breasts and cheeks. Her nipples were engorged, crimson and hard. Her eyes shone with ado-ration as she drank in the sight of him towering above her. The smooth hard muscles on his chest glowed with sweat. Above the tight ring of flesh that gripped his cock, her wet lips glistened. Tangling his fingers in the damp hair, he pushed his fingers back inside, shoving in as many as he could, three, almost four, his thumb rubbing hard against her clitoris. Sinking down on her, he trapped his hand between them, encircling her with his arm. He held her tightly to him as he began to piston his hips against her arse again. His fingers scrabbled in her juicy well, forcing most of his hand inside her. His thick rod filled her other entrance, slipping rapidly in and out, and his tongue filled her mouth. He felt her orgasms racking her as he pounded, fondled, and kissed her warm, wet openings.

'I love you,' he gasped, the words drowned out by her screams. 'I love you, come for me, I love you...' He screamed it louder and louder, abandoning all control. Pinioned to him, she thrashed in his arms, coming with every stroke of his cock. He had lost all sense beyond her welcoming, shuddering body and the joy of flinging himself, as hard as he could, into her. His hand was soaked with her cream, stuffed into her stretched pussy. He felt the sap rising in him. Unable to stop, he shoved himself deeper, and faster. 'Come for me again, come for me, come with me,' he howled. His unbearably stiff shaft began to shudder inside her, in time to his cries of bliss. He felt her gripping hard around him as she joined him. Sobbing, he spurted jets of hot seed deep in her bowels.

They lay inert, listening to the sound of each other's heartbeats gradually slowing. A warm cloud of well-being surrounded Sarah, as her mind drifted back over his words. *Yes. Darling. I love you.* She wanted to ask if he'd meant those wild words, but how could she? And even to ask would break the spell of oneness.

'What were your visions this time?' he murmured against her ear. He loved the way his body made pictures spring into being for her.

'The hut, again,' she whispered. 'I saw the forest of dried herbs hanging from the ceiling, all clustered together. Everything was – dark, sort of shadowy and rich. And the wooden beams, sort of rough and smooth at the same time. Like they'd been cut roughly and been smoothed out by age.'

His lips touched her cheek softly. 'What do you think it means?'

'I don't know,' she said uncertainly. 'I'm not sure they mean anything – in that sense. It's just how it is.'

She ran her arms over his back, clasping his buttocks closer against her and feeling his smooth skin. He lifted himself on one elbow, and gazed down at her. His emerald eyes filled with softness.

'You know –' he whispered, but before he could continue the doorbell rang. She hesitated.

'Go on, get it,' he said ruefully. 'I'll pull some clothes on.'

Throwing her dress over her head, she moved on bare feet over the cold hall floor, wondering who could be visiting unexpectedly. She threw open the door, and froze in dismay.

'Good evening,' said Jo, smiling seductively.

'Who is it?' called Adrian from the lounge. Jo raised an eyebrow, and scanned her flushed face and dishevelled hair pointedly.

'It's – um . . .' She didn't know what to say. Someone I shag from time to time, who might be a ghost? My invisible friend?

'Shall I leave?' murmured Jo, his face expressionless.

'Hi!' Adrian strode over, hand outstretched.

'You must be Adrian,' said Jo smoothly, shaking his hand. 'I've heard a lot about you. I'm Jo.' He glanced at Sarah.

'Come in, come in, yes,' she said hastily. Her mind was reeling with confusion. And how had Jo found out his name, when she hadn't seen him since – since the Phoenix party?

'You have the advantage, I'm afraid,' Adrian was saying, leading the way back to the lounge. 'Are you at college with Sarah?'

'No, I'm a Balliol man. Theology.' Sarah stayed standing in the hallway, holding the door open, as the usual litany of Oxford small talk unwound in the lounge. She could not believe she had forgotten about the full moon. The discovery of Adrian seemed to have obliterated everything else. And here was Jo, just as he'd said he would be. Except, that meant he had been in the library, so she was sane and he was a ghost, but Adrian was talking to him quite happily. It could all just be a bizarre coincidence.

'Sarah? You OK?' Adrian stood in the hallway.

'Fine,' she said, coming to and closing the door. 'Fine.'

'Shall I open some wine?'

'I'll get it,' she said. She couldn't face entering the lounge quite yet. Uncorking the bottle, she wondered if Jo would be able to drink it. Surely it should just fall through him? She giggled, faintly hysterical. Another alarming thought occurred to her: what would Adrian think? She'd only been with him eight days, she didn't owe him retrospective loyalty, but still – he'd just said he loved her, even if it *was* a moment of madness.

The two of them seemed quite at ease when she returned, chatting comfortably.

'So if you're finished, what are you still doing in Oxford?' Adrian was asking.

'Oh – I still have a few loose ends to wrap up,' Jo said casually. 'Thank you.' He accepted the glass Sarah offered him. 'Besides, I rather like the place. I'm finding it hard to leave.'

'Not quite ready to face the real world?' Adrian chuckled.

'Something like that.' He glanced slyly at Sarah.

She sat quietly through their conversation, struggling to reconcile all the confusing thoughts and feelings in her head. She found herself wishing they would both leave, so that she could sit in peace with a coffee and her tarot cards, and question by question unravel the mysteries. *Ask the tarot cards if he's a ghost?* She laughed aloud at the irony.

'Sarah doesn't believe me about the meanings of plants, she thinks I'm making it all up,' said Adrian, misinterpreting her laugh.

'Sarah doesn't believe in much,' said Jo. He drained the last sip from his glass. 'I must go, I only came to pass on a message. Well, a little gossip – I believe you both know Clara?'

Adrian flushed, and Sarah nodded. Jo's face twitched, although whether with discomfort or amusement was hard to say.

'She and Dr Piedmont seem to have developed a – liaison. I'm not sure how close they are, but I'm certain it bodes ill.'

'From what I've seen, they deserve each other – no offence, Adrian.' Sarah glanced uncertainly at him.

'I'm not offended. I don't know what I ever saw in her,' said Adrian quietly. 'A week with you,' his eyes met hers, intimately, 'and it's like the scales have been lifted.' She gazed back at him.

Jo, watching their exchange, frowned in concern. 'I'm not sure how much to tell you. You should be careful. She's vindictive.'

Adrian barked a brief, humourless laugh. 'You know her then?'

'A little. You might like to think about leaving Oxford, for a bit. Until you know more. And it's probably best not to say where you're going. Well, I only came to warn you, and I have.' He stood up, straightening his gown.

At the front door, he turned and laid his hand on Sarah's for a moment. His eyes lowered, almost as if they flickered shut, and she was reminded of the first time he'd touched her – so hesitantly and longingly, as if unable to believe it were possible. With a small, sad smile, he was gone.

'He's in love with you,' said Adrian softly, gazing after him.

'Don't be jealous.'

'I'm not.' He dropped his eyes to hers. 'My heart breaks for him.' He pulled Sarah into his arms and held her tight, rocking her slightly. She closed her eyes against the feeling of unbearable safety. She wanted to say that she felt she'd been looking for him her whole life. She wanted to say that she'd come home. She wanted to tell him about all the frightening things Jo had told her, and what had happened in the library, but right now his arms were around her and who knew what might happen if she said any of those things? Don't look a gift horse in the mouth, she told herself.

'So what about those paintings? They're in your studio?'

'In Mother's room, yes. But it's dark – the light doesn't work.'

'We'll take a candle, then.'

Sarah shuddered. She loved the room in daylight, but at night . . .

'Come on, fraidy-cat.' He kissed her forehead. 'I'll hold your hand.'

The old, shallow steps creaked as they ascended slowly, the candle flame quavering with their steps. A rectangle of moonlight lay in the hallway from the spare bedroom opposite, falling just short of the doorway. Sarah opened it hesitantly, and followed Adrian in. He nodded gravely, and walked towards the mantelpiece. Behind them, the door swung shut, and he put his hand on her arm as she started. He was staring ahead, his mouth open. Sarah looked up at the portrait, and shifted uncomfortably.

'It's you,' he said flatly.

'It's very like . . .' said Sarah, and looked at it through his eyes. In the darkness, the concentric pools of gradually dimming candlelight illuminated the features, blending the unfamiliar hairstyle and dress into obscurity. 'Yes. I figured . . .' She began to stumble over the explanation she had concocted for herself, about freak likenesses and family prejudice and the landlord choosing her on account of that. Adrian compressed his lips, shaking his head silently.

'The plants are there,' she whispered, gesturing towards the floor. He knelt down, lowering the candle to examine them closer.

'Almond, bay leaf, bodhi, iris, sage, sunflower,' he muttered, gazing intently at the first one. She crouched down beside him, hating the feeling of the empty, dark room behind her. He shuffled further on his knees. She looked at his face, starkly lit by the naked flame. 'Caraway, cinnamon – and a mortar and pestle.' He smiled, a faraway look glossing his eyes. He crept along further, studying each one carefully, muttering the names and nodding knowingly. 'Anise, black salt, cinnamon, pine – the mortar and pestle – what's that?' He peered closer. 'A frying pan. Look.' With his finger almost touching the paint, he traced the shape. He turned to look at her, his eyes shining with excitement. 'Sarah, do you know what these are?'

She shook her head in mute bewilderment. 'They're just pictures – pictures of plants.'

'Not just pictures!' He leapt up excitedly, the candle dimming to a tiny blue glow before regaining its strength. Stepping back, he looked at the whole row, running the length of the wall. 'These are recipes. Look – there!' He pointed at the last picture he'd been looking at. 'Read it!'

She felt frightened by his excitement and by the eerie

feeling this room always held for her at night. The window pane rattled in a gust of wind, and the rocking chair in the corner creaked. She looked, but couldn't understand.

'From left to right,' he said, 'just like words. There's the star anise and the cinnamon, in the pan. That picture over there has oil, but not this one. So you dry fry them. The mortar and pestle is a little to the right, with the black salt in front of it. So you grind those up together, next. And on the far right, the pine needles, with a knife. So you chop those up and add them to it.'

'What does it make?' asked Sarah in a small voice. She wanted to leave, and come back in the calm pale light of day.

'It's cleansing,' he said, his face relaxing with joy and understanding. 'It's a spell, for cleansing. That one over there,' he gestured, 'is for passion – that's for wisdom, there. That one's against evil spirits – that one's to see the small folk. That's to see the dead. It's a treasure trove!'

Her unease was increasing steadily. 'Please can we go?' she said. 'It scares me in here, I don't care if I'm being a fool – I want to go . . .'

'But . . .' he began, carried away with his enthusiasm.

'Please!' she wailed, spinning around towards the door. 'I'm scared, I . . .' She got no further. Sitting in the rocking chair by the door was an old woman, her hands folded on her lap, her black eyes watching. Sarah began to scream. With each scream, her fear trebled. Cold icy terror unrolled across her skin, biting into her stomach.

'It's OK!' she heard Adrian yelling, as if from a far distance. He grabbed her and she fought against him, trying to move away from the motionless old woman. She couldn't stop screaming, her eyes wild with terror. A part of her stood outside, watching, waiting for it all to stop, for the woman to be a trick of the light, or a figment of her imagination.

Adrian managed to pinion her arms to her side, and pull her roughly against him.

'I can't get out, I can't get out,' she was howling. The terrible spectre was sitting by the door, she couldn't approach. His voice was echoing in her ears, trying to calm her, telling her that everything was alright. She struggled, screaming afresh as the woman stood, and began to clutch her way towards the window. One aged hand was clasped to her hip.

'My darling, hush, it's OK, she's letting us out, it's OK...'

'It's not OK!' Sarah was wild with hysteria. 'What's she doing here, who is she, who is she?' Adrian was manhandling her out the room. As the door slammed behind them, she saw a last glimpse of the old woman standing by the window, looking after them with sorrow in her eyes.

Adrian carried her downstairs to the lounge. Sitting on his lap on the sofa, a fit of sobbing overcame her. He stroked her hair and held her tight, still murmuring that everything was fine.

'There's some wine left,' he said, when she had calmed down a little. 'It's restorative – I think you need it.'

She took the glass, her hand shaking, and sipped it.

'Adrian,' Her voice came out in a husky squeak, and she cleared her throat. 'Who's upstairs?' The question sounded unnaturally calm.

'I'm sorry – I should've warned you when we came in. I didn't think you'd see her. I think it must be Mother.'

'Mother,' repeated Sarah dully.

'You know – Mother's room – that Mother.'

'My landlord's mother. Upstairs. But . . .' She wanted to say, but she should have told us she was coming, but I've rented the house, OK not for much, but it's still my house. Then she thought of something else. 'But she's dead.'

'Yes.' He took her free hand in his. 'I haven't told you this before . . .'

She listened in silence, sipping the wine, while he spoke. He'd always been able to see ghosts, he said, right from childhood. It was second sight. It took him years to realise they even were ghosts. Often, out walking with his mother, he would wave and greet people he knew, and be mystified when she asked why he was waving at an empty bench. As he said that, Sarah remembered Tim accusing her of talking to bushes at the Phoenix party, and she shuddered.

His grandmother, Adrian said, had explained it to him when he was six, just before she died. She was already bedridden and the end was very near; he was sitting on the bed chattering, swinging his legs. He saw her face light up with a smile of pure joy, and following her eyes, realised a young man in uniform was standing outside the window, peering in. The boy waved, and with a quizzical smile the man waved back, and was gone. Gran's smile softened and faded a little, but the warm pleasure stayed in her eyes.

'You saw him, then?' she said. He nodded, surprised at the question. 'He's come to check on me,' she laughed. 'He's waiting. It won't be long now. Ah . . .' She stroked his cheek. 'You have your granny's gift.'

It didn't frighten him, to learn that some of the people he saw were ghosts. He knew them already, they'd never harmed him, so what was to be frightened of?

'Will you be a ghost, granny?' he asked, hopefully. 'Then you can stay with me forever.'

'No, when I'm done, I'm done,' she said, 'No unfinished business on this earth for me. Besides, I've got my young man waiting for me.' Her eyes sparkled, and for a moment the face of a pretty girl shone through again. 'It won't be long now,' she repeated with satisfaction.

The next time he saw her was the last, but she passed on what she could, to help him with his gift. She waited till his mother left the room, and told him to feel under her mattress and pull out the book beneath it. He withdrew a yellowing, hard-covered book, fat with pastings and interleavings. Turning the pages carefully, he saw they were filled with her elegant, copperplate script, interspersed with strange symbols.

'I can't read cursive yet, Granny,' he said, looking up in disappointment.

'Not yet, you can't,' she said, 'but you just put that in your schoolbag before your mother comes back, and hide it somewhere safe at home. You'll be able to read it soon enough. It'll help to remember my name.'

It was her Book of Shadows, filled with her spells, recipes, and sightings. On the outside of his bedroom window, the wooden cover of the air vent had rotted slightly, creating a small, cubic compartment that he could just reach by stretching his hand up and out. He put the book in a tupperware container, and hid it there. He took to smiling all the time, so that the smiles he directed towards the Others, as she called them, went undetected. As he learnt to read the old-fashioned writing, he began to pester his mother about plants, wanting to recognise the herbs and weeds that his granny's book recommended. His mother, however, was a Londoner by birth, and could hardly tell a nettle from a dock leaf. At twelve, he tried to joined the local botanical society. The matrons and retirees that formed the bulk of it were so amused that they let him.

'It was like losing one grandmother and gaining

twenty,' he said. 'And I hadn't even really lost my grandmother, because I had her book.'

Sarah gave a small, tired smile. 'So I have this – gift, as well?' she said.

'Maybe,' he said. 'Granny's was always stronger at the full moon, so maybe yours is, too.'

'Would you believe me if I said I think Jo is a ghost?'

'Yes,' he said slowly. 'To be honest, I usually can't tell the difference, except sometimes by clothing.'

'And now there's a ghost upstairs as well?' She thought she was dealing with it all incredibly well, now that the initial fright had passed.

Adrian shifted uncomfortably. 'Actually, she's been here the whole time. Um – she's usually in the spare room, in the day time.'

'You might have told me.'

He grinned wryly and stroked her cheek. 'Would you have believed me?' He kissed her tenderly on the lips, the eyelids. 'Why do you think Jo's a ghost?'

Wearily, Sarah smoothed her forehead with her hands. Should she tell him everything, including what she had done with a ghost?

As if to spare her, Adrian said, 'You slept with him, didn't you?'

She nodded, embarrassed. 'Do you mind?'

'Mind? If it were in the last – what, ten days? – then yes, I might mind. Go on, tell me the whole story.'

With an immense feeling of relief, she did.

'Well, that makes one thing clear,' said Adrian, when she had finished. 'We should leave Oxford.' She looked at him in surprise. 'He knows things we don't, Sarah. If he's warning us, we should take it seriously.'

'But where would we go?'

'I can return your hospitality for a bit. Term finishes tomorrow. We can miss ninth week, it's not serious. How would you like to spend Christmas in Cornwall?'

5 Tiphareth

Sarah stared out of the window, transfixed, as Adrian navigated the twisting coastal road with easy familiarity. His profile was silhouetted in the setting sun which shot flames through the gathering clouds, across the Atlantic ocean. To her left lay miles of crumpled, hillocky scrubland, interspersed with small villages of sombre grey stone.

'Over there,' he said, his face soft with pleasure. She looked in the direction he had nodded, and saw the waves breaking on the cliffs, the spume pink and grey in the failing light. 'When I see that, I know I'm on home ground.'

The house, he had explained on the train trip down, had been his grandmother's, left in her will to him rather than to his parents. The old woman knew her daughter-in-law hated the tiny, quiet village and would have sold off such an inconvenient property. Still, the bequest had done nothing to ease the ill-feeling that had always lingered.

'Now that I'm older, it sits more easily,' he'd said. 'She can say "my son's house" to her friends, and pretend I'm a fine feather in her bourgeois crown.'

'No resentment there, then?' said Sarah, raising her eyebrows.

He shrugged. 'Not really, no. It's just the truth. She'd rather I were earning a salary, like everyone else's sons.'

When they collected his car from his parents' empty house, Sarah understood a little better. The characterless façade, deep carpets, and heavy brocade curtains were all in strict keeping with established, careful taste. It was an environment that should have produced a son working in a top-notch graduate job in London, not mucking about with plants and struggling to live on scholarships.

'Not that they want me to struggle,' he'd added. 'They're always offering me money, but I want to make my own way. I'm not doing what they want, so why should it cost them? Scholarships are different – those committees want me to spend my life knee-deep in mud.'

He slowed the car down to just a few miles an hour as he turned into a narrow, hedge-lined road, onto a gravel drive, and eased it to a halt next to a low, grey-stoned cottage. Ahead of them lay the boundless seascape, the last flecks of sunset lapped wildly at the clouds, the crimson turning to baby pink and violet even as they watched. The rough, crevassed stone of the walls was flecked and patchy with white lichen and dark moss.

'Welcome to Morvah,' he said. 'Population 65, unless someone's had a baby recently. No pub, no shop, no post office. One church.'

'It's perfect,' murmured Sarah.

His thoughtful gaze evolved slowly into a smile, and he pulled out a huge, wrought-iron key. 'Let me show you around.'

The door led directly into the biggest kitchen Sarah had ever seen, but she had only a moment to marvel at its size before she gasped in shocked recognition. From the beams hung thick bunches of dried herbs, a dim, desiccated overhead forest in dim light. He squeezed her hand in silent understanding.

'I collected them in the summer,' he said softly. 'I thought of them when you told me your dream – I'm sorry, I didn't think to say.'

'It's OK – it's beautiful.' She meant it. However frightening the dream had been, the sight of the rustling bunches were nothing to do with that fear. Rather, they felt comfortable and homely.

He lit an oil lamp, the flare momentarily blinding them before he replaced the glass shield and turned the wick down. Through the long, low window above the sink, the sea was being overtaken by twilight, the burning light of the wick replacing the sun as it slipped below the horizon. In its burnishing glow, she saw a blue and white farmhouse plate in the centre of the wide, wooden table. Two dried lemon halves lay on it.

'Room freshener,' he said, as he saw her glance.

Heavy, copper-bottomed pots hung from hooks above the Aga, next to a heavy string of garlic and another of threaded, dried chillies. A series of shelves was filled with old tea-caddies and glass jars, all unlabelled and unbranded. She wandered forward and touched them lightly, wonderingly.

'My herbs and spices,' he said timidly. 'And teas.'

In the dim light, she could see the small beads, seeds, and tiny, dried curling leaves, their colours varying along a palette of soft, natural colours – greyish greens from the palest to the darkest, a swathe of beiges, browns, russets, and black.

'How do you remember what they all are?' she asked, gliding her fingertips across the serried ranks. He shrugged, shyly.

'Do you want to see the rest?'

The cottage consisted of just a few rooms: a bedroom and a bathroom that each competed with the kitchen for size, and a spare room converted to a study. The dark red, polished flagstones and white roughly plastered walls of the kitchen continued throughout. A deep, claw-footed bath, fed by copper pipes, stood in the centre of the bathroom, beneath a deep-ledged window. Through the leafless vine curling across the pane, Sarah could see the coastal path and the sea beyond.

'That's wild jasmine,' said Adrian. 'I don't like cutting it back too much, it's wonderful in the summer, sitting in the bath, staring through the flowers. There's a boiler, but no heating. The kitchen has the Aga, though, and the bedroom has a fireplace, I'll show you.'

She followed him as he carried the lamp, watching how the light warmed and softened everything it touched. He set it on the mantelpiece, next to a small, carefully formed doll. She exclaimed in delight, lifting it up. It had the sunken, characterful face of an old woman and was dressed in a painstakingly sewn old-fashioned outfit. A black dress, with a red overskirt and white apron, a lacy bib, a black headscarf, and trim black boots adorned it. In one hand, it held a small wooden staff. Seeing him watching her anxiously, she replaced it with care on the mantelpiece. Her fingers tingled.

'What is it?'

'A chimney doll. It protects the house,' he said. 'So does this.' From the wall, he lifted what looked like a bracelet of crumpled orange beads from its hook. 'Rowan berries,' he said. 'I only found out what they both were from Grandma's Book of Shadows.'

They began to read the Book of Shadows together the next afternoon, after a morning spent dusting, scrubbing, and chopping wood till their muscles ached. Sarah collapsed at the kitchen table, resting her elbows on the wood she'd scoured and rinsed repeatedly with boiling water. Adrian lifted the kettle from the stove, poured a little water into the teapot, and began selecting tins from the shelves.

'Divination tea,' he explained. 'It's one of her recipes.'

He emptied the teapot, and began spooning in dried flowers. 'Mugwort, rose hips, lemon balm, eyebright,' he said, 'and some China black tea.'

Sarah pulled the book towards her and began to flip through it. *Jennie Cunnack*, it said on the first page. Her years spent poring over manuscripts made the cramped, old-fashioned script easy to read. It was obviously a treasure-trove of folkloric knowledge, listing in full the healing properties of local plants and where to find them, how to prepare different herbal infusions and wines, how to make candles, and a variety of other forgotten household arts. Here and there was a name, a date, and a place – these, presumably, were the sightings that Adrian had spoken of. On one double spread was a list of sayings and aphorisms. The strength of the ink and the handwriting changed just enough to show they had been collected over some time. She glanced up at Adrian. He was standing by the counter, holding the teapot handle, staring out at the approaching storm across the water.

'This is so pretty,' she said. 'Listen. "Like influences like. Will controls action. The stronger will controls the weaker. A symbolic act is a real act. Repetition brings strength. The breath can convey power. Not all that is, is seen. Not all that is seen is real." What lovely sayings. I'd like to write them on the walls of my house. And this one: "Never forget to clean up after yourself and not just physically."'

He turned from the window, his face pensive. 'You see what I mean, I didn't really lose her at all.' He put the teapot and two cups on the table, and sat down. 'All the same – for a moment there, I couldn't help hoping that maybe I'd see her. She said she wouldn't stay, but . . .' He shrugged sadly. 'It would be nice.'

Sarah looked down at his grandmother's sayings, wondering what she would have said to comfort him.

Jennie Cunnack, she mused, an old knowledgeable woman with a heavy Cornish accent. 'The bones of this land are not speechless,' she said lightly, her accent thick and local, her voice deepening. His body went rigid with shock.

'God, that's uncanny!' he said, his arms pimpling. 'How did you do that – her voice?'

'Just a Cornish accent,' said Sarah, alarmed. 'Sorry.'

'That was her voice,' he said, shuddering, looking around.

In silence, they returned to the book. As she turned the pages, the cursive script grew rarer, and the pages were filled with the geometric symbols, each line closed with a small node.

'I've never been able to figure out that stuff,' said Adrian. 'It must be some kind of code, but I haven't figured it out.'

Sarah looked closer. 'It's the Malachim alphabet,' she said. 'I've seen it in old manuscripts before.'

'Can you read it?' he asked excitedly.

'Yes – not fast – hold on . . .' She began to trace the page with her fingers. After a few minutes' silence, she frowned. 'Some kind of substitution,' she said. 'Can you get me a pen and paper?'

He sat in silence while she scribbled rows of strange symbols underneath each other, criss-crossing grids and crossing letters out. Her tea cooled slowly, and she sipped at it as she struggled to decipher the code.

'She didn't give you any clues?' she said, looking up. 'Anything to tell you how to read it?'

'No,' said Adrian. 'She just said I'd be able to read it soon enough, I think she meant the cursive.' He drank from his cup, thoughtfully. 'She said it would help me remember her. As if I could forget my granny. Or maybe she didn't mean just me, maybe she meant she'd be famous. She said, "It'll help to remember my name."'

'That's it!' said Sarah, scribbling a new grid hastily. 'That's it, the name, of course! It's a personal code, it's so obvious.' He watched in mystification as, with small jabs of the pen, she outlined the curious shapes and dots beneath each other. Leaning over the book, she began to copy the symbols under the grid.

'There!' she said, triumphantly. 'It is a substitution code, using the same alphabet, and her name's the key! Look!' She saw his bewilderment, and hastened to explain. 'You can do it with any alphabet,' she said. 'Here.' She quickly wrote out the Roman alphabet from A to Z. 'And then I take my name – Sarah Kirkson.' Underneath, she wrote 'S A R H K I O N'

'I leave out the letters I've already used, so only one S, one A, one K, one R. Then I fill in the rest of the alphabet. B, C, D, E, F, G, J . . .' She dashed it down. 'Now I'll write you a message.' She looked at the grid, thoughtfully, her pen hovering. Her hand trembled slowly, as she carefully wrote, 'BEJVKYJU' and handed him the paper. He studied it, his finger keeping track of the letters as his eyes flicked back and forth between the message and the code. She picked up her tea, to keep her hands from shaking, and studied the amber water intently, not daring to look up. He put the paper down. She could feel the air pressure dropping as the storm approached. The light was yellowing rapidly, and beginning to darken. He leant forward, his hand cupping her cheek to turn her face. Reluctantly, she looked at him and his lips closed on hers. Their arms moved around each other as their lips rubbed gently, parting to let their tongues delicately flicker. They stood in silence, clasped in an unbroken kiss. The hair on their arms prickled and stood with the electricity of their bodies and the looming clouds above.

'Come,' he whispered against her mouth, and she followed him down the dark corridor to the bedroom.

He pushed the curtains wide open. Outside, a different curtain of dark grey and whipped water approached steadily. The tension crackled between them as they faced each other. There would be no boundaries this time, she knew. There were no possible excuses for what they were about to do. She realised, as she looked at him, how much the physical pleasure of sex could be a protection, a wall against the extraordinary intimacy of unpeeling someone's clothes and placing their secret parts inside you.

They stepped closer. Slowly, they unbuttoned and took off each other's clothes, shocked at the nakedness that was revealed. She felt the familiar yearning that glowed between her legs, and let go of it This wasn't about the greedy selfish glut of lust. Side by side, they lay down on the bed. Knowing she had no right to do so, she began to touch his body. Her fingers traced every part of it, not just the sensitive places she knew would bring him pleasure, but the whole of it – his elbow, his shoulder blade, the jutting bone of his hip. Her body, taut with fear, ached for him. She wanted to retreat into simple feeling, to rub his penis as if to say: This is all it's about, the pleasure we can give each other, how me straddling you makes us both feel great. His hand was running slowly up her flank, warm on her chilled skin. The black shadow of the storm was above them now, blotting out the light from the sky, but their eyes still shone with their own dark light. Fat drops of rain spattered against the window, a staccato drumming that increased steadily into a torrential downpour. All the while they lay, side by side and naked, touching each other cautiously. His hand was learning her shape, like a sculptor remaking her out of clay. He stroked her breasts with the same deliberate care as her shoulders. Her palm gliding down his chest slid over his engorged shaft and continued down his thighs. A sheet of lightning illuminated them for an instant: their bare, pale skin; his hand sliding up her breast towards her collar bone, her skin taut with goose bumps; her arm curving around as she felt her way up his haunches; the dark curls that hid her cleft facing his heavy erection; their pupils huge and black as they stared at each other. Thunder echoed against the cliffs as she caressed upwards over his bottom and his fingers entangled in the curls at the nape of her neck. His hand began to slip back down her body, between her full breasts, and over the soft curve of her belly. His fingers trickled slowly through the curling hair of her mons, delicately brushing the full lips, and ran tantalisingly between her thighs. They drifted away from her skin at her knees, and came to rest on her hip.

'Shall we?' he said quietly.

'Yes.'

They inched their bodies closer on the bed, until they could feel the tubular imprint of each other's thighs, and the soft flesh of her breasts squashed between them. The deliberation of each movement made it exquisitely tense, as they trembled against each other's skin. She pulled her leg up gradually until her inner thigh rested on his sharp hip bone. Her tender lips unfurled like an orchid, exposing her entrance to the cold air. The swollen head of his stamen nudged against her small bud. They both shuddered, lying motionless, feeling the electrical storm raging between them. They breathed deeply, in unison, and with each breath their bodies shifted a fraction against each other, the tiny movements a raging tantalisation. She could feel her opening, between her wide spread lips, calling for him, as she looked deep in his eyes. With their eyes locked on each other's, full of the knowledge of what they were doing, they moved their bodies together, until his ripe erection pressed against her sheath. Gradually, he penetrated her.

Their chests heaved as they inhaled steadily, her slippery passage contracting around him. Flashes of white lit up the tiny beads of sweat on their skin and their parted mouths as they ground their groins languorously together. Thunder echoed in their ears and in their loins. Her depths clutched at him as he pulsated within her, their slow circular plunging keeping perfect time. Between them, she felt flames licking up their bodies, a wild raw heat that no deluge could dampen. Faster and faster they slithered, pumping their hips to the beat of their hearts, feral cries rising from their throats. Her eyes were full of his, yet she saw something else, as well. Towering, smoky, sunset colours, dancing together like flames and entirely dwarfing the doll-like little bodies with their pale limbs that lay far beneath, at their base. The land of these two inner, other beings was dark and smoky, too, as forbidding as an industrial wasteland at night under a threatening red sky. She had always imagined the soul as a pure, thin, pale-blue wisp, when she had thought about it at all. But this – these – were so severe, so terrifyingly big. In his eyes, she recognised the same look of awe as their hips pistoned harder, his thickness stoking the fires that fed their frenzied dance of body and soul. His solid rod seemed to swell with each thrust, cramming her to her limits, forcing wails of bliss from her constricted throat. As the fires raged fiercer between them, she watched the ruby-coloured beings' dervish. With an excruciating howl, her eyes drowning in his and his in hers, they came together, their fluids mingling as he poured his cream into her.

They lay quaking with elation and love, at the centre of a warm cocoon, their flesh still throbbing and spasmodically contracting. The flames around them seemed to die away little by little, like a hearth fire burning down. Every few minutes, their bodies would clench again, spasming as she bathed his still hard cock with her juices, as he spurted more nectar in the depths of her womb. They came peacefully and ecstatically, again and again, and lay speechless in the interludes, listening to the rain falling steadily in the twilight. They drifted into sleep, their soaking private parts still tangled, and woke in the utter dark of night to find their bodies moving steadily back and forth, making love in their sleep. Adrian groaned with urgent pleasure as he glided in and out of her, his body resting heavily on hers

'How is this possible?' he moaned. His cock was unbearably stiff, aching sharply with his need.

'The spirit is willing,' sighed Sarah. The powerful joy of orgasm rippled over her, sizzling on their skin. She parted her legs wide to him, lifting herself up to meet him. Grabbing handfuls of her breasts, he pummelled harder, her shouts of delight lifting him through waves of want.

'I need you,' he yelled hoarsely, 'I love you, you know that!'

'Yes!' she said, 'Yes, I know, yes, I love you!'

He plunged into her like a maddened beast, driving as deep as he could, slamming roughly against her. Her orgasms crashed over him with each violent shove, the animal in her meeting his. His groin battered hers, sending the piercing rapture deeper into them. He moved quicker and quicker, until he was galloping on top of her. Her frenzied legs clutching him deeper, her hands clasping his buttocks, she pulled him rapidly into her. With a roar of love, he froze, far inside her, all his muscles taut and straining. The paroxysms of his raging shaft, deluging her with love, brought her to a final peak with him.

The coded writing opened a new treasure-chest of knowledge in Granny Jennie's Book of Shadows. The plant lore and folk remedies written in cursive were only a fraction of what it contained, the rest hidden from inquisitive – or inquisitorial – eyes. After all, in the days when the book had been started, witchcraft had still been illegal. Sarah found herself drawing on the full range of her mediaeval lore as she decoded its secrets: not just the Malachim code, but old alchemical and astrological symbols for the elements, the planets, the signs of the Zodiac, and time. The pentacles, those five-sided stars once revered and since despised by Christianity, were carefully hidden in elaborate, apparently artless drawings. A pen and ink sketch of gnarled, interwoven trees disguised the familiar pattern; the leaves, on closer examination, showed the symbols of the five elements it unified: earth, air, fire, water, and spirit.

They spent hours drawing and painting the Wheel of the Year, marvelling at its brilliant complexity and simple obviousness. At the centre of the circle were the eight Sabbats, the main festivals. These were the four solstices, and the sacred days in between: only Lammas was unfamiliar; Candlemas, Halloween, and May Day, or Beltane, all lingered in common belief. Next came the twelve signs of the Zodiac, carving up the solar year like calendar months. Finally, they drew the thirteen full moons. They learnt the names of the moons and that, although it was already December, they were still under the waning Snow Moon of November. Only on the twelfth would December's Oak Moon begin. Until then, while the moon shrank, was the best time for banishing spells. When the moon began to wax, it was time for invocations. Using soot from the fireplace in the bedroom, they mixed ink and painted protective spells on the doors of the cottage. In the dark winter and almost empty landscape, it was easier to believe Jo's warning.

All the same, there was so little to banish, and so much they longed to invoke. Each day, their passion grew wilder and more inventive. Each day, they discovered new ways to tangle their limbs, mixing skin, sweat, and soft sticky secretions, and new ways to play with each other's souls. After the apocalyptic vision they had shared in the thunderstorm, they learnt other dances and a whole palette of colours. They lay in each other's arms in bed, on the rug in front of the fireplace, clasping thighs at right angles on the kitchen table, knowing they had seen the same pictures, and that they were real.

They made candles, while they waited for the new moon. For hours a day, they dipped the long cotton threads into wax, let it cool and harden, dipped it again. Rainbow rows of the slender, tapering rods built up in the study. The book gave instructions how to make them, but also how to use them: the meanings of the colours, the grammar of their layout, how to light and extinguish them, how long to burn them, when to perform the different rituals. They made astral candles for themselves with a single piece of string, each with a golden yellow core, Sarah's layered in red and Adrian's in black.

In the bedroom, they set up an altar, spreading linen over a low, oak table. It fitted so neatly that they felt sure Granny Jennie had sewn it for the table, probably for her own altar. On it, they laid a small dish of salt, a censer with a stick of incense, two white candles, and one of the copper goblets filled with fresh water. That was earth, air, fire, and water; they debated what icon to put on it for spirit. Every idea they had seemed too narrow, too limited, and so they left the space waiting for several days. On the eleventh of December, reading tarot for each other, the Empress card came up.

'Of course!' said Adrian, 'It should be Her – the Goddess!'

'What about the God?' said Sarah. 'He's her mate, her lover, isn't he?'

'And her son, of course,' added Adrian, and they exchanged a wry, naughty smile.

They chose both, and spent that evening making two ornate little pictures. Adrian painted a voluptuous, full-figured Goddess in flowing and revealing gowns, like Botticelli's Venus, sitting in splendour of verdure and water, and a lively, Puckish figure of ambiguous age, either a lithe young lover with fiery veins or perhaps a maturing son, stag horns on his head, playing a flute. When the paint had dried, Sarah wrote their many names around the edges in a calligraphic border. They placed the two icons at the back of the altar, in the centre, using pebbles they'd collected from the beach to hold them up.

'Let's wait up till midnight and then light the candles and incense for them,' said Sarah.

They lit the fire and Adrian fetched some rose-brandy liqueur he'd made in April. Watching him pour the fragrant liquid into two more of the copper goblets, she marvelled that she'd ever doubted his plant lore. Over the last fortnight in his house, almost everything she had eaten and drunk was from his handpicked, home-made store. The coffee and wine that had started and ended her days before had given way to his blends of herbal teas, which themselves tasted nothing like those she had bought in the past.

The first few sips of the liqueur went straight to her

head and loins. Rolling on the rug with him, their tongues deep in each other's mouths, she tore at his clothes.

'It's another of your aphrodisiacs, isn't it?' she gasped. Without the usual cocktail of toxins in her blood, the herbal remedy created a conflagration in her veins.

'It seemed right,' he spluttered, choking on his words as she unleashed the thick wand in his trousers. 'To toast the Goddess and her mate . . .' His words drifted into the hungry sounds of pleasure as she guzzled greedily at his cock. Her tongue massaged his shaft as she sucked, pressing firmly and wetly along the length. She crawled onto her knees, tilting her head to take him deep in her throat, her bottom in the air. With one hand, he seized the heavy fabric of her skirt, tugging it up. Shifting his body at an angle to hers, he could see the bared orbs clenching and rocking as she sheathed him in her throat. Her pelvis bucked slightly with each motion, her thighs parted. Hypnotised, he watched her lustful curves, tearing his eyes away only to stare longingly at her open petals half-hidden and glistening in the firelight. He craved their loving, sticky grip, but the sweet warmth of her mouth was too irresistible to leave. She was savouring his full length in long, clasping mouthfuls, tasting the salty drops that escaped from the tip, and sinking back down slowly. At last, the erotic sight of her rocking buttocks was too much and he scrambled to his knees behind her, both facing the altar. She arched her back eagerly as she felt the blunt tip pressing between her splayed lips.

'My love,' he whispered, as he glided into her honeyed passage. As he pushed, slow and hard, impaling her fully, watching her shudder in bliss, feeling the welcoming clutch of her eager pussy, they heard the church clock begin to chime. Both of them held still, trembling with desire, as it tolled twelve times.

He lifted the matches from the base of the altar, and lit one. With her one hand on the floor, his one hand clasping her breast, they put their free hands together and stretched across to light the two candles, and the incense. The sweet-smelling beeswax and curls of woody smoke filled the room as he plunged in and out of her, bringing her to one ravenous climax after another. Each time she came, he felt her orgasm in his own body, as if he were pouring himself into her. Still he kept driving his rigidity into her, imploring her with his body to come again, and again, to keep washing the joy over them. Their eyes were on the leafy pictures and delicate script of the icons, glowing with reflected flames, when her complete ecstasy overtook him.

She was a tiny node of light, lying in the lap of the Goddess. All was safe and dark, here. Warm soil surrounded her. The brilliant gems in the earth passed their strength to her. The long fight was over. Rest, said the roots of the trees. She could feel them stretching their vast, thick roots into the ground all around her, tingling with life and sap, questing for water. Be calm, said the water, rushing silently through its subterranean tunnels, smoothing the rock, washing back and forth to the call of the moon, driving its powerful currents from one side of the globe to the other, oozing gently through the grains of loam. The infinitesimal white point that was still her burned brighter, hard and small, and said, No. It is not finished. *The earth bore down heavily on her, but she would not give in, she would not disperse. Harder and harder it crushed her, and still she fought back, clinging to the thin line of silver that still spiralled upwards, up to the surface, where it was bound to a node of light as powerful as her own. I will not, she said, though here there was hardly a* her *to speak. A brilliant calm came upon her, then. The Goddess had felt her struggle, and had turned her lovely face to the little struggling thing. She longed desperately to stretch out to that massive, peaceful soul, and she begged.* I have always done Your will, I have always worshipped You, I have always loved You. My work has been interrupted, I am not finished. *She could feel the power that ran in her still, as she pleaded. The Goddess smiled then, and Her words emanated through the earth:* So mote it be. *The burden of soil lightened. The node barely had thoughts, barely had a self, but it burned like a hard diamond with pure will, and with something even stronger. And it waited. Roots sank into the ground, lengthened, and died. Roots vanished. Back and forth across the distant surface, the water lapped. The planets tugged, as the world spun and swung around and around on its orbit; the moon circled. It felt the pull of the cosmic energies, it kept watch over the lights of the dying as they entered the soil and dispersed into particles that rejoined the Goddess. It waited.*

She opened her eyes. The candles on the altar had burnt low; the stick of incense was just a long thread of ash. She was leaning against Adrian's chest, his legs around her, her hands in his.

'Did you see that?' she asked.

'No,' he said. 'I could feel it – I could feel you drawing on my strength. I didn't know where you were, you weren't here. I just kept holding you, and feeding you my strength, so you would be strong enough to come back.'

She turned her face into the curve of his neck and felt his arms encircle her naked body.

'Thank you,' she said.

'I think that was a bit dangerous,' he said guardedly. 'I think we – invoked Them. We should have cast a circle, first.'

* * *

They began to practise spells after that, learning how to cast and close the sacred circle that would keep them safe. Before dawn and sunset, they lit the log fire and rinsed each other in the deep, claw-footed bath. Clean and naked in the firelight, they would open the circle and learn their magic. They chose their spells carefully, wary of attempting anything they couldn't yet control. They learnt to meditate, to scry, and to see each other's auras, amazed at the rainbow of colours that revealed itself. They discovered their special strengths: the fire energy of the candle-burning rituals for Sarah, the earth energy of potions and powders for Adrian. One dawn, they sat cross-legged next to each other, each with a palm upraised and touching the other's, supporting a tiny down feather. As it floated gently upwards, their bodies rose from the ground. They hovered, feeling the air all around them and the faint touch of each other's hands, hardly daring to speak. At last, Sarah spoke the words to end the spell, and they settled back to the ground once more. Any scepticism that had lingered in their hearts up to that point now vanished. They closed the circle and dressed without speaking. At the kitchen table, they sat with their tea, looking at each other in silence. Wintry, morning sun was already sparkling on the sea. Eventually, Sarah spoke.

'It works,' she said flatly. 'We can actually do this. But I don't know what we're trying to do – I mean, why we're trying to.'

Adrian nodded. 'It's all very well floating,' he said.

'It's amazing,' interjected Sarah.

'But you're right, there has to be some sort of point.'

'If only your gran could have taught us herself. Someone must have taught her, and explained why, but she didn't write it down.'

'There's always Chun Quoit,' he said slowly. 'I mean, if all this stuff actually works – and now I'm pretty convinced it does – then that should work too.' Chun Quoit, he explained, was one of the many sacred stone formations in Cornwall – the landscape was liberally dotted with them. As an ancient burial site, it was also purported to be a place from which to communicate with ancestors. 'It's just over a kilometre away.'

They walked together, their long shadows rippling on the tussocks of grass in front of them. The dying sun touched the hill ahead with old gold, and fell on the heavy slab that topped the dolmen, supported by a cluster of leaning stones beneath it. It looked set to topple over, leaning heavily to one side and seeming to curve downwards beneath its own weight. The cold, salty breeze whipped around them, reddening their cheeks and chilling their hands. As they drew nearer, Sarah felt the heavy, earthy force around it, like gravity. It stood almost as tall as her; she could lay her arms over it, and rest her chin on the rough stone. Standing like that, as if hugging it, she felt its ancient strength spilling over into her. Next to her, Adrian rested his back against it, shading his eyes against the setting sun.

'It's almost sunset,' he said, squinting. He looked around at the empty fields. 'We don't want to be interrupted.'

'I'll cast a wide circle,' she said, her cheek lying against the stone. She drew away reluctantly, her arms dense with its borrowed power, to a distance of about ten metres on the far side of the stone. With her right forefinger pointing at the ground, she began to walk in a wide circle, chanting as she walked.

'I consecrate this circle of power to the Ancient Gods. Here may they manifest and bless their children.'

Adrian watched her tall figure moving clockwise around him. She was imbued with a new strength and confidence he hadn't seen before. It changed the tilt of her head, the carriage of her spine, the way her hips slowly swayed, filling her with sensuous grace. When she returned, smiling, he was beglamoured by the light in her eyes.

They crawled through the slit in the rocks, into the narrow chamber inside. Sitting cross-legged, they laid out the altar in the small space between them, repeating the now-familiar words as they did so.

'This is a time that is not a time, in a place that is not a place, on a day that is not a day.' One by one, they placed the items between them, the water, the salt, the incense, and the four coloured candles, finishing with the litany, 'By the powers of the Ancient Gods, I bind all power within this circle, into this spell. So mote it be.'

The small space echoed as their voices died away. A russet gleam of dying light slowly lengthened, darkened, and began to recede as the sun slipped down. Between them, they lit the white and pink candle of Granny Jennie's star sign. Their faces glowed in the shadowy flicker of the five flames as they took each other's hands, glad of the human warmth, and began to say the words of the spell. As they ended, they looked around expectantly. No-one was there but themselves. They met each other's eyes, and shrugged.

'Perhaps it didn't work,' said Adrian.

Outside, they could hear steps on the grass. 'It seems my circle didn't work either,' whispered Sarah. They glanced nervously at their occult paraphernalia, hoping that the flickering candles wouldn't draw the passer-by. Sarah's heart was beating wildly with fear of being caught. Would it be taken as defacing a monument? The sound drew closer, and she bit her lip, closing her eyes.

'Dynnargh dhis,' said Adrian, his voice choked. Sarah opened her eyes. A young woman's face, pale and shadowy in the moonlight, was watching them through the crack.

'Gwra'massi,' replied the woman. Without climbing in, she was sitting with them in the stone chamber.

'So, you deciphered my book,' she said. 'I expected you would be calling on me soon after.'

'Sarah did,' said Adrian. 'Granny, this is Sarah, Sarah, this is Granny Jennie.' His voice was thin and unnatural. Granny Jennie's face was young, younger-looking than Sarah's, but with the wisdom and certainty of a much older woman. She looked long and hard at Sarah. Apparently coming to a conclusion, she nodded her head firmly.

'He's sat there with his mouth abroad,' Granny said, cocking her head towards her grandson. 'So, you have all your granny's power. Whatee goyn duwidden?'

'That's what we wanted to ask you,' said Adrian.

'You get three questions, by tradition,' said Granny, 'Three each, mind.'

Adrian cleared his throat, nervously. 'We've been learning how to do all these things, but we don't know why we're doing them. What to do with them. What are we learning magic for?'

Granny shook her head thoughtfully. 'Ordinary things, for the most part. Keeping the bad away, encouraging the good. Helping the earth to tick round as it should. Worshipping the Lord and Lady. Making your life the prettiest and best thing it can be.' She studied Sarah again. 'You're learning together, that's a special bond already. That's reason enough, if it's reason you're after. This young lady has a fair bit of power in her, though, you too. Combined, that's a lot. Using sex magic, are you?'

Both of them blushed. 'Not really,' said Adrian. 'Once – by accident . . .'

'Don't be cakey, you have the chance to share your power. There's a lot that can be done, with that amount.'

As she spoke, they both relaxed a little. The notion of speaking to the dead had unsettled both of them, but Granny's ordinary appearance and salty sense calmed them. They broke in occasionally with questions, keeping careful count. She explained the three realms to them. Most people divided things in their heads into Good and Evil, if they thought of the spirit world at all, and as the Church had defined itself as Good, that meant pretty much all else was Evil, 'dabbling in the occult'. But there was good and bad in all things, and the Church had taken up plenty of the bad – burning people at the stake, making harsh rules, hurting the Earth – as well as good. Heaven and hell are real, she said, but that doesn't mean we have to have any part of them, it's not one or the other. Rather, both were invaders, fighting over a planet that didn't belong to them, which belonged to *itself*, to Herself, the Goddess. The Goddess didn't tell people what to think and do, when to have sex and how much money to give away. She asked only for her gifts to be treated well and appreciated, and all of life, all of its experiences, were her gift. She was the Great Mother, giving us the flesh on our bones and the earth under our feet. Both heaven and hell opposed her, and hell fought dirty, disguising itself in the Church's cloth to do its worst.

'That was a trick,' said Granny. 'The devil using God's clothes to tell people that witches were on the devil's side. Burning and drowning Her best and innocent children. At least that stopped.'

'What should we do, now?' asked Sarah.

There was no 'should' about it, Granny explained. Anything they chose to do was out of love, the way they did things for each other. If they wanted to serve Her, there was much that they could do, from just helping people to showing like-minded souls how to take care of the world. They weren't to go proselytising, though, or working their fingers to the bone and taking the world on their shoulders as their duty.

'Remember the first law,' she said. '"An' it harm none, do what ye will." Love life, love the Lady and her Lord. And do what ye will.'

With those words, she was gone.

The night was clear and cold as they wound their way home across the field and down the empty ribbon of country lane. The dreamily heavy silence of Chun Quoit lingered with both of them. For the first time, Sarah had had a taste of what pure earth power was. As their footsteps swung rhythmically, she realised she had considered it a safe, comfortable energy, warmly reliable but without the stirring power of fire. Now, she understood. It was that, but it was also tombs, earthquakes, massive rocks far more ancient than the oldest manuscript she had ever reverently opened. It was quiet, but like a slumbering giant. She had thought earth energy wasn't her 'thing', somehow, but the strength of the rocks had flowed so easily into her arms.

'It's the first quarter,' Adrian said softly.

'Oh yes,' said Sarah, following his eyes, her train of thought broken. 'Yule in two days.'

'That too – but something else. That spell for increasing power, it said to start seven days before full moon.' He tightened his arm around hers, where they linked together. 'Tonight, in the chamber, when we lit the candles, I felt the fire, I felt what it could do, magically, I mean. Do you think we could – I don't know if it will be strange . . .'

'Share each other's power?' Sarah completed the sentence for him.

They walked on through the freezing air, in unspoken agreement. Scarcely able to see his face in the darkness, she felt as though a new person were alongside her, half stranger and half familiar beloved. Her loins ached, her small bud dancing at the thought of erotic ritual. When they entered the kitchen, she stood uncertainly, watching him light the gas lamp. It flared, showing the rigid bulge beneath his jeans, lying along his thigh. Involuntarily, she was fantasising him pushing that rod into her, until his hips squashed hard into her soft, inner thighs. How was it possible, she wondered, to square her lust with a sacred ritual?

He touched her arm gently, and she lowered her thumb from her gnawing teeth.

'Don't be scared, my darling.' He pulled her into his arms, rocking her in his embrace. 'Remember the thunderstorm?'

She nodded, her cheek rubbing on the soft wool of his jumper. Her body trembled against his, and his hand running through her hair lit sparks in her flesh.

'It'll be like that – or like when we put the icons on the altar. But we'll be in a circle this time, and it'll just be you and me, safe and together.'

'I'm not scared,' she said, lifting her lips to a breath away from his. 'I want you so much I don't know what to do with myself.'

He laughed, digging his hands into her buttocks to press her against him. 'Then light the biggest fire that'll fit, and I'll fill us a bath.'

The bathroom was lit by lots of little candles when she came in, their brilliance softened by the steam rolling from the clear water. Adrian's beautiful body was already naked. She laughed in delight at the gorgeous sight of it all, and felt the tension in her body ease. They bathed for a long time, washing each other slowly. The hot water worked deep into their muscles, until their very bones felt warm again. Mischievous fingers and toes crept over sensitive flesh. By the time they entered the bedroom, the fire in the hearth and in their bodies was blazing. Adrian knelt at her feet as she stretched out her arm and, slowly spinning, intoned for the second time that night, 'I consecrate this circle of power to the Ancient Gods. Here may they manifest and bless their children'. They turned eastwards, their backs to the dark sea behind them, and said together, 'This is a time that is not a time, in a place that is not a place, on a day that is not a day. We stand on the threshold between the worlds, before the veil of the Mysteries. May the Ancient Ones help and protect us on our journey.'

They bound the elements one by one into the circle, feeling the energy inside it increasing and changing with each vital force. When the circle was sealed with the final words, they turned to the altar. Looking at the icons, Sarah realised that they were not, as Adrian had said they would be, alone. Adrian's two small paintings were imbued with palpable life; the Lady and her Lover were watching them. Looking into her dark, soft eyes, Sarah knew that the ritual they were about to perform was the closest to the Lady's heart of all. She was the Queen of the Earth, and what everything on and under the earth craved, from the smallest amoeba to the most complex mammal, from lichen to oak trees, was life. To live, and to reproduce, was the purest aim, from which all else sprang.

They turned to each other, and ran their hands lightly down each other's arms. 'May we share our power as we share our bodies,' they chorused softly. Their hands began to wander over each other's bodies slowly, as they repeated the mantra, out loud and in their heads, at different times and together. He found the heavy weight of her breasts and supported them, his fingertips roaming the soft skin of the globes. Her palms pressed against his chest, she felt the compact fullness of his muscles, and the tiny hardness of his nipples. Sinking gradually to his knees again, his hands traced the full, sumptuous shape of her body, from her generous breasts to the concave of her waist and over the swell of her hips. She felt her body being redefined as he explored it, becoming fuller, richer, more womanly. Her thighs swayed towards him, offering herself to his mouth. He accepted gladly, and as he pressed his lips to her slit she felt herself growing taller, flickering upwards like a flame from that burning point where his tongue danced over the tiny glowing coal of her clitoris. Tilting her head back in bliss, she moaned aloud, letting her sounds of pleasure form the words of their mantra. He drank deeper, pushing his tongue into her and lapping at her juice. Her little whimpers were barely louder than the crackle of the fire or the succulent slurping of his tongue. At the gentle pressure of his hands, she placed her feet further apart.

He sat at the base of the triangle formed by her legs, licking eagerly, pressing his tongue between her cheeks against the tight hole of her bottom. She shuddered violently, molten lava coursing through her as he pried. His fingers rippled across her fleshy lips, and she grabbed his raised knees for support. He gripped her hips, pulling her closer to him, and her knees yielded. Crouched over him, she pressed her face against his fiery shaft, half-sobbing while his tongue lovingly violated her privacy. She wriggled above him, parting his thighs, sinking her mouth down to taste his own small aperture. His cry was muffled, his rod danced against her breasts. She tongued him wildly, losing herself in the long kisses, until his thrusting tongue had her quivering dangerously close to the edge. She turned to face him then, kneeling between his legs. His eyes were half-glazed as he murmured again with her, 'May we share our power as we share our bodies.'

She lay on top of him, rubbing her body against his, feeling the magnetism of his skin. Their warm flesh and bones shifted together, firm and soft, hard and yielding. As she writhed slowly against him, his staff slid closer to her tightly sealed passage. Soon, too soon, it was slithering between her creamy lips, butting insistently against the entrance. She felt sweet spasms of joy rising, and forced herself to lie still, quelling the waves of feeling.

'May we share our power as we share our bodies,' he said again, and with sudden strength in his arms, he swirled her around and beneath him. She shook violently as he shoved slowly into her, stretching the taut, aching walls of her pussy. When he was scarcely halfway in, she cried out with anguish. Her mind and limbs flailed helplessly, as he slid his battering ram back and forth, spreading her juices and deepening his thrusts. Slowly, fiercely, he consolidated every quarter-inch that her tight passage gave him. Her voice howled out the words of its own accord, maddened and lost in the unstoppable strength of his penetration. Her mind filled with earthquakes, violent chasms swallowing trees, boulders thundering down storm-filled rivers, tree roots slowly tearing up the foundations of ancient buildings. Her whole body was arched, flung out beneath him. She dreamt again how the earth had crushed her once, trying to blot out the determined bright spot that she now knew had been her. This time, the same massive pressure was flowing into her and filling her. It was becoming her own strength. As she bucked her hips against her beloved, she felt her own fire and destruction licking through his veins. His head was flung back, his arms rippling with power as he supported his scorching plunges into her. Their orgasm flowed upwards through them, a volcanic fire erupting through their mouths as his lava flooded into her welcoming cave.

She lay, drained and sated, feeling the warm weight of his body upon her, staring dreamily at the uneven ceiling above her. She thought of the stars and planets spinning beyond them, unimaginable distances away but really there, held in orbit by gravity, imposing their strange forces as they swung past.

'The ritual said for seven days...' she murmured quietly into his ear. Her voice was soft, half-lost in thought. 'In two days' time we move from Sagittarius to Capricorn – Fire to Earth.' she added. 'And it'll be Yule, and we can marry for a year and a day.'

His warm arms clasped her close to him.

6 Geburah

Sarah pressed redial on her phone, and listened once more to the tense, tinny shrilling, its mute screams at last cut off again by the voice message.

'Hi, this is Adrian, please leave a message and I'll ring you back.'

She hung up. She was sitting hunched against the cold on a bench on the college quad, watching the bare, jagged branches judder in the stiff wind. Turning to the phone in her hand again, she redialled. She had almost given up hope of him answering, but just to hear his warm familiar voice promising to ring her back was something.

Henrietta came out with two cups of coffee and sat next to her on the bench, waiting while the ringing subsided into voicemail.

'Still no answer?' she said gently.

Sarah shook her head. 'I get to hear his voice,' she said. The effort of speaking made her lower lip twist and her eyes rushed with tears again. Her face distorted as she forced the storm of sobs back down. 'It's been a week,' she said, her voice struggling for clarity. 'I'd just like – to know what . . .'

She broke down, covering her face with her hands from the curious glance of two passing undergraduates. She felt Henrietta's arm pull her closer, and she wept harder.

'We floated,' she choked out incoherently, 'we – we saw souls, we . . .'

* * *

A week and a day before, they had returned from Morvah and Adrian's college had offered him a room in halls. He'd accepted it and moved out of Sarah's – on the same impulse, she had presumed, that made him refuse money from his parents. He had been as gentle and loving as ever, kissing her on the doorstep and promising to return the next evening for dinner. That was the last time they'd spoken. She'd waited. She'd phoned. She'd walked to Christ Church to knock on the unyielding wooden door that the porters assured her was his. When she left, she stood outside and counted the windows at least five times, unable to believe that his light was on, his silhouette against the curtains. She went back in and beat on the door until one of his neighbours threatened to fetch the porter. At home, she cried until she vomited. A week without his kisses, without the shared rituals at dawn and sunset, without the heat of his body in bed. With each day that passed, the comforting disbelief faded into more grief. Every morning she was further away from a world where it was impossible for Adrian not to love her, not to want to speak to her. She'd heard his voice, at least. She heard his voicemail several times a day, though she'd given up leaving messages. When she phoned his department, she heard his voice in the background, asking who it was. Her heart smashed against her ribs as she said her name, and then she got to hear his voice again, muted from across the room, telling whoever had answered the phone that he was a bit busy, and would ring back.

'Everyone will be coming for formal hall soon,' said Henrietta. 'Do you want to eat in a pub, instead?'

Sarah nodded, wiping her face on her coat sleeve. 'A dark one,' she said, trying to smile. She was grateful to leave the college and all the eyes in it, but as they walked through the streets she longed to hide her face from the whole world. A paper bag over her head would do nicely. As they crossed Radcliffe Square, she veered from shadows to shadows. Anyone might know Adrian – anyone might report her swollen, blotched face. Adrian, who had held her as she sobbed, wasn't supposed to care, but ... She sniffed, trying to clear her nose and her head.

They sat at the back of the White Horse, in a quiet, gloomy alcove. Sarah laid out the cards on the round, wooden table, its surface pitted and streaked with use. She felt, if not better, at least more human after the solid pub meal that Henrietta had insisted she eat. Her hands moved across the table with fateful sureness, setting each card in its allotted space. For these moments at least, her mind was filled with just one question. For now, it crowded out the snapshots of Adrian's naked body in the silvery morning light, the sudden smell-memories of his skin, the snippets of conversation, that usually invaded her mind.

What will happen next with Adrian and me?

She completed the Celtic Cross, turned them all over, and looked away abruptly. The future column showed a heavy stripe of black. The outcome was the Tower.

'Wait,' said Henrietta, 'wait till I read it – maybe it's not all bad.'

Sarah looked at the cards, her jaw stiff with revulsion. She wanted to sweep them all back into their bag and tie the drawstring, but she waited. Maybe Henrietta could find some glow of hope, even in this.

'It's a very powerful reading,' Henrietta said at last, pulling at her cigarette.

Powerful bad, Sarah wanted to say, but she restrained the bitter words.

'Seven Major Arcana – it's important. OK, you weren't wrong about the past, that is certain. The Sun and the

Lovers – and the Sun lightens the whole reading, don't forget that.' She began to weave the narrative from the pictures.

'You're feeling right now like you're completely defeated, that's the ten of swords, because you've been tricked in some way – that's the Magician. And in the near future, you feel – um...'

'Outcast and unbearably grief-stricken,' put in Sarah dully, her eyes on the three of swords.

'Well, yes,' said Henrietta reluctantly. 'And you're confused, you don't know what's going on, that's the Moon upside down – then, in the general future – oh. Well, you feel like your worst nightmares are upon you, but that doesn't mean they are – and your environment is...'

'The worst aspects of the Devil.'

'Yes. But it might not be so bad – you're overlooking the High Priestess, your own strength, and the outcome is the Tower, but it's the right way round, so it's cathartic in the end, things are destroyed that need to be destroyed...' Her voice petered out.

Sarah smeared her rolling tears across her cheeks and gathered up the cards again with damp hands.

'Sorry I seem to be a waterworks,' she said. 'Can we just forget the future and get another bottle of wine?'

'Sure. Tomorrow might be better.'

'Tomorrow is another day,' muttered Sarah, pulling out her purse. 'Tomorrow and tomorrow and tomorrow, creeps on this petty pace...' She pushed the money across the table. 'Do you mind getting it? I can't face the world.'

Sarah tried, in the ensuing days, to throw herself into her work. She spent longer and longer in the library, trying to deaden the grief of her heart with the joys of the mind. Not many joys were to be had. Dr Piedmont hadn't returned her chapter or replied to her emails, all her sense of focus had evaporated, and increasingly she just surfed manuscript images at random, looking for something she no longer knew how to define. As if to rub salt into the wound, the texts she found all seemed to echo back to experiences shared with Adrian. She was badly upset, rereading Julian of Norwich, by the hazel-nut passage.

'a lytil thyng þe quantite of a hasyl nott . . .' she read. On the screen, the parchment glowed like gold. 'It is all þat is mad. I merueled howe it myght laste. for me þought it myght soden ly haue fall to nought for lytyl-lhed. & I was answered in my vnderstondyng. It lastyth & euer shall for god louyth it.'

The little round thing, containing everything, which will last forever because God loves it, brought back powerfully the vision she had had of lying beneath the earth, fighting for existence. Adrian had held her and given her his strength, had helped her find her way back. How could she ever find her way back to anything now, deprived of her guiding star?

Apart from obsessive tarot readings with Henrietta, all of them uniformly black, she eschewed anything to do with magic. She let the altar gather dust and deter-minedly ignored the rising and setting of the sun. She dreamt, however, of little else. Night after night, she visited the dark, herb-ceilinged shack and mixed potions in her wooden mortar. Each dream was fragmented but lucid, like scraps of memory with the connections miss-ing. One night she was painting symbols on an old house, her face wrapped in fabric, and had to hide suddenly. She remembered standing in the deep shadow of the doorway, shaking with fear, as footsteps passed. Another night she was casting a circle in a meadow, around a group of cowled people, under the light of a brilliant moon, and turning back saw Adrian among them. His face shone with love. Her stomach jolted with excitement, and she woke up to her empty bed. A few times, she dreamt again of Adrian walking across the meadow, the terrible horsemen gaining speed, and her futile attempts to cast a spell of protection fast enough.

She began to write the dreams down, in the hope that it might stem the tide. She found she could remember the exact name of every herb she selected from the ceiling and ground into her bowl. She also knew the purpose of what she was doing in the dreams – combinations for healing a skin disease, for legal matters, for and against miscarriage … Her dream diary came to resemble a book of spells and herb-lore. She tried to work out the dream-logic behind it. The obsession with plants pointed to Adrian, but the spells themselves seemed to have no connection with her feelings.

She avoided the west wing of the house, with Mother's room and the guest room where Adrian had spent a single night. She told herself there was no such thing as ghosts, and anyway she could only see them at full moon, but nothing could persuade her to set foot there. She watched with dread as the moon waxed.

Dr Piedmont's reply finally came towards the end of third week. Sarah had walked to college through a restless storm, the wind lashing the rain so vindictively that her umbrella was only an encumbrance. Staying at home was out of the question – the moon would reach its zenith today. She would stay over with Henrietta, or if need be in the MCR, but not alone in the house. She was soaked from the waist down, and stood dripping in the lodge as she tore the envelope open. Her work was returned, aggressively annotated, with whole passages scratched out – no explanation – and lots of heavy underlining, with the word 'NO' scrawled in the margins. 'Bastard!' she muttered sharply, her outrage increasing.

'Is that from Adrian?' Henrietta had just entered the lodge, equally soaked, and hurried over eagerly.

'No, it's my sod of a supervisor! Look at this!' She brandished the sheets and launched into a tirade against his attitude to supervision, tardiness, lack of explanation, patronising attitude, and stupid greasy hair. 'I mean – where's the sense of fucking profession-alism?' she spat out. She turned to the final item in the envelope – a photocopied invitation to a supervisors' dinner at Christ Church, with her name highlighted. Her stomach turned over violently. Henrietta took in her white face, and looked down at the sheet.

'Not a very polite invita...' she began, and stopped abruptly. 'Oh.'

In the list of supervisees' names was Adrian's.

Sarah's anger collapsed like a quenched fire and her shoulders began to shake.

'I can't cope, Henrietta,' she whispered through her veil of tears. 'I'm cold and wet, my work's going terribly, Dr Piedmont just slashes at me with his horrible claws instead of helping,' I'm too scared to go home because there's a ghost in the house, she thought, 'and Adrian...' The tears fell faster as she got to the true cause of her tears. 'Adrian doesn't love me,' she managed to say, 'and I haven't seen him and I want to and I'm going to, and I don't know what to do. I'm sorry.' She sniffed, and tried to wipe her eyes with an equally wet sleeve. 'There just doesn't seem to be a reason for anything, a reason for going on, you know?' She dabbed at her face again, blinking furiously. 'I don't mean I'm suicidal or any-thing,' she added hastily, 'I'm just – um...'

'Heart-broken?' supplied Henrietta gently.

With lips tightly compressed, Sarah nodded.

* * *

Too cold to work in the library, she spent the day with her books in Georgina's, a snug little coffee shop with brightly coloured walls and a ceiling of old film posters. Sitting right next to the radiator, she felt the warmth slowly return to her veins as her clothes dried out. Grateful to think of anything besides her pain, she steeled herself to go through Dr Piedmont's comments one by one and check if any of her more recent research notes shed any light. There was a curious logic, she found – he seemed to be steering her away from any examination of the Old Religion. She had included it as just another aspect of alternative thought, something contemporaneous which threatened Church dogma. She reread more carefully the passages he'd deleted. At the back of her mind, a rebellious decision was forming – this was the focus she'd been lacking, this was what she'd hone her topic in on. Whatever his objections might be, they didn't seem to be academic.

When the waitress said they were closing, Sarah looked up in surprise at the emptied café.

She walked out into the covered market, the lights a cold dead colour on the brick floor, the shops already mostly shuttered. Outside, the storm had cleared, night had fallen, and a fat moon was already rising. Despite herself, she thought of the last full moon. She and Adrian had made wands, celebrated with a feast, and made love by the fire. She had looked up at the silver coin of the moon that night, full of joy and wonder at its beauty. Now she stared at its swollen white face with fear.

'Sarah?' said a familiar voice behind her.

She spun round, hope soaring, and found herself face to face with Jo. He must have seen her face fall, because he grimaced wryly, saying, 'I know your heart's engaged elsewhere these days, but I hoped you might invite me home for a little conversation, at least.'

'I wasn't going to go home,' she said, flustered, 'I'm afraid of seeing – a ghost,' she finished, lamely.

He raised his eyebrows incredulously, his little smile mocking her. After a few seconds, he took pity on the look in her eyes.

'Take my arm,' he said, extending it. She slipped her hand over his forearm, and he squeezed it tightly to him. 'Are you frightened of me?'

She shook her head mutely.

'Then who?'

'Mother,' she mumbled. 'She lives in the house, I didn't know before. And I know it doesn't make sense, because I'm not afraid of you, but I'm afraid of being there alone, tonight.'

They walked up the Banbury Road in silence. The solid pressure of Jo's arm and the way his head leant tenderly towards her was almost unbearably comforting. After the constant presence of Adrian in her bed, in her arms, by her side, the last month had been bewilderingly isolated. She couldn't think of touching Jo as she had before. She couldn't bear the thought of anyone touching her as Adrian had ever again, but she revelled in the closeness like a starveling as they walked. When they were sitting together on the sofa, she couldn't resist resting her head on his shoulder. His hand stroked her hair gently. Her relief at being touched again, cared for, was like sinking into a soft bed to sleep after days and nights of exhaustion. She put her pained loyalty not away, but to one side, and let herself snuggle her head closer to the curve of his neck, as if laying down a heavy weight that she knew she would have to pick up again – but not yet, not right now.

'Where is Adrian tonight,' he murmured, 'when he should be looking after his beautiful, scared darling?'

The pain came rushing back. Sarah sat up, and moved

into the corner of the sofa, her knees pulled up. She massaged her forehead wearily, hiding her face, as she said, 'Adrian's not coming back, and I'm not his darling, and I doubt he thinks I'm beautiful or cares if I'm scared.' Her face hardened, to avoid crumpling.

'What?' exclaimed Jo, horrified.

'He's ditched me. Dumped me. Left me. Whatever you want. Or so I assume, because he just left and hasn't deigned to speak to me since. I mean, maybe I should've guessed, when he left his last girlfriend so easily and jumped straight into my bed, it doesn't exactly demonstrate a loyal character. Don't know what I was thinking, really.' The acid bitterness rolled off her tongue, voicing at last all her worst and least true thoughts, smashing the golden idol of her dreams.

'And you let him?' Jo was appalled.

'It's not like I had much choice, is it?' Sarah snapped. 'He won't even speak to me, Jo! I wasn't given a vote, you know. He fucked off without a word and I'm in smithereens and that's pretty much that. Get it?'

Jo leapt to his feet and paced restlessly up and down the lounge.

'He's alive and well?' he asked abruptly.

'I've seen his silhouette and heard his voice across the room from the phone in the lab. And a few friends assure me he's still walking and talking. I haven't been able to make any closer observations.' Her tone was increasingly sarcastic, as her mute sorrow at last found a banshee's voice.

'This isn't good. This isn't good at all.' He shook his head gravely.

She stared at him disbelievingly. 'Not for me, no,' she said sharply. 'Don't know what you're so upset about, you might even get your easy lay back.'

He spun on his heel. 'Don't even think about betraying Adrian,' he said angrily, brandishing his finger.

'Betrayal?' Sarah's voice rose. 'Jo, I'm the one who's been betrayed, in case you hadn't noticed. Maybe you think I should be some kind of Miss Havisham in a wedding dress and lock myself up and never so much as look at another man...'

'That's not what I meant!' Jo interrupted. 'Sarah, you're a witch, stop thinking in terms of that horrible hypocritical prudery, betrayal is your motive, not your deed.'

Sarah jumped up. 'Stop preaching at me,' she yelled. 'You have no idea what I've been going through, you have no idea what kind of god-awful thing my life has turned into! I've been trying, goddammit! I've been trying to get on with life, let myself heal somehow, focus on my work, and even that's going to shit.' She pulled her annotated thesis chapter from her bag, and flung it at Jo's feet. 'That's what my supervisor thinks of my work, and right now my PhD is the only other thing I have in my life!' She flopped back into the sofa, arms tightly folded, quivering with rage. Jo stooped and picked up one of the scattered pages.

'The printing's on the other side,' said Sarah sarcastically.

'No, it isn't.' Jo turned the sheet around and showed her the reverse. It was his own handwriting, the message he had written in the library. Sarah stared at it in horror.

'I gave that to Dr Piedmont?' she said, appalled. 'I couldn't have!'

Jo was shaking his head in bewilderment. 'I can't believe you could be so careless!' he said. 'Why don't you just use your power, you have it, just use it for once! The man is –'

'Shut up!' screamed Sarah, snapping. 'Stop it! Adrian printed that out, not me. Adrian ended our relationship, not me. Everything's going wrong, and all you can do is moan at me, like everything's my fault, just get out!'

'Please, Sarah, don't!' said Jo, anxiously, 'Please.'

'Get out! Get out!' she yelled, her eyes screwed up. He said nothing. She felt the withdrawal of his presence even before she opened her eyes and saw the empty room. She sat very still, trying to absorb what had happened. 'I'm sorry, Jo.' she whispered, but she knew she was alone.

There was a soft tap at the lounge door.

'Come in,' Sarah said softly, wonderingly. Had he just vanished from the room, not the house? The door swung slowly inwards, and she sat up, ready to apologise. But walking hesitantly around the door and holding awkwardly onto it, was Mother.

'Don't be alarmed, my dear,' she said, her voice quavery with age. She fumbled with the door handle, looking for something else on which to steady herself. Sarah stared as the old woman's hands moved uncertainly this way and that. Without intending to, she leapt up to offer a supporting arm. The small, wasted hand that rested on her clutched with brittle strength as Sarah walked her slowly to the nearest chair.

'Thank you very much, thank you,' the woman repeated as she lowered herself clumsily. 'I do hope I'm not intruding, I heard raised voices. I couldn't help overhearing, I'm afraid.'

'I'm sorry,' said Sarah confusedly, 'I didn't think – I didn't mean to disturb you.'

'No, no, that's quite alright, it is your house, after all. I'm just a guest. And a rather unwelcome one, I fear.' She settled her thin legs at last, adjusting their position with her hands. 'Now, I won't keep you long, but I think we need a word. That Adrian, your young man –'

'He's not my young man,' interrupted Sarah, but a look from Mother silenced her.

'He has the Gift, as do you. As did I – not to the extent you have, but something of the Second Sight, at least. Now, foresight was never my gift, so I won't pretend it was, but something is very seriously amiss. For one thing, you have just thrown out a true friend in your hour of need. For another, you are neglecting the craft.'

Sarah opened her mouth to speak again, but Mother raised her hand.

'I am not chastising you. I have known something of heartbreak, too. But it seems to me that something else is at work. Consider. You find a young man with the Gift, power that matches your own in strength, and complements it. You fall in love, go away, come back with all the tools of the trade and suddenly – mystery. The man vanishes. You stop working at the craft. He stops as well, he must do, because it would be impossible for him to continue and still do you such harm – not even an explanation. You are too blinded by sorrow to consider it rationally, I understand. That, too, hinders your fighting back against – well, whatever has caused this.' Her hooded eyes softened as she looked at Sarah. 'I grieve for you, my dear, I do. I try not to intrude, you choose not to see me except when it's inescapable, I try to respect that. But my hearing never suffered with age, whatever happened to the rest of me.' She waved disdainfully at her shrunken body. 'I hear you crying at night,' she said pityingly. 'Fit to break a soul's heart, that sound. A fair few times I've crept in, hoping to calm you a little. I'm sorry if that frightens you,' she added, taking in Sarah's widening eyes. 'But there you are, fast asleep, and weeping like a freshly widowed bride.' Her rheumy eyes glistened with tears, and she sighed. 'And the advice I must give you is the hardest and most painful possible.'

Sarah had curled up again, tucking her legs in, in the foetal position. Her chin rested on her knees as she watched the old woman and listened to her words. That sympathy had brought moisture back to her ever-wet eyes, but it was a sweeter sadness for being so genuinely pitied. All the same, her heart sank heavily at the thought of the advice to come.

'I know,' she said tiredly. 'I have to put it behind me, move on.'

'No, my dear,' said Mother sadly. 'It's worse. You have to hold on. You have to return to the craft, you have to keep hold of your love, which means every day's pain will be as bad as the first.'

All the wisdom that society could offer contradicted what Mother said that night. The time of epic romances had passed. Looking around her, Sarah knew that love could scarcely conquer a few years of the ennui that comfortable routine generated, much less all. Holding firm to your true love was just clinging on to the warm blanket of delusion, the sweet consolation of foundless fantasy. Let go. Get over it. Move on. Get on with your own life. Forget him, he's not worth it. Anything else was Denial, which would then be surely followed by Anger, Grief, and Acceptance. She thought of Spenser's *Faërie Queen*, and how Janet had clung fast to her own true love, Thomas the Rhymer, while the Queen had turned him into a serpent, a lion, a giant spider, burning fire, and every other painful or monstrous thing she could devise. How easy it would be, to pretend that her everyday misery was part of a magnificent quest, that all this was just a test of her love and she would win her darling back, his blindness cured, if she just held on. But it wasn't easy.

She began the rituals again the next morning. She wiped the dust from her tools and set the altar up in Mother's room, by candlelight. If Mother was there, she neither saw her nor felt her presence. At a quarter to eight, she sat cross-legged at the centre of the magic circle, tears streaming freely down her face, while the dull grey light of a faceless dawn crawled into the room. Her eyes stayed on the picture of the Goddess, while her lips murmured quietly, 'Grant me insight. Grant me insight.' She didn't know what spells to perform or what to ask. The one thing she wanted above all else was to ask for Adrian's love back, but not to beglamour him or blind him with lust. His own true self looking out of his own eyes could only come back of its own accord. And yet, she had to hold on. Eventually, she closed the circle, feeling as if she had only reopened a wound.

Cutting short her day at the library, she repeated it at sunset, with no more result. The next morning, as she closed the circle, she remembered that the following day was Imbolc, one of the eight Sabbats of the calendar. It was the time of cleansing, of newborn lambs, one of only eight uniquely sacred days, and without Adrian, with whom could she celebrate it?

'I don't know how to say any of this,' she began, fiddling with Henrietta's packet of tobacco.

They sat in the downstairs room of Café Nero, in a fug of cigarette smoke, dark wood, leather, and purple walls. Most of the small, round tables were occupied by individual students, their laptops whirring quietly. Soft classical music fell gently through the cigarette smoke that drifted towards the ventilator. As Henrietta gently released her tobacco, to roll a cigarette, Sarah transferred her intense attention to her mug of coffee.

'This much is clear,' said Henrietta, after a long silence.

'I'm a witch.'

'Oh-kay . . .' The cigarette slowly rolled itself between Henrietta's narrow fingers.

'So is Adrian.'

She nodded slowly.

'We're married. Sort of. For a year and a day. A sort of pagan trial marriage. And when I said we floated, I meant it literally, not just great sex. We actually sat together in the centre of the circle and lifted off the ground.' Of everything they had experienced, the floating had been the most meaningless – pretty, but nothing more. Now, it was the only definite proof to which she could cling.

In staccato bursts, she poured out every detail of their time in Cornwall, from seeing each other's souls to seeing his dead grandmother, from the Book of Shadows to the sex rituals. Her sentences were abrupt, for every word was a betrayal of their privacy – but she couldn't carry on alone, and she was trying to carry on at all costs. At last, the flow faltered, and the silence resumed.

'Why didn't you tell me any of this before?' said Henrietta, eventually.

'Because you wouldn't believe me – I didn't think you would believe me.'

'Sarah, I read your cards almost every day!' she retorted, looking hurt. 'How can you keep this from me? Why do you think I wouldn't believe you? I even told you I believe in witches, but . . .' She stopped abruptly.

'I'm sorry, Hen – I didn't believe me, I – you do believe in witches?'

'Yes. At least, I think so. My mother was a witch, I think. I don't really know, I only read the court judgements – they got divorced when I was two, and my father got custody, because my mother was a witch, but then she died a year later anyway. I don't remember her, really, but I found the papers. Either way, my dad would have brought me up.' She shrugged. 'So, the tarot cards. I don't really know anything more about it, but . . .'

Sarah was staring at Henrietta with delight and hope etched on her face. 'Would you like to learn?'

'I consecrate this circle of power to the Ancient Gods. Here may they manifest and bless their children.' In the dim glimmer before sunrise, Sarah's naked body glowed in pale planes as she walked slowly, her hand extended, marking the circle. She smiled faintly, as she passed the most westwards point and the portrait, so like her, that stood as a dark rectangle above the fireplace. Returning to the opposite side, she raised her wand, saying 'This is a time that is not a time, in a place that is not a place, on a day that is not a day. We stand on the threshold between the worlds, before the veil of the Mysteries. May the Ancient Ones help and protect us on our journey.'

Henrietta stood at the centre of the circle, also unclothed, watching with eyes full of enchantment as Sarah opened the ritual. When each of the elements had been introduced and each of their powers called upon, she finished, saying, 'This circle is bound, with power all around. Between the worlds I stand with protection at hand,' and the two sat before the altar. At the centre of the white linen cloth, stood Sarah's golden-yellow candle, its red centre already revealed and its wick blackened from previous lightings. Next to it rested a newly made white candle with a green core, its wick still untouched, for Henrietta. Around these two, were another four candles: white behind, for truth and sincerity; purple in front, for power and divination; and orange on either side, to attract these towards them. Their right hands clasped as Sarah guided Henrietta's hand to light each candle, while she whispered the words of the ritual herself.

With all the candles glowing and the first whispers of light gold whispering about the room, they turned to face each other, cross-legged, the tarot pack lying between them.

As Sarah began to shuffle the cards, musing on what question would best answer her confusion, her eyes rested peacefully on Henrietta's beautiful body. *Not one wen did I spye*, she thought lovingly. How many men would give away years of their life to sit with her like this, and how few would be able to do so and still adore the loveliness of her soul more? The cards fell lightly from hand to hand as she considered her question, and it began to take shape around her friend. Her eyes absorbed the sweet, small curves and narrow shoulders barely touched by the hesitant, new sun. Between her crossed legs, a narrow pink slit peeped out of her pale, fluffy hair. What is Henrietta's story in this? she thought to the cards, and began to shuffle more intently. When she laid out the Celtic Cross, and turned each card over, the bright, pastel colours of the chosen cards made her catch her breath.

Henrietta helped her dress for the dinner at Christ Church, fixing her hair and make-up with expert fingers.

'You are so beautiful!' she exclaimed, stepping back, delight on her face.

Sarah smiled anxiously, but turning to the mirror she saw herself through Henrietta's eyes. Her eyes gleamed like deep pools, huge and dreamy, shining with purity. Her face glowed with peace. Her top followed the inward contours of her waist sensuously, and held up her cleavage like a gift. Between her breasts, nestled a ruby, held in filigree, on a thin silver chain. It belonged to Henrietta; the two girls had consecrated it as a talisman for protection against evil that morning.

'Now remember,' said Henrietta as they parted at Carfax Tower, 'whatever happens tonight, nothing can touch you, they can't take anything away from you!'

She fingered the ruby like a rosary, as she walked through the gates of Christ Church and towards the Senior Common Room, where the pre-dinner drinks were to be held. Would Adrian be there, in the clumsily mingling crowd? *Nothing can touch me*, she repeated like a mantra as she crossed the quadrangle, and it seemed she glided above the ground without stepping on it. The first face she saw as she floated into the SCR was Clara's, pinching with disgust. She couldn't see Adrian's face – Clara was already tugging him with her, following the head porter into dinner.

She stood motionless just inside the room, an elegant statue in her flowing skirt and fitted top, her face expressionless. *Nothing can touch me* echoed in the hollow chambers of her mind, as she watched the back of his head moving away from her. The hair she had held between her fingers. The head that had bent over her breasts. The shoulders and back that had lain naked beside her, to which she had sleepily clung, dreaming of planets and stars, gods and goddesses, knowing that he would see into her dreams if they so wished. A desolate hall of echoing marble and empty floors had replaced her mind, and Dr Piedmont's sardonic witter was like the clanging of a far distant bell, to which she nodded vaguely. She let her supervisor take her arm and lead her into dinner, her eyes unseeing now that Adrian had passed beyond her view. *Nothing can touch me*, she thought, and remembered vaguely that she was furious with Dr Piedmont, somewhere in a distant universe beyond the outskirts of her soul.

'Yes, quite,' she said vaguely, when his intonation suggested he had asked a question. Like a beautiful automaton, she took her place opposite Adrian, and rested her calm eyes on him as she laid her hand on the ruby, holding it closer to her skin. She could only see part of his face, as the rest was blocked by Clara's enthusiastic kisses. She observed his ear. She broke her bread roll, and buttered it.

'Hello, Adrian,' she said, when he emerged from the embrace. 'Clara,' she nodded. 'So you did need his razor in your bathroom, after all?' She smiled distantly.

Clara looked as if she was determined to ignore a bad smell, but the ruby's spell held and Sarah felt the hostility wash over her. Her heart should have been beating like wildfire, but it pounded as steadily as ever. Water off a duck's back, she thought calmly, and her thoughts turned to the ducks of Oxford as she prepared another mouthful of roll, watching the creamy butter turn the fluffy interior slick. She didn't yet dare test the power of her talisman against Adrian's eyes.

Dr Piedmont slid onto the bench, coming to rest beside her. 'How lovely,' he said, bringing his hands together. 'A chance for all my students to get to know each other – Sarah, this is Clara and Adrian; Clara, Adrian...'

'We've met,' cut in Sarah placidly. If she broke her calm now, she thought, she would fling the heavy table away from her, scattering the crockery and crushing people beneath it. If she started screaming, she would never stop. The three of them were ranged against her, waiting for a crack in her armour into which to stick their spears. She would be as sealed as an egg, and they would never know how fragile, but she couldn't avoid Adrian's eyes all evening.

She raised her lids, and saw again the full perfection of his beloved face. She could feel the tingle of magic across her skin as the ruby redoubled its protection, and she didn't gasp or stare. He was more beautiful than she had remembered in her weeping, idealising dreams. In the low light, his smooth skin swept gently across his cheekbones and curved in. Across his brow, it knitted slightly; his mouth was faintly pursed. His eyes were open, but shuttered and hard. Never before had she seen this expression on his face – was this anger, she thought wonderingly? Was it directed at her? The field of the spell quivered violently; she felt it like a fabric stretching almost to tearing point.

'Why did you come?' he said hoarsely.

She glanced at the others – the attention of each was directed towards their neighbours for a moment. Could she tell him honestly, that she had come to rescue him, to prove her love whatever it cost? What did Janet do, to save her Thomas from the Faerie Queen? *I have to win him back*, she thought desperately, *I don't know how. Show me.*

Clara turned back sharply, her eyes whisking from one to the other in suspicion. The soup was placed in front of them.

'Delicious,' murmured Sarah as her nose wrinkled at the over-salted smell. 'What herb is this, do you think, Adrian?'

'How should I know,' he scowled.

Interesting, thought Sarah. You can love a face so well and so attentively, and still see new expressions on it. She could feel the pain clattering at the boundaries within the magic, but she paid it no heed. Her inner self screamed hysterically as she scooped her soup neatly towards her mouth. *It's like turning and running in the dark, that's what lets the demons in. Stay calm.* They ate their soup in silence.

'How is your research going?' asked Clara stiffly, as the bowls were collected.

'Well, I've had a few setbacks,' said Sarah easily, 'but I think Dr Piedmont has pointed me in the right direction.' She smiled graciously at him. His face was contorted in a sneer. 'I forget what field you're in?'

'Law,' supplied Dr Piedmont. 'And doing rather well – she's one of the shining stars of our college, I believe.'

His tongue darted out as he spoke, moistening his lips so that they shone lasciviously.

'How privileged we are, to be sitting with you then,' said Sarah mildly. 'I take it your father's a lawyer?'

'A judge,' snapped Clara.

'He's been very good to Adrian, I understand,' said the supervisor. Sarah raised her eyebrows in polite question, but no more was said.

When their attention was turned to the main course, Sarah focussed unseeingly on a point just beside Adrian's head. Silently, she invoked the Goddess's help, and a thin white band came into view around his head. She shifted her eyes slightly to the side, and colours glimmered into being around him. Like an iris, it was flecked with colours that all seemed to be one, but as she studied them the different shades emerged: a dull, dark brown with spatters of greyish yellow and specks of brick-red. She had never imagined his energy could sink to such low levels – he was weary to the bone, tinged with fear and anger. As she stared, she felt the ruby's enclosure split and spread. Her inner eye saw tendrils of brilliant wine-coloured fog reaching out towards him, curtaining them from Dr Piedmont and Clara. From the base of his aura crept a degraded, melancholy blue, like the sea as storm clouds gather. However cavalier his behaviour, his spirit was sick with misery, dreary and scared. My love, her heart cried, let me give you back your joy and brilliant colours.

'Is the food not to your taste?' broke in her supervisor's voice.

The cloud hands of love that had almost touched Adrian whipped back, enveloping her again in unnatural calm, and she began to eat.

The wind whirled frantically around her head as she walked home and the clouds reached down to tear at her clothes with rain. She felt their fury with relief, their anger that of a mother who's been driven to rage with worry. The streaming water washed away her tears, disguising them. She strode as fast as she could, away from the place where she had seen Adrian so cowed and curt, towards her altar, where she could see inside him again. Mother was right: something was deeply awry and was cutting into his spirit. She could not say goodbye.

'I'm coming, my love,' she whispered, as her feet carried her speedily away from where his body stood. 'I will protect you, whatever it takes.' She could see herself towering over Oxford, the storm clouds hurtling about her, arms outflung, electric with power. *You will not touch him.* First, she had to know who, or what, she was fighting. At the altar, she could be with him again.

She tore off her wet clothes as she walked up the stairs, lit the fire hastily, and stood in front of the icons of the Goddess and Her mate. She didn't need a ritual bath, when the Goddess Herself had washed her all the way home. With stiff, cold fingers she unclasped the ruby and laid it on the altar, saying as she did so, 'Thank you for your protection.' As her fingers relinquished it, she felt tidal waves of tears threaten to engulf her, but stilled her heart. Later, she could cry all she liked. Right now, she needed the spirit of Diana, the huntress, a warrior. She cast the circle with a sense of sharp power she had never experienced before. '. . . in a place that is not a place . . .' She felt her position between two worlds and the irrelevance of physical placement in the words. Her body was here in north Oxford, bare and goose-pimpled. Adrian's was in Christ Church, but tonight she would see with his eyes, feel with his skin, penetrate his mind and look beneath.

She felt the words of the spell returning to her as she

sat at the centre of the circle, her legs crossed and her hands upturned on her knees. She had always known, she had only to remember. In calling them up, she glimpsed a storehouse of knowledge deep in the recesses of her mind. Now was not the time to wonder where it came from.

'His eyes are my eyes,' she intoned, lowering her lids. 'His skin is my skin. His ears are my ears. His thoughts are my thoughts. I will see as he sees, feel as he feels, hear as he hears, think as he thinks, and he shall have no awareness of it. From this hour to the next, I will inhabit him, and then by the grace of the Goddess I will return.' Her head swam. Dimly, she felt herself sinking to the floorboards in a dead faint as her spirit turned away from her body. The light of the fire through her closed eyes darkened, and with a lurch she felt herself flung forwards. Her fingers sank into soft flesh and a hot musky taste filled her mouth. Her head rose. Her eyes opened. Clara's prone body lay spread-eagled before her, breasts sloping sideways and nipples erect, her thighs wide open, her eyes staring at the ceiling, her mouth gaping and gasping.

'Don't – you dare – stop,' croaked the girl fiercely. Her legs rose, her heels dug hard into Sarah's shoulders, forcing her back down. Revolted, Sarah fought to get away, flailing backwards from the dark orifice. Her heavy limbs wouldn't obey her, her muscles refused to stir. Instead she felt her head lower obediently, and saw her hands spreading – no, not her hands – Adrian's. They opened the folds of her gash, and ducked down to taste her again, lapping obediently. The girl's taut thighs pulled closer, half-suffocating him inside her. Sarah felt her lungs pounding without oxygen – at last, Adrian pulled his head free.

'At least let me breathe.'

Sarah wanted to scream, recoil, vomit, weep, but each

of these required a body under her control. She floated, powerless, inside Adrian's skin as he obeyed Clara's curt demands. She tasted as he did, when he pushed his tongue between her buttocks. The fingers that shoved viciously into Clara's slippery pussy felt like her own. She felt the clutching, clenching orgasm of her rival as if on her own hand. Worse, she felt the degrading lust that built up inside her – inside Adrian – and the desire to plunge into that slick sheath or the other, to grab those small tits and twist them hard, to bite deep into her neck.

Adrian, she howled inside him, *this isn't you, this isn't how you make love, you don't use women, I know, I've seen your soul*. She had cast her spell well, however. He was oblivious to her visiting spirit as he gave into his lust. She felt his throbbing hardness in his hand and in his shaft, and the agonising tension as the tip pushed hard against Clara's anus. Its blunt end poked unavailingly at her wrinkled hole, determined to wrest gratification from it. The rubbery opening yielded a quarter inch, pulling back the skin from his head. His shudder of fierce delight mingled with Sarah's horror. She felt the thrill of that constricting passage, the ache to push harder, how Adrian's spear danced with excitement at Clara's wail. His hand seized one of the small breasts, using it to pull himself up from his knees onto her. His weight lodged his weapon deeper inside and the girl howled to be fucked. Each shove was an act of revenge as he forced the little aperture to accept his swollen erection. His roar of pleasure seemed to come from Sarah's own throat as he lay at last half-way encased, shifting back and forth, the tight passage massaging his head. His arms grabbed her tightly, pinning her to him, holding her in place as he hammered deeper in. His teeth sank into the side of her neck, his thighs bucked up and down, his buttocks clenching, his mind filled with lewd fantasies. These, too, Sarah could see and feel as if they were hers – Clara encased in shiny latex, her breasts and vagina framed and exposed by the glistening black. A whip descending on her bare buttocks, as she lay tied to the ground, impaled on a monstrous dildo, spasming with pain and ecstasy. Clara struggling against him, trying to fight him off, too scared and powerless to scream for help, while he used her depths and yielding flesh to bring himself off. Hatred seemed to fill them both as they heaved violently together, fighting their way to orgasm. Drowning in despair within Adrian, Sarah felt his mounting pleasure. Each thrust wedged him deeper, until the girl's sticky lips were rubbing against his crotch. She wriggled against him, using his body as he used hers. The shifts of her flesh against him, her breasts rubbing, stomach heaving, arms fighting for freedom, sent him to a higher pitch. He clutched her harder, redoubling his pummelling of her arse. Sarah could feel the piercing sharpness of orgasm approach. Through all her disgust, she felt it too, and longed to come – but Adrian held off, forcing Clara to lie still, letting the tide abate. Breathless, Sarah felt the violent twinges of his cock threaten to break control, then still, and subside. When it had calmed, he lifted himself up and began to move again, sodomising her slowly and pleasurably, withdrawing almost his whole length before stabbing it back in, watching her breasts judder. Clara's arm, pinned at the elbow, twisted so that her own hand could tweak her bead and push inside her. She fingered herself frantically, her palm rubbing at her hard clit, while Adrian filled her arse. They began to move faster, both groaning and rocking furiously, Clara's butt cheeks slapping against Adrian's thighs as he thrust. The current of lust carried Sarah with it, sinking and struggling, hungry for the ecstasy that would make it all stop. She felt the pitch rise higher and higher, as the sap mounted in Adrian's cock. Like the snap of a light switch, every sensation vanished. She lay stiff and cold on the hard floor, staring at the low-burning fire, sick to the stomach with revulsion. A mile to the south, in a room in Christ Church, Adrian was spurting his seed up Clara's backside.

7 Chesed

At the sloping desk, by candlelight, the dark ink glistened as Sarah's wedge-shaped nib moved carefully down the page, shaping each letter as a work of art. She was recording the ritual in her dream diary, which had become, of its own accord, her Book of Shadows. As she reread the words she had used, a heavy calm fell over her heart. She had been blinded by her pain, just as Mother had said. She longed so much for Adrian's body, his thoughts, his soul – so much that it had misled her, but she couldn't even retreat into saying too much, not if she were to hold fast to him. *His thoughts are my thoughts. And he shall have no awareness of it.* It had been the wrong ritual. If he were trapped, all she had done was join him in the trap, without even bringing him the comfort of her company. What he didn't know, she couldn't learn from inhabiting him like that. She watched the writing dry, remembering the disgust of being forced to participate in such a sordid, loveless fuck. *His thoughts are my thoughts.* Her heart beat and leapt, realisation striking her instantly like lightning. Everything she had thought and felt inside him had been his thoughts, his feelings – her longing to bring him true bliss again had been his longing, for her. For the first time in seven weeks, a smile of pure joy lit her face before being wiped away with renewed horror. Let them be my thoughts, she thought wildly, frantically, I got out, I'm strong enough, I can take it, don't let him be feeling like that, always, every day, let them have been my thoughts. Her mind writhed, like a mother who will twist as she falls, preferring to break her own back on the rocks rather than drop the baby she carries. She had to stand between him and danger, she had to fight tooth and nail for him, she could not leave him lost and appalled, helpless to resist. How had Clara done this to him? Sarah's mind rushed back and forth, hunting for a spell that could have caused such harm, but she could think of nothing. She needed to know more, she needed power, wisdom, a campaign plan, guidance – she needed Adrian's grandmother's Book of Shadows. She needed to know more about those visions Adrian's body had summoned up in her. Blotting the ink of the ritual's shadow, she turned to a clean page and began to compile the most extraordinary to-do list.

Henrietta shook her head in bewilderment, staring at the cards. They sat in the circle together, as before, except now the sun was setting behind thick walls of cloud, and premature darkness had fallen around the glowing altar candles.

'Something is wrong in the past,' she said at last, her eyes tracing the hexagram. 'Something big – the world off kilter. You can't see what it is, it's shrouded in a dark world of – it's the unknown, beyond knowledge. And it's urgent. You need to dream – that's the Seven of Cups, there – and you need help, or you have help.' She gestured at the Knave of Wands standing at the top of the hexagram. 'A loyal companion – maybe even a lover – and there, at his base, Death – and the Devil, but upright, sex and instinct and lust, something profound and carnal. Death is upside down, so not letting go of something. Does this make sense to you?' She lifted her puzzled eyes to Sarah's, which glowed with excitement. 'What did you ask?'

' "What is my first step?" – yes, it makes sense. It's Jo. He'll help me dream, he'll light the dreams up inside me and keep me safe while I explore – it's almost full moon, but I sent him away, I need to call him back, I need to find where he's buried.'

'Buried?' squawked Henrietta, terrified.

'I haven't told you about Jo?' Sarah was astonished.

'No! He's buried?'

'It's OK – Hen, it's OK.' She stroked her friend's bare shoulders gently and ran a soothing hand over her cheek. 'He's a ghost. I didn't know when we met – we had sex, made love even, twice, and I still didn't know. Or I wouldn't believe him. But he's on my side, he warned Adrian and me before, about Clara.' Sarah's palm rested against the curve of her friend's neck, her fingertips calming her with little strokes. The softness of Henrietta's skin made her want to slide her hand down, and cup one of her breasts, to feel the warm smooth weight of it in her palm. She withdrew her hand reluctantly. 'If you're too scared – if it's all too intense for you, I'll understand. I don't know if all this is what you wanted to learn. I hardly know enough to teach. Maybe this is all the wrong way round.'

'I do want to,' said Henrietta. 'To learn, and also to help. But I think finding Jo – uh, being with Jo – maybe that should be a bit, um, private.' She glanced at the cards and blushed. 'I could read it more clearly than I said, I thought I was inventing nonsense, but it's quite simple, really. That is why I just said the card meanings. But what I read was, a man will help you by refusing death, and with sex. Next time I will believe the cards more.' Sarah was blushing now too, and they shared a naughty smile, their eyes sparkling.

Sarah drifted from sleep to waking in a dreamy haze of titillation. She lay still, savouring the duvet against her bare skin, and thought of how Henrietta's shapely breasts might feel in her hands. She imagined Jo stripping her clothes again, of him kissing her own breasts with delight and awe, and gliding into her. Her groin twinged and ached with hunger, her lips tightening against each other rhythmically and her nipples tightening. The slippery cream of ovulation trickled from her. *Adrian, forgive me.* Tearing sorrow and bitter regret mingled with her arousal. She had to do this to help him, and not for a moment could she let go of her love for him, not even to ease the grief of infidelity. Tonight was full moon. She could look up death records – how had he first introduced himself? Mr ... Her heart sank, as she remembered how she had interrupted him before he gave the surname she now needed. Nor did she know his birth date – or death date. 'Jo' wasn't a lot to go on. Well, that she could think about while she cleaned. The Storm Moon was full, and it was time to spring-clean.

By the time the sun was descending, the whole house sparkled and she had dredged her memory for every word Jo had said to her, without success. The best she could do was retrace the steps of their walk together, her hands plunged deep into her pockets against the cold, the last sunlight throwing long, violet shadows and shafts of shimmering radiance across the Banbury Road. They had crossed the road here, she thought, before they'd reached the brightness of North Parade with its faded bunting and little restaurants, before the glittering glass restaurant. She passed the Engineering and Physics buildings, and remembered how he had argued that alchemy couldn't possibly be just a metaphor. At the bus stop, she navigated round a little knot of people and down the few stone steps into the church yard. They had sat in the muddy grass, smoking – she remembered the angle of the tree, as the car lights had lit it in brief brilliance. She had been right here, leaning against this grave, and he had spoken from behind it.

Once again, she traced the letters slowly with her fingers, but not to read them this time. Deep as the shadows were, the sun had not fully set and she could still see clearly. Her fingertips moved over the rough, lichenous stone with marvelling tenderness. 'Jonathan Montjoie, 1790–1811, As I Am, So Will Ye Be.'

It was one minute to sunset, fourteen minutes to moonrise. She sat on his grave to wait, stilling the thrill of terror in her at the thought of his bones beneath her. Through the open door of the church, she could see an elderly woman fiddling with one of the large flower arrangements. One troublesome flower refused to point as she intended, and her bird-like hands fussed around it, trying to fix the stem without hurting the bloom.

'Jo,' she whispered softly as the twilight deepened. 'I'm sorry.'

Car tyres skimmed across the tarmac, the pedestrian crossing emitted little beeps, and a bird chirruped in the trees, settling down to sleep. No other sound came to her ears. The moon had surely risen, hidden by the buildings to the east, and she leant against Jo's grave again, waiting for it to appear above the rooftop. A few early worshippers arrived at the church, and she reached deep into her memory for help, into that treasure trove of forgotten spells she had glimpsed before. She closed her eyes, imagining white light enclosing her in a shining bubble, and slowly beginning to blur, taking on the shadows and shapes of the gravestones and muddied grass. More people trooped past, neatly dressed and heavily wrapped against the cold. Whether it was the shadows or the spell, she sat unseen while the last of them arrived, the doors closed, and the choir began to sing. The high, pure voices of boys and deep tones of men rose and fell together in the songs of what was, after all, a men's religion. She wondered at the women sitting in there, excluded from the choir as they were excluded from God's likeness. And yet they stayed – she could sense some important truth there, on the edge of her consciousness, the thought hovering without falling into place. Before she could arrange the ideas symmetrically in her head, she saw the first, bright sliver of the moon rising, just a little north of east.

When the moon is at her peak, then your heart's desire seek, she thought, a pang in her heart for Adrian. This was the first step, she reminded herself, to bring him back to her.

'Jo,' she murmured again, 'I'm sorry. Please come back.'

Against the church roof and trees, the moon appeared impossibly huge and she shivered at its power. Still, she waited in vain for a reply, unwilling to give up her vigil. As the last drops of it drew themselves away from the silhouetted building, rejoining that perfect giant circle, she repeated her plea again. In the silence that followed, she stood slowly, stiff with cold and waiting. A movement under the tree caught her eye. Wrapped in his black gown, Jo was leaning against the trunk, a smug little smile playing on his lips.

'Beautiful moon, isn't it?' he said.

'How long have you been there?' demanded Sarah.

'Long enough to hear you beg,' he replied, smiling, and opened his arms to her.

'Your soul seeks Adrian's,' objected Jo when she explained her plan. 'How will I be able to keep you safe? You went back to him, sure enough, but I can't be your light in the darkness like he can. Not if you love him, and not me.'

'Your body – the warmth of your body. Jo, I need your help,' she pleaded. She knelt at his feet in the lounge, her hands entwined with his. As always, she had lit soft candles to spare his sensitive eyes the bright electric light.

He shook his head stubbornly. 'Impossible.' She began to argue, but he cut her short. 'What body, Sarah? You sat above what remains of it tonight.'

The brief spasm of horror on her face, quickly masked, was enough. He stood up abruptly and turned to look out the window, where the full moon flooded the lawn with white light.

'Those are really my bones,' he said, answering the question in her mind, his back to her. 'My flesh has rotted many years since. That is what being dead means. I am a staring, grinning skeleton under a weight of soil. For all the love in the world,' his voice choked, 'I cannot give you the warmth of my body.'

She was behind him now, and turned him gently with her hands. Her hands ran, marvelling, over his thin face, looking deep into the pain of his eyes. His loss was so evident. She couldn't show him the terror she felt, and so she pushed it away, letting her eyes fill only with strength and tenderness.

'But I feel you,' she whispered in wonder. 'Your skin against my palm – your muscles beneath it.'

He shuddered in longing as her hands ran down his arms, massaging their strength, but he held still, only his eyes filling with tears.

'Your gift to me, Sarah,' he said. 'It's your gift. I walked the streets unseen until you saw me, untouched until you touched me. I can't give you what Adrian can. I bowed out gracefully for him, did I not?' The jump in his throat as he spoke betrayed what that had cost him, and she felt his misery tear at her heart. 'I can't give you what he can, I can't even help you back to him. I would die for you, but . . .' His face wrinkled up in tears which he covered with his hands. Together, her arms around him, they sank to the floor and she pulled his head to her breast, soothing and rocking him as she had once before. I'm comforting a man two hundred years older than myself, she thought, and yet I feel older than the hills themselves, not younger than him. She crooned gently to him, his tears wetting her breasts. She had, then, a sense of her womanliness come so powerfully upon her that her eyes blurred; it was as if she could cradle the whole world in her arms and ease its pain. Slipping her hand beneath his head, she eased one breast from within her bra, exposing it to the air, and guided his lips to it. He took her nipple hungrily in his mouth, suckling as she cradled him and stroked his hair, drawing life from her that flowed through him, strengthened and stiffened him. He sucked more fiercely as tender lust drove his heart's pain away, and grasped her other breast with his hand, fighting to free it. He drew back then, staring at her bared bosom and stroking the sides of its fine curves.

'You still have so little knowledge of your own power,' he said, marvelling. 'People study for years to see what you see by accident. They spend their lives trying to do what you do unwittingly. You have so much power, how can you need my help?'

'The cards said you,' she said breathily. His fingers were still stroking paisley patterns across her naked skin.

'If the cards said so...' His eyes burned with fire a moment, and he turned away, struggling to master himself. 'You don't know what you're asking,' he said in a strained voice. 'My dearest wish is to bury myself in you again. You are begging me to. But if the price of that is to strand your soul, because I can't give you the link you need...'

'The link was my thought,' she murmured softly. 'The cards just said we should have sex.'

'And did you look for me just because they told you to?' he asked, his voice still taut with restraint. 'Or did you want to?'

'I want to.' She met his eyes. 'And I want you.' In that moment, lost in tenderness for him, it was true.

Swiftly, his hand dived beneath her skirt and pressed against her panties, feeling the wetness that had seeped while he had been kissing her breasts. 'You speak the truth, my lady.' The light of his soul was back in his eyes and he was once more the masterful womaniser of before as he threw her skirts above her waist. 'And I will teach you the truth of your words.'

With practised hands, he stripped the flimsy knickers from her and opened her thighs as far apart as they would go. Her legs and lips spread before him, he lapped gently at the soft skin at the sides of her knees, watching the small shivery touches send their heat through her.

'I will light such a fire in you,' he whispered, watching her breasts, still constricted in her clothes but bared.

His tongue was slowly approaching the apex of that sweet scent and juice as he licked slowly up her thighs. Wide open for him, she felt his hair brush her lips and almost wept with longing. To be filled again and have him thrust his weight into her. Unable to bear it, she seized him, hauling him up to her, and flung her legs tightly around him. She wailed as his thick shaft butted against her entrance through his clothes, and rubbed her wetness against him, wild with lust.

'Yes,' he hissed fiercely, 'you need me, but you will need me more . . .'

They wrestled wildly as he struggled to throw her off, arms and legs colliding. At last he pinned her down, panting. Standing up, he tore his clothes off and she stared in lust as he revealed first his pale, shimmering torso, then his narrow hips and thickened rod.

'Before we solve the problems of your soul,' he said, kneeling between her thighs, 'I think your sweet body is demanding its own satisfaction.' With one abrupt thrust, he forced himself into her slithering depths, tight with weeks of unsatisfaction. She howled with pure joy and delight, like a waterfall's ecstasy at throwing itself off a cliff. The earth's strength welled up into her, through the floors of the house from the soil and sturdy rock beneath. Fire burnt her eyes clear as he brought her to orgasm after orgasm.

'I can see,' she yelled, at the peak, 'I can see again!' Gratitude soared through her as she wept uncontrollably, and bucked continuously against him. The grey mists that had covered her soul since Adrian had left were torn away by his repeated piercings and far below she could see again the territory of herself, taste the power of her undiminished magic. Once more, the sharp lemon flavour of alertness filled her. She gloried in her strength, stretching out her abilities like muscles long unused, pulling Jo closer and deeper into her. The flames licked at her again with the fire that was her special strength, but she felt too the immutability of the rocks, the crushing power of the avalanche, the unremitting strength of soil, and realised that Adrian's abilities, too, had stayed. She wept harder then, her face crushed into the curve of Jo's neck as their hips bucked. It had all been real. The power they had shared in the cottage in Morvah still rested in her and welled up in her now, summoned by her ecstasy.

'I'll give you everything,' Jo said against her ear, 'anything I can, everything, my soul!'

'This,' she screamed, clean and sharp, 'This is what I need, Jo.' At the new pitch to which he brought her, she fell into the death-sleep of trance.

* * *

The rooftops of Oxford were dark, but in the windows of the colleges far below the candles of late-working students still glowed, sprinkling the town with faery lights as the Goddess had sprinkled the skies with faery lights above her. She was caught between the twin realms of light, laughing with pleasure as she spun through the air. A thin fragment of cloud, lit by the moon, drifted above her and for sheer pleasure at being alive with the chill air goose-pimpling her skin, she dived upwards through it. Far below, in the streets, a staggering drunkard caught sight of her silhouette against the moon and shuddered with fear, crossing himself. She flew on, north-west now, not needing to look at the town when the stars themselves could tell her all the directions she needed.

She landed gently on Port Meadow. Tonight was Ostara, and the witches would dance. Tomorrow the children would run into the meadows and forests with their prettily coloured eggs, offering them to the spirits and the little people, and new beginnings and abundance would pour forth into the earth. Tonight's celebration was for the adults, to celebrate those aspects of the Goddess which came later in life, after the childish games.

Already, a small group was gathering near the mound, skirting down from the sky. As she walked forwards to join them, she lifted her face to the full moon and felt the radiance filling her, imbuing her with the spirit of the Goddess.

'Well met by moonlight,' she said, her face glowing with pleasure as she strode into the group. The others made signs of respect to their leader, and for a little while she walked from one to another, asking about their spells and advising on herbs. She was as ready to learn as to teach, and listened with eagerness to their reports. What was a coven for, after all, if not to share their knowledge? One of the witches was speaking about the properties of the orange, a new fruit to their shores but now freely available in the Wednesday market, when her attention was distracted by a lone figure walking across the meadow in the moonlight. His uncovered head shone, the hair cropped short, and his gait was unmistakable. Her heart beat wildly. This was the youth she herself had found, when she had nursed him to health from fever, summoned to his lodgings by his servant.

Mistaking her distraction for alarm, the witches gathered around her.

'Is he a stranger?' asked one, anxiously.

'Should we fly?' said another.

She stilled them with a gesture. 'He is the man of whom I spoke, he is here at my invitation.'

Until she saw him approaching, she hadn't known how anxious she was whether or not he would attend. It had been foolish to rely on a stranger. The rites of Ostara required a man, and one pure of spirit. The Goddess asked so little and gave so much. It was normal to ask someone tried and tested, who would join for joy of the Goddess and not for the ordinary joys which Christianity denied its men. And so many of its men feared the Goddess's women. Should she have gambled the outcome of a sacred day on a hunch? But here, he came, her hunch had been right.

He climbed the mount with a few long strides and stood before her. 'My lady.' He bowed deeply. She wondered if he gave her that name out of courtesy, or if he knew more of the Old Religion than he had said.

'Hadrian,' she said, arms outstretched in welcome. 'Well met by moonlight. Will you celebrate the true Lady with us, and give us her due, as she gives us a new year of abundance?'

He bowed again, in acquiescence. 'But you must show me,' he said, colouring. 'I know little of Her rites.'

'Little enough in this life,' said one of the witches dreamily. She was part seer, and spoke with the drowsy assertion of sacred knowledge. The others smiled, and relaxed a little.

Sarah was still wondering over the true meaning of his words and his blush. *Is he so untaught?*

Earlier in the day, the four fire spots at the cardinal points had been cleared of grass that might catch fire and spread. Now, the witches moved from one to the other, laying firewood and kindling ready for burning. Sarah led the beautiful youth into the centre.

'Do you remember what I said before?' she said seriously, gazing into his eyes for any sign of avarice or cruel lust.

'Yes,' he murmured. He was shy, but met her eyes frankly, marvelling at the poise and strength of this woman. In his father's household, she would not have been let beyond the kitchen. No, he reminded himself truthfully, she would have been chased away with stones if they knew what she was. Her demeanour, however, was queenly, and the night's light upon her cheeks gilded her in beauty.

'Repeat to me what you remember, then.'

As he would've to one of his tutors, in his childhood, he recited back what she had said. 'The fires will be lit, and the circle opened with the four elements, and the witches will dance doesil and widdershins, and . . .' He faltered, but not from lack of memory.

She smiled inside at his blushes, but kept her face stern. 'What do the elements represent?'

He marvelled inwardly. Here he was, a student at the University of Oxford, being tutored in the elements by a commoner! Yet she knew things he was too shy to utter, and her very posture promised a world of knowledge none of his tutors could offer him. He repeated the lessons she had given him while he lay convalescing in her care. As he did so, he remembered how he had burnt at the sight of her moving about his room, hips swaying and breasts spilling over her bodice. Only his honour had kept him from pulling her into his bed and having his way, as most of his fellows would have done. Only my honour? he wondered, now, seeing her in her element. She has power.

'I don't know how . . .' he muttered miserably.

She raised her eyebrows, waiting for him to continue.

'I don't know how to take you without lust!' He burst out. 'I stand at the sight of you, I can't sleep for dreaming of you! Of course I agreed, but I don't – I don't want to – turn it all to sin,' he finished miserably.

She let her smile show, finally. 'That is the truest sign you can give that you will not,' she said quietly, standing on tiptoe to kiss his forehead in blessing. 'Our Goddess is not as cruel as your Christian God. She will delight in your delight. And if you only wanted to take what you could, you would have forced me while I nursed you, as you longed to.'

He began to protest, but she laid her finger on his lips. Their full, red succulence trembled against her finger.

'Stay here, and listen to the Goddess while I open the circle.'

She moved away, and took the lit torch from one of the waiting witches. Walking round, she cast the circle, laying the elements at each of the corners of the compass, lighting each fire as she did so. When she rejoined him, his face was flushed in the firelight.

'It begins,' she whispered.

Around them, the witches joined hands around the circle and began to sing, dancing widdershins. She laid her body close to his, clasping her arms around him.

Much more slowly, like the centre of the circle that they were, they twirled in the same direction. When the witches ceased and began to dance doesil, she showed him how to reverse direction. As they slowly spun between the fires, now at the centre, now along the spokes of the wheel, their bodies brushed. She let her hips deliberately swing against his crotch, and his stiffness was answered with corresponding tension in her own groin. When the others began to turn again, she held him still, her arms raised to rest her hands on his shoulders. He was so tall, standing near to her – tall, strong, and full of youthful vigour. Pulling out the clasps at her shoulders, she let her gown drop to the ground and heard his little gasp at her nakedness. With a skilful throw, her gown went flying and was caught in the clasped hands of her dancing companions. She undressed him then, knowing that he felt the eyes of the witches as intensely as the heat of the firelight, and the nearness of her own naked body more than anything. His clothes, too, were caught by the outstretched arms of the witches, whose hands never left each other's. Moonlight and firelight mingled on his young flesh. He was already a man, but with spring's lifeblood in him, and his stiff branch sparkled with early dew.

They resumed their twisting dance around the centre, as the witches around them sang. Voices clear as bells heralded the return of warmth to the world as their hips twirled. His shaft was heavy with its own blood-weight, and jutted out at right angles to his gracious flanks. His mouth shook with longing. His very eyes were anxious with wild desire and the longing to prove himself worthy, by which she knew he was.

The flames licked high into the air, the heat almost searing her bare thighs. The power of the Goddess was flowing into her from all directions now. The fire's warmth coated her spinning body, the earth's strength flowed upwards through her dancing feet, the moon poured its clean light down into the crown of her head, the evaporating dew of the grass coiled in steam around her calves, and the brush of the young man's skin made her spirit dance. The Goddess was expanding her senses, so that she too saw, tasted, smelt, heard, and felt through fire, earth, water, air, and spirit. The men were approaching across the fields. She felt their heart fires approaching through the dark, as she had earlier seen the tiny lights at college windows, and she searched through their souls for any trace of impurity. They were fewer in number than ever. With every passing year, that men's religion bit more heavily into their rites, chasing and hounding, cursing with fear the things that should bring joy. All the same, the hearts of those who came were clean and bright, keen with joy and anticipation, with no flicker of scorn for the women who would play the Goddess to each man tonight. They were closer now. If she took her eyes off the youth, she could see their shadows cast on the rippling meadow grass. The sweet, flushed lines of his body enraptured her. It was right that she couldn't tear her eyes away from him – now, when all were ready to witness, he would play the Puck to her Queen, lead her a merry dance and delight her with his flute.

She smiled slowly and pulled him closer, standing on tiptoe to reach his rosebud lips. He kissed her nervously at first, and then seemed to realise he had, at last, been given licence. Suddenly his mouth pressed harder against hers, drowning her in bruising kisses. His hands grasped her flesh, running fast over her. He seized her buttocks, the flesh filling his palms, and pulled her tightly against him. He groped her thighs, ran his palms hard over her swelling breasts, then pressed close again, rubbing his still-smooth chest deliciously against them. All the time, his tongue never stopped delving deep in her mouth, locked in an unending kiss. She was becoming, now, the Goddess, and he the Horned One, son and lover. Around her she sensed, rather than saw, the men and women mingling, their eyes fixed on the sacred scene but with sidelong glances and small steps moving closer to whom they wished. As he lowered her to the ground, she heard the quiet whisper of a bodice being unlaced and saw past his head how the woman's breasts were slowly exposed to the moon. In knots and couples, the witches and the men stood around. Over the crackle of the fires, she could hear the shortening breath. Impatient hands were straying into bodices, down breeches, under skirts, but all would wait and watch. Only when the Horned One had had his Queen would they give in.

Her beloved was kneeling over her, his long hair falling over her as he nibbled at her breasts and pulled one nipple then the other into his mouth. With her back pressed against the earth, she felt its impatience to burgeon riotously into spring, breaking out in blossoms and sunshine. She felt the avid haste of the coven, waiting for the moment they too could succumb. Why wouldn't he sink into her? She ached for him, her legs parted, unbearably empty until he filled her. He was slow and gentle, savouring the taste of her skin, the glory of his freedom. Truly he has the spirit of the Goddess, she thought, so patient and slow – *if the warmth comes too quickly, the early blossoms are nipped by late frost – he will not give into all our impatience any more than She will speed up the spring*. Never had she felt such fever at Ostara. Tears were streaming down her face as she begged incoherently for who knew what, for him to do exactly as he was doing and never cease his patient exploration.

When his tongue found her crevice, she screamed, flailing her arms on the steaming grass and arching her breasts high, holding them up to the moon. He lay curled up between her thighs, drinking thirstily as a kitten. All her nakedness and his thick erection were displayed to the hungry eyes around them, lighting their lust, putting the spring fever into them just as the Goddess did, with her teasing daffodils.

He lifted his mouth at last and met her eyes. His lips shone with her juice, his eyes with joy.

'My lady,' he said. Lithe as a deer, his body slid over hers, wedging his engorged pole in her entrance. It stuck fast, hardly an inch deep, and she groaned in pleasure. 'Forgive me, my lady, but I must,' he whispered, panting, and with a sharp thrust forced himself deeper. Her shrill screams of '*yes*, *yes*', sounded like pain, but he knew better. He had more wisdom than his years. His eyes glowed with love and tenderness as he battered her cruelly, immersing himself in her forgiving sheath while she yelled like a banshee beneath him. Like a storm hitting the cliffs, he pounded into her, sweat glowing on his brow. Broken sounds, deep as thunder, fell from his mouth into hers. She was lost to all the world but him, she was the world and felt its rocks churning beneath the plates of soil. She felt all the universe, which had shrunk to that dazzling point of light between them, so close to explosion. All life would restart when that taut, tiny, straining point burst open, worlds would be recreated, it was him and nothing but him – his hands driving her beyond the abyss into violence and ecstasy. Nails clawing at his back, her legs soared high above them both, clenching and spasming, her hips rising from the ground, her shoulders following. Now, in mid-air, nothing could stop the fury of their hammering. They floated above the fires, meeting each other's slams in perfect time, until – all their limbs stretched out, their muscles straining – like an eight-pointed star they pulsated together, beyond sound, feeling the bliss tearing at them. At the height which is usually agony, or frustration, or too soon subsiding into loss, they floated outside of themselves. They stood outside the world, hand in hand in the stars, looking into each other's eyes and knowing that they, too, were made of stars. Around them, they heard strange deep chimes and gentle tinkling drifts, like harps, strings, all playing at once, but far more than any of those. Both knew, without speaking, it was the music of the spheres.

'Why, there is wisdom to be found here.' Neither knew which of them had spoken. 'We could bestride the stars forever and never be sundered.' The air was dark, deep blue, as rich as velvet, and sang as they moved into each other's arms. Their glittering lips were close enough to feel the soughing wind of space on each other's mouths. His sceptre still lay deep inside her. 'The Lovers . . .' One touch of their lips, and they would never leave, never return to their little bodies, their separate skins, their skulls that held their thoughts apart save for the clumsy mechanisms of speech. Lost in each other's arms, eternal in the skies, they would be a constellation to lift the spirits of lovers forever, sliding across the heavens locked in their embrace.

'No.' Again, they didn't know which of them had spoken, but both felt cut to the core with loss and resentment, and knew they were right. There was work yet for their bodies to do. Slowly, they let the thin cords of light draw them back to where they still hung suspended in the air, and then sank gently back onto the ground. The last of his sperm seeped into her womb as they lay still together and the rites of spring were unleashed around them.

For a long time they lay together, stroking each other's faces and gazing into each other's eyes. Both were grieving for the world they had lost, weeping inside that even such a moment could fade as time resumed its whirl, but still lost in the joy of having found each other.

'You must go,' she said at last, kissing his forehead. 'You are the Horned One tonight, you must bring delight to everyone, not just me.'

Despite the love and longing on his face, she felt him rise against her thigh at the thought, and laughed with delight. 'Truly I chose well,' she said, pulling him down for one more languorous kiss. As he stood, he was drawn away eagerly by two of the youngest witches. They had come maidens to the rites that night, she knew, and would leave women. She watched their young hips pressing close against him, their hands roaming, as his clasped their breasts. Two shadowy heads, a man and a woman's, bent over her own nipples. Hadrian's eyes met hers. His smile answered hers.

All that night, they felt each other's presence like two magnets, the space between them taut with energy. Grass rubbed against her belly and breasts while the honeyed strokes of an unseen man filled her, rhythmically rocking her hips against the soil. Ahead of her, she saw Hadrian's buttocks clenching between the sweet thighs of one of the maidens, his muscles bunching as he withdrew, and releasing as he sank gently back inside her. The girl lay with her head pillowed on her friend's spread thighs, as Hadrian shared his kisses between her mouth and the other girl's still virginal slit. One arm cradled the girl he was bringing to womanhood, the other busied itself at probing her friend, teaching her to want his shaft inside her. And so, she thought, spring becomes summer. Abruptly, her own body blossomed with joy, bringing a responding deluge from the man with her.

As he withdrew, she was again covered in kissing mouths and stroking hands, drawn to the Goddess residing in her tonight. The dark shapes of bodies blocked the dying fires, hiding Hadrian's body – but not his presence. She would know his spirit forever now, she could find it in a snowstorm, in the darkest mists, in the lands of the dead. She heard the girl sobbing in joy and felt his release thrill through her. She rolled over, offering her breasts to the multitude of loving palms that ran all over her. From the gasps around her, she knew some of the hands were otherwise occupied, writhing and twisting in slippery folds, and some of the people whose mouths kissed her held their hips gleefully entwined. She felt the tides rising again inside her and closed her eyes, letting the Goddess guide her choice of heart fires. She reached towards one whetted with anticipation, fraught with longing, and found in her arms a shy, untried lad. She kissed him lovingly, letting him feel the smoothness of her bare body against his and how his own replied with stiffness. He was dizzied already with the novelty of fondling naked bosoms, sharing deep kisses, touching and being touched in intimate places. She mounted him, sliding slowly down. He would savour that first, engulfing slipperiness forever. His head was flung back, his eyes closed, as his hands explored the weight of her breasts. The cluster of lovers had parted again, now that she had made her choice, and she could see Hadrian leaning against the breasts of the new-made woman. With strong hands, he guided the other girl onto his girth so that her legs wrapped around both him and her friend. His arms supported her swaying back – she was near fainting with the first shock of penetration, but his fingers had done their work well and willingly. Watching all three of them join their parted mouths and flickering tongues, she knew with sudden certainty that the two girls had been each other's lovers a while already.

Her own hips rose and fell, easing her young lover into the steady rhythm he needed to learn. She bent over to kiss him again, then let her breasts fall against his face. He lapped at them eagerly and rubbed his smooth jaw over them till both face and bosom were slick with saliva and her breath was fast and ragged. She ran her body faster up and down his pole, rubbing hard at the base. She had meant to teach him slowness, but his tongue on her nipples was driving her into a frenzy.

'You like this?' he panted in delight, as she groaned and shuddered against him. His hands found the globes of her buttocks and tugged her faster and deeper against him. She gasped her assent, thinking, So be it, so be it – he will teach me instead. His fingers had found her crack, and pressed against the small hole knowingly. She flung her head back and saw Hadrian's eyes again, his face masked in ecstasy, his arms heaving the girl up and down on his lap while she squealed in delight, the other's teeth and lips clasped on his neck, hands groping the breasts pressed against Hadrian's chest.

Sarah sank down again on her lover, feeling his finger slip deeper with every shift of her thighs. Her breasts were crushed against his chest now, their thighs lying flat on each other's while they rocked to and fro like pistons. Their mouths joined again and she tasted his pleasure, moaning with unbearable excitement. He probed far inside her with his slim finger, matching the movement to his proud cock's gallop. Feeling his own penetration through the thin membrane of skin, massaging and pumping her, he brought them both to a quivering peak, clutching and trembling with rapture.

Some of the witches had already laid out the feast near the edges of the circle, away from the joyful flails of lovers' limbs. He fetched her a cup of wine and she sipped it gratefully, leaning into the circle of his arm. Together they relaxed, sated for the moment, watching the delight around them. Her eyes rested on Hadrian's perfect body as he thrashed in a tangle of arms and legs and orgasmic bodies.

'You love him, don't you?' said the boy with her, a trace of bitterness in his voice.

'Yes,' she answered in wonder. She stroked his cheek lightly. 'But tonight is a night of generosity and joy. We witches don't bind those we love to us. Nor,' she added, with a hint of sternness, 'are we bound by those who love us.'

The night passed in feasting, merrymaking, and love-making. At dawn, weak and overcome with ecstasy, she leant on Hadrian's arms as she made her slow circuit of the hill once more, closing the circle. With it, their loaned power of being the Chosen Ones passed. When that was done, she stood with her arms wrapped around him, lips glued, and knew that whatever had been born between them had not passed, and never would.

The kiss continued, but another voice was whispering frantically into her mouth.

'Sarah, my darling – come back, come find me.'

Her arms still clasped a man's body close, but its shape had changed, her legs lay wide, and her back dug into the floor. Opening her eyes, she saw Jo's face streaked with tears in the first dim blue light before dawn.

'I'm here,' she croaked.

'I didn't know what would happen,' he wailed, clutching her tight. 'It's almost dawn – all night I lay with you, you hardly breathed – and I waited and waited, but it's sunrise, you never see me in daylight, it would be another month, and what would happen to you?'

She kissed his anxious outpourings quiet, murmuring her love and thanks.

'The sun is close,' he said, pressing his head against her neck. 'Any moment now, you won't see me or feel me anymore.' He lifted his head abruptly, and stared into her eyes. 'For pity's sake, learn to use your own power!' In that instant, he vanished from her eyes and arms. Only a faint disturbance in the air, the barest hint of a mirage, betrayed his presence.

She closed her eyes, ashamed that she was unable to meet his. 'I will,' she said to the empty room.

Sarah sat in Meltz waiting for Henrietta, watching the rain hammering the empty night street. It was seven on a Saturday night, but she was the only customer, and the waitress leant on the counter staring at the clock, sunk in profound boredom. This was the end of term, the end of ninth week, and the tourist season had yet to start. Oxford felt deserted, abandoned to its interminable rain. She shuffled her cards absent-mindedly, wondering again where Adrian was right now. Please have gone home, she thought over and over. Surely in Morvah, in the protection of that spell-bound cottage, he would return to his senses. A house provides more protection than I can, who love him so much, she thought bitterly. Clara would certainly not let him escape from her clutches to Morvah, though, and the colleges happily evicted their students in holiday time, so where was he?

Henrietta broke into her thoughts, smiling, her hair caught in little damp curls around her face. Another girl was with her, and irritation stabbed Sarah. She wanted to tell Henrietta everything, her vision, her frustrations and inability, not make polite conversation with strangers.

'Hi,' she said, making an effort to smile.

Henrietta beamed, and Sarah felt her mood shift a little. 'This is Caitlyn – we're trying to persuade her to stay in Oxford for the holidays.'

'Not quite,' said Caitlyn, slipping into a chair. She had a soft, Welsh accent and a narrow face around which her fair hair hung listlessly, in need of a wash. Her clothes looked like a poor box assortment, badly combined and shapeless, but all this neglect couldn't disguise her startling beauty. 'I'm sorry to spring in on you, if you wanted to be alone with Henrietta, but I had to meet you.' Her words, so close to Sarah's own thoughts, chased away the lingering resentment.

'I told her you were a witch, and you were teaching me,' said Henrietta.

They asked for a platter and two more wine glasses, and picked at the food as they chatted. Caitlyn was an astrophysicist at Queens, working on dark matter.

'As you can imagine, I keep my interest in astrology pretty under wraps at the department,' she said dryly. 'To my mind, it's not very different – we know there must be something there, but what it is and how it works is a grand old mystery.' She wanted, she said, to learn witchcraft as well – how to use this theoretical knowledge she had. 'I know the times down pat, but I don't know what to do with them,' she explained.

'The times?' queried Sarah. She had listened mostly in silence, intrigued by Caitlyn but still desolate with her own sense of ineptitude.

'Well, we're under Pisces now, Sun sign, that's the time to work with intuition, empathy, your subconscious – it's a brittle sort of time, skins are very thin, and that's difficult. The Moon's just come into Pisces now too, so that energy's inside and out. It's Saturday and almost fourteen hours from sunrise, so we're under Mercury right now, but the Moon will be dominant soon. And then there's Saturn, today's planet, which is a slow, heavy planet of discipline, responsibilities, control – frustration – and of course the moon is waning, slowing the energies down even more – we've all got PMT, I take it?'

Surprised, Henrietta and Sarah nodded. 'Well then, all

the more proof that all of this works together. The drag of the moon, the sensitivity of Pisces, the heaviness of Saturn, the restless energy of Mercury, our bodies have their own time-honoured way of manifesting all this.' Her explanation stopped abruptly. 'I've learnt all this and I don't know what to do with it. Are you really a witch? Can you really teach me?'

Sarah looked down, pushing her olive pits around her plate. 'Do you work with moon phases at all?' she asked eventually.

'A little, yes.'

'Well, the moon's waning right now and I'm finding there's sweet fuck-all I can do.' Her mood was finally spilling over into her words. She found herself blinking away tears, hardening her mouth to speak. 'It's not really a time for magic. Banishments, yeah, but I can't access my spells.'

The last two weeks had been painful. She had been so sure, that first morning, that she had finally found the key with which to unlock everything. She knew for certain that she'd been a witch in Oxford hundreds of years ago, that she'd met and loved Adrian there, and bonded with him far beyond the confines of the flesh, that the briefly-glimpsed treasure trove of spells in her mind was her own knowledge, carried into a new life. She didn't need Granny's book – she had her own Book of Shadows locked inside her. She would dig deep, pull out the relevant spells, fight with every weapon she had, rescue Adrian. And yet nothing came. Her mind yielded nothing. Her dream journal held nothing useful, just cures for ailments like some spiritual Boots Chemist. Her to-do list demanded all sorts of spells, such as seeing the dead, increasing her power, finding lost objects – she had no idea how to perform any of these. Everything seemed to have slipped from her grasp. It was as if she had never learnt any witchcraft at all, except that she knew some form of terrible magic had stolen her love from her.

Caitlyn was looking at her tenderly, as if she heard the pained thoughts. 'Two more days,' she said encouragingly.

'But I'm trying to fight, I'm trying to find things out, there isn't time,' exclaimed Sarah despairingly.

'You can't fight the moon and the planets,' said Caitlyn. 'The waning moon is a time for learning, yeah?'

'Yes, but I can't learn anything!'

'Oh yes, you can. You can learn to wait for the moon to wax again, and to explore your subconscious while Pisces gives you that opportunity, and then in two days it'll start to kick off again, and when the Sun goes into Aries, you'll perk right up – it'll all come back. And I can learn about witchcraft – if you'll teach me.'

Sarah felt Caitlyn's and Henrietta's eager eyes on her as she scowled moodily at the table. She wanted to say she had nothing to teach, but already her mind was formulating what they needed to know – the Wheel of the Year, the tools, the altar, the Goddess and Her Son, the different rites ... She wanted to say she was no expert, and remembered her own thoughts from that dreamlike vision. A coven was no teacher-led school – it was for learning from each other. And the minimum for a coven was three. 'OK,' she said, smiling a little. 'We can teach each other.'

Henrietta breathed out in relief. 'So ... when shall we three meet again?'

Caitlyn pulled out her diary, and opened it to pages of hieroglyphs. 'Let's see,' she said. 'New moon – the Sun, Moon, Mercury, Jupiter and Venus in the twelfth house – Saturn in the sixth, so our studies can wait. I'd say Monday is very auspicious.' She grinned.

8 Binah

'This is a time that is not a time, in a place that is not a place, on a day that is not a day. We stand on the threshold between the worlds, before the veil of the Mysteries...' The familiar litany of words calmed Sarah's mind, lifting it out of self-consciousness. She felt the awareness filling her again. A soft breeze played over her bare skin, the dew wet her feet, and the morning star shone brightly on while all the others softened and hid themselves as the sky's blackness eased into blue. The night before, they had quietly welcomed the New Moon and sat talking into the small hours. When the others went to bed, she had stayed by the altar meditating.

It seemed so long now since Adrian had been with her and they had explored this together. Alone with the Goddess, she sought out her memories of him, revisiting her pain. She was creating a coven, but her Horned One was so far from her. She was learning her past, their past, but he knew nothing about it. None of this seemed to bring him closer, and the only spells she could think of were not allowed. Love spells, harm spells. The Wiccan Rede chafed. Every day that passed was another day he spent in that hell she had so briefly visited – if indeed, it was hell to him, not just her own revulsion and jealousy. How could Clara have such a hold over him when she, with all the power of their past link, had none? How could she get him back, did she have any power at all?

Now, as she cast the circle, she felt the power

imbuing her again and her doubts eased. She was moving forwards, after all – she had asked for power, and now she had the power of three, not one. As she called upon the elements, she felt also the reawakening of her old powers, a faint stirring of the times she had flown above the clouds, healed the sick, and kept the innocent from the clutches of the court. That life which she remembered in confusing dreams and trances still seemed unreal, the stuff of fantasy, but in her heart she recognised it as strongly as her own childhood.

She stood by the altar once more, in the dawn, facing the east where the hidden sun was turning the clouds to fire.

'This circle is bound, with power all around. Between the worlds I stand, with protection at hand.'

They sat together around the altar on the grass, and Henrietta laid out the Tarot cards to ask for guidance and purpose for this new, small coven. She studied the hexagram in silence. The pale light of the sun slowly drowned the golden glow of the candles.

'We must help you,' she said simply. 'You must get Adrian back. For now, that's all we need to know. After that, we can ask again.' She gathered the cards back up and handed them to Sarah.

Sarah knew her question before her hands touched the cards, and she shuffled slowly, the words blazing across her mind. *How can I break the spell?* She laid out another hexagram, and Henrietta frowned, lapsing into quiet once more. Several minutes passed before she spoke, and then it was fluent and unhesitating.

'It's too dangerous, you don't know what you're fighting, you mustn't do this. You must dream again, find out more. Celebrate Ostara with us, joyfully. But whatever you're planning, don't do it.'

Sarah felt her heart rebelling violently. 'Clara can't be

that strong!' she exclaimed. 'She is nothing to Adrian, she had some cheap love-spell, I can break it!'

Henrietta shook her head sharply. 'No, not yet. It's too dangerous. There's a much stronger force at work than a glamour.' She looked at Sarah's mutinous face. 'Promise me, Sarah, promise by – by the moon, swear by the Lady. Don't try yet.'

Sarah took a deep breath, wrestling inwardly. How could she not even try? But Henrietta, usually so easy-going, was compelling her fiercely.

'OK,' she said reluctantly. 'I swear – not yet. Not until after Ostara.'

'Not until the time is right,' pressed Henrietta.

'But how will I know when the time is right?'

Caitlyn spoke for the first time. 'When we know more, when we know what you must do, I can help you find the best time.'

It was eleven weeks since Adrian had left, five since she had seen him at Christ Church and flung herself like a fool into his body. She felt further than ever from getting him back. Perhaps it would all turn out to be a consolatory delusion after all, and even the visions just fantasies of splendour. Perhaps she was a fool to ignore Tim. She had so little material proof against her doubts.

She sat up abruptly from the sofa, and began to pace the room. A witch shouldn't need physical proof, she told herself. Of her time with Adrian, the only empirical evidence she had of anything supernatural was their shared levitation, and that had been the least meaning-ful of all their experiences. She wanted to beat the walls with frustration and let her face twist with tears at all she had lost. She wanted to feel the misery as purely as she had the first day, so that the accompany-ing disbelief in his faithlessness would return as well. She could try a ritual ... try to break the spell ... but

Henrietta had made her vow not to. What could it bring upon me worse than this? she thought angrily. To lose not only my soul's other half, but all certainty of being one with him. Time, the great enemy of grief, was eating away at her faith. Learn to use your own power, Jo had said, but how? She was teaching Caitlyn and Henrietta what little she knew, but who would teach her? Without Granny Jennie's book, with nothing but fragments from her own memory, where would she even learn the spells? She halted midstride, her eyes wide with realisation.

When sundown approached, she was prepared for a ritual, but not the one she had forsworn. She was more careful in every detail than she had been since Adrian had left. Her body was rinsed and glowing, sky clad. Her tools lay ready on the grass. She opened the circle with her wand, asked for blessing from all the elements and the Great Mother, and knelt down to build the fire in a cast-iron pot in the centre. While the flames subsided into coal, she sat meditating, beseeching the vast spirit of the earth beneath her to help. At length she opened her eyes, to find the sky flaming and the coals glowing. She looked again at the painting, which she had laid in front of the altar, to check the order. In the daylight, she had been able to make out what she hadn't seen with Adrian – a chiaroscuro skeleton worked into the background. Now it had retreated into the shadows once more, but the plants were still visible, laid out in neat order. It had taken her more than an hour with a copy of Culpepper's from the downstairs shelves to work them all out. Her fingers trembled as she sprinkled over the coals aloe, pepper, musk, vervain, and saffron. In the painting, a tiny scroll lay curled next to the dim coals. She lifted the little fragment of vellum on which she had carefully written the name, and as she threw it onto the fire said aloud,

'Jonathan Montjoie, I summon you. Great Mother, give me eyes to see.'

She watched the thick smoke rise, fragrant with the herbs and spices, faintly acrid with the burning vellum. As it curled, she saw the shimmer of a face appearing in it, flickering in and out of sight.

'Jonathan Montjoie, I summon you,' she repeated. 'Great Mother, give me ears to hear.'

Through the haze, the face came clearer, but still as translucent as mist.

'I'm here.' The voice was a faint sough of wind in her ears.

'Jo,' she murmured, her eyes filling with tears. Until now, she hadn't really believed he was a ghost. Even when he vanished from on top of her, he had been completely, physically there and then utterly gone. Seeing him now, like a wisp of smoke, her heart ached for him.

'Use your power!' It was barely a whisper, but she could hear Jo's insistent tones.

She forced herself to relax, drawing up her spine and feeling the energy rushing up her from the damp soil beneath. Opening her palms to the fire, she let its force penetrate her, its spirit soaking into her just as its warmth did. Her eyes shifted as they did when she looked at Adrian's aura.

'I summon the power that is mine by right,' she intoned. Her voice sounded dead and monotone, but it rang with strength. Looking again into the fire, she saw Jo more clearly, like a light projection or a hologram.

'It's only your power you need summon,' he said softly, his voice ringing more clearly in her ears than before. 'I hardly leave your side.'

'I have so little power.'

'You have so much!' he retorted. 'Sarah –' His hand

reached out towards her, above the fire. She reached out to grasp it, but her hand passed through the insubstantial mist and his eyes darkened with sadness. 'You don't even know,' he said sorrowfully. 'I know something about witches, more from my studies than personal experience. I've stayed close to some of the fine-looking witches, since my death, but none have been able even to sense my presence when they strain every power they possess. And then, without even knowing what you are, you see me – touch me. I've only ever heard of one witch with your kind of power, apart from in myth.'

'But how, when I can't even see you clearly?'

'You can, when it's by accident,' he reminded her. 'Sarah, you must understand. Do you think I magically gain a material body at the full moon? But that is the time when you are most receptive. You give me form, because your own body and spirit are so intensely entwined – that is the strength of a witch, not dissolving the bond. Dissolving that bond is the Church's teaching, and the Devil's, they can do nothing with bodies, only with souls, and they're fighting over the souls of the earth, hating all material form – do you understand?'

She shook her head mutely, ashamed.

He sighed. 'How could you, in a world which believes in nothing? And I made it my life's research – my short life's research. Your spirit needs your body as much as your body needs your spirit. And where your spirit leads, your body follows – this is true of everyone, even to walk from one place to another, but powerfully true for you. Beloved, my darling . . .' His misty eyes beseeched her across the smoking fire. 'When I carried you to your bed – you remember?'

She nodded.

'It was your spirit I carried, only. You were the one who brought your body with us, so indissoluble, with such belief and power that the heat of your skin filled my spirit. Do you know what anyone else would have seen?'

She thought of herself, clasped in his strong arms, lifted up the stairs. She thought of herself, floating, arms entwined around empty air, drifting upstairs. A thin chill ran through her.

'For you – when one rejoices, the other does too. I wonder if you even know how to cut your body away from your spirit as everyone else does, so routinely. Your spirit made love with mine, but nothing can separate your body and spirit. The two combined are the greatest power on earth, that is the most important teaching of witchcraft. And that is why sex magic is your greatest strength. Some people would never master it – they would see it as a great chance for their body, and tie their spirit up, cut it off. They would have the Devil's sex, and he would gloat. But for you, the union is so effortless, your magic is unintentional. Now you must learn to make it intentional. Sarah – you must be careful. The Devil hates witches – God, the Devil, they both hate them. The Devil has crossed your path already, he must know what you are, but he doesn't know you know. You have to be wiser, you have to know what you're doing, so you can hide it. Whatever happens, he mustn't know you know.'

The garden had grown dark while he spoke, the sky purple and laid across with thick bars of black, approaching cloud. Jo's face was growing dimmer. Sarah took a deep breath, dipping her hand in the consecrated water, concentrating again on the strength of the earth and the fire. She was bathed in their material form, the soil supporting her, the coals warming her, the air filling her lungs, the water dripping from her fingertips. She focussed on opening herself to their spirit as well. It was true, what Jo said. She had never been able to touch anyone as just a body, without loving their spirit as well, even if only for that time. By instinct, she responded to the natural world around her the same way, her heart singing joy to the magnificent displays that the clouds put on, her fingers stroking a tree as she passed. Now she must learn to do that consciously, invite those elemental spirits, and cup those massive powers in her tiny hands.

She sprinkled the herbs and spices once more on the dying coals, each in order. 'Mother, let me see . . . Mother, let me hear . . .' she whispered. She felt an inkling of the leviathan strength of the Earth, as her own minute spirit implored. In comparison, she was infinitely small and brief – exactly as tiny as her own body contrasted with the planet, as abrupt a flicker as her own life compared to its. Jo's trembling shape firmed a little again, in the renewed smoke.

'Is it meant to be, that I will get Adrian back?'

'Nothing is meant to be, Sarah. Am I meant to roam Oxford like this?' He spread his arms. 'We choose. And I think you have already chosen, and I think you are strong enough. But I cannot guarantee anything, and I don't have any special spirit wisdom to grant you. Only the fruits of my research. But one thing I can do for you.'

Her eyes filled with hope, and he grimaced faintly. 'Perhaps more than one thing, but if we are successful, you won't need me by then. You will not see me this full moon. I shall haunt Adrian. Whatever spells this Clara has put upon him, I doubt they will keep his natural ability from him at the full moon. He will see me.' He looked deep into her eyes, his own no more than smudges of smoke now, nearly an optical illusion. The smoke was fading, and her ability to see him with it. His voice was growing fainter. 'Perhaps I can remind him of the truth. Fight with body and soul, Sarah. Don't let anything separate them. I will be close to you all the time, you will see me whenever you are able, but not at full moon.'

In the days before Ostara, the three girls were hardly apart. Henrietta and Caitlyn were learning to see and interpret auras, Sarah's own skill at the tarot and knowledge of astrology were advancing, and all three were discovering a multitude of useful, domestic spells. They talked endlessly about the tarot, astrology, and witchcraft, but also about their life stories, love stories, mothers, clothes. They did each other's hair and makeup before going out, like teenagers, and lazed around giggling in their underwear. Sarah's academic research was slowly advancing again, as well. She needed to forestall the criticisms Dr Piedmont would raise against the direction her thesis was taking. No doubt, his acerbic nature and razor-sharp intellect held nothing but contempt for the amorphous collection of myths and hearsay that was the Old Religion in literature. But surely, Sarah reasoned, that also is the point? If none of it could be safely committed to paper, what other way to safeguard the information than encoded in manuscript? These monks would have come from the same English villages as the wisewomen whose persecution had already begun. She needed an iron-clad argument to present to him, proof that her research had not already been done, and some evidence of material to work on. Without some central manuscript, however, she had nothing.

Low fires flickered around them on Hurst Hill as they danced around at the centre of their invisible circle of power. The shelter of the trees, and the spells binding the circle, kept them hidden from prying eyes. All three had worn long skirts, which swirled around their legs and whipped against their legs. Their hands were clasping each other's tightly as they spun around faster and faster, and Sarah was irresistibly reminded of the Three of Cups in Henrietta's pack, the three laughing maidens. Beneath their twisting feet, the mud was churned, splashing their ankles and skirts. Their toes dug in deeper, relishing the grainy squelch. They slipped and slid as they whirled more quickly around, until they were twirling so fast that their centre of gravity was between all three of them. The brilliant fires and perpendicular strokes of the tree trunks were streaming into a blur, mingling the reddish-yellow and black, the brilliance and darkness. Caitlyn was the first to lose her balance, shooting feet first into the centre, pulling the others down in a laughing, panting heap. They lay tangled in the mud, catching their breath and still chuckling. Lying across Sarah's thighs, Caitlyn propped her arm up on her elbow, which dug deep into the sludge.

'What does the ceremony say now?'

Sarah thought hard, trying to send her mind down those mysterious paths to her old memory, but could find nothing. 'I don't know,' she said truthfully. 'I don't think we need stand on ceremony too much.'

'So I can kiss you now?'

Her heart held still for a moment, the flames playing in slow motion across Caitlyn's face and delicate lips. She felt her body rush with heat and cold. She glanced at Henrietta, whose head lay on Caitlyn's lap. She nodded.

Sarah slid down through the mud, and pulled Caitlyn's head tenderly towards her. The other girl seemed so small and fragile in comparison with herself – or was she just comparing with the men she had been with? It was like holding a little bird, whose delicate wings she might bruise. Caitlyn's small mouth pushed her own apart. The sweetness of her kiss and the softness of her lips was dizzying, she wanted to tear the girl's clothes off, seize her breasts in her hands, hold all her naked body at once, but she didn't dare be rough. All the metaphors she had always disdained came rushing to her mind: flowers, fine porcelain, butterflies. She lay on her back, her hair tangling in the wet earth, and held Henrietta to her. Their three mouths met, their tongues shifting against one another's, sliding to and fro. Sarah's arms slipped under their tops, around the smooth warmth of their backs. She marvelled at how easily she encircled their narrow bodies, her hands reaching around to stroke the sides of their breasts.

Caitlyn broke free first, lifting her top over her head in one movement, throwing it to one side, and unclasping her bra. In seconds, they were all naked to the waist and pressed close again, back into their lingering kisses, their breasts rubbing against one another's. Their hands ran over one another, leaving trails of mud which didn't seem dirty anymore – just clean, gritty earth and pure rain. Sarah shook with longing as Caitlyn and Henrietta reached under her skirts, drawing her knickers down her legs. Her palms ran up their sides to touch their breasts, so perfect and different. Henrietta's were small and rounded, not even creasing beneath, her nipples tiny, pink, and crinkled. Caitlyn's were heavier in Sarah's hands, fuller, with pointed nipples as dark as the tawn of tiger's eye. Sarah rocked her hips as she savoured the different shapes, and drew them to her mouth. Their nipples touched one another's before her lips reached them, and she suckled both at once. Her eyes closed, her lips nibbled, she heard their small gasps and the wet, succulent sounds of them kissing passionately. Her skirt rose, baring her parting legs, and slender fingers ran up her thighs. She felt the juice rising and brimming in her and sucked harder, clasping and massaging a breast in each hand.

Round and round the circle they went, taking turns to clasp one another's nipples in their mouths, drown their tongues in deep kisses. One by one their knickers were drawn off and the soft flesh of their thighs stroked, and teased. Again, Sarah held each girl's curves in her mouth and hand, then she was once more locked to Henrietta's lips while Caitlyn lapped at their nipples, and then she pressed her mouth and bosom to Caitlyn's, offering their nipples yet again to Henrietta's tongue. Their legs slid against one another's. Their breath came quicker, each brush of their thighs was sweet agony, their hands roamed faster and more avidly over each other's near-nudity. Their skirts rose, and the grainy soil rubbed between their calves. Caitlyn arched up, holding herself on her hands above them, her dark points disappearing into their mouths. Her thigh pushed closer between Sarah's, who shuddered, spreading and closing her legs to hold it closer. She sank down heavily, gasping as Henrietta's teeth grazed her nipple, her flank rubbing the material of Sarah's skirt hard against her slit.

Feverishly, they tussled, hauling each other closer, plaiting their legs, till Sarah's thigh pushed against Henrietta's apex, and Henrietta's own legs fought to get closer to Caitlyn's wet entrance. Impatiently, Sarah pulled her skirt out the way, groaning as the fabric chafed against her swollen bead, and then at last she felt it – the sweetness of skin on skin. Her creamy lips slithered on Caitlyn's thigh as Henrietta swayed against her own. She clutched at them with arms, legs, hands, mouth, and pussy, sinking into the abundance of bare flesh. Maddening arousal danced between them, rushing forwards and eluding their grasp as they bucked more fiercely. Their cries rose unashamedly through the night air. Forgetting all thoughts of fragility, Sarah sank her teeth into Caitlyn's neck and gloried in her wails of delight. Henrietta's manicured nails raked her back. Her arm caught up Henrietta's bottom and pulled her more roughly down, forcing her thigh harder against her. Femininity be damned, she thought. Womanhood was the drumming of blood in their veins, the wells of creamy juice, the crush of breasts, and ferocious desire. She could feel her orgasm so unbearably close, hovering forever at the cusp, and abruptly Caitlyn pulled away.

'No – please!' she exclaimed, but the girl was already turning on her side, pushing Sarah's legs wider apart, reaching for her entrance with fingers and tongue. Henrietta followed suit, making a new triangle, so that Sarah lay facing her glistening valley as Caitlyn's fingers began to probe.

She was unsure of herself, of her own desires, as she leaned forward and let the tip of her tongue drift over Henrietta's glistening bead. She tasted the fresh, salty creaminess as her own passage spasmed gleefully around Caitlyn's exploratory digit. She savoured it hesitantly, running her tongue around the frills, bringing each drop back to her mouth curiously. Caitlyn was kissing her gently, a single finger inside her. The quivering sensations combined with the taste as she drank more deeply, and reached gently inside Henrietta's squirming sheath, copying Caitlyn's movements. Their caresses travelled around the trembling, lustful circle. The way she nibbled at Henrietta's pearl and licked her hood was repeated by Caitlyn's tongue. As Caitlyn pushed a second finger into her taut opening, her own middle finger pierced Henrietta, and she felt Caitlyn's gasp at being filled against her lips. Languorously, they pumped their hands in and out of one another's dripping sheaths, feeling the dew coating their hands, as they suckled the sensitive buds and ran their mouths over each other's petal-like folds. Deliberately, she forced her ring finger into Henrietta, who moaned wildly, opening her legs wider to receive it and shoving harder against Sarah's hand. When she felt Caitlyn's hand impaling her with still more thickness, she screamed and began to buck, clutching with her spare hand at Henrietta's hips to hold the girl's delicious mound against her mouth. Caitlyn's hand tore at her breast and Sarah's hand reached eagerly for Henrietta's small mounds, pressing hard against the yielding flesh. Her passage was being stretched wide by Caitlyn's hand, she couldn't count fingers anymore, just the unbelievably ecstasy of being pummelled and stoked with such thickness, such knowing skill. She plunged in and out of Henrietta, feeling the ecstasy rising, watching the shudders of Henrietta's thighs. She heard the squeals and gasps muffled by Caitlyn's own vale, as hers were muted by Henrietta's mons, and the same spasms that seized her held them all frozen, quaking, thin wails of eerie sound drifting constrictedly from their mouths.

When she woke, the dawn was pure and cold. She walked outside to kiss her hand to the morning star and the slowly descending moon. Her limbs were stiff and chilled. Back inside, she picked up the broom, besom twigs tied firmly to a staff of wood. As she did every morning, she shook out the bed clothes and swept the scattered herbs into a small pile. She scooped them into a small earthenware pot. Later, she would offer them back to the Goddess, either sprinkling them in the woods or tossing them onto the fire. They would return to the earth or crackle in the flames and release their healing fragrance. Then she began to clean and scrub with a vengeance. This evening, her beloved would come to her. He would find a haven of beauty to light such a fire in his heart. From pure happiness, laughter bubbled up inside her.

That was the morning of the riders. She saw Hadrian walking across the meadows when she went out to refill her pot at the river, and stood for a moment, gazing at him. His shoulders had broadened in the last two years, but the blinding light feathered around his body. For a few moments, he seemed again the thin man-child she had nursed to health with herbs. He had called them her strange concoctions then. Now, he knew almost all her plant-lore – and all her body, all her soul and heart, all her ways. In turn, he had taught her to read and write, not only in the common tongue but in Latin and Greek as well. They learnt each other's skills so easily that they wondered if their unearthly fusion, that first night on Ostara, had given them each a portion of the other.

'When I inherit from my father,' he said often, 'we will not be apart for a single hour. We won't meet in secret, but out in the market, and in our home.'

She laughed, and stretched out her arm to encompass the wooden shack, the fields, the river, and the forests around it. 'I have already inherited from my Mother,' she always replied. 'I have no secrets from her.'

She saw the riders before he did, a moment after he saw her. He was already waving as she raised her arm to warn him. She fell to her knees, drawing a circle of protection, but it was too late. Why hadn't she given him an amulet, as she had so often thought of? They had seen him wave, they had seen her standing by the shack – it was too late for a spell of invisibility, also.

Tears were running down her cheeks as the riders reached him. The Sight had struck her a blow in the pit of her stomach, she saw it all before it happened. Death, the Tower, agony, and anguish. The Sight she never used for them, because they were so happy, could have saved them if she'd used it. They could have run, they could have hid. She retched as they kicked him, reaching out to his soul. Over and over, she whispered, 'My love . . .'

She had more than enough time, later, to work everything out in her head. She thought through it all, as she lay manacled on the dirty straw, bitten by fleas, in all the filth these so-called Children of God allowed to exist. She was chained in the grossness that bred the pestilence and disease they blamed on those like her, Children of the Mother, who only walked from house to house undoing the damage by the power and gifts of the Mother. Even so, at night a shard of moonlight fell through the tiny window onto her foot. They could lock her away from the Mother, but She would always find her.

The first night, she cried with gratitude to see that silver square touch her skin. As her sobs eased, clarity returned. She had seen no one cross the river, from the wide vantage point of her door. The constables must have been behind the shack already, or hidden in the forest. The riders' livery was that of Hadrian's father – of Hadrian himself, come to that. His father's men had kicked him down, then. The constables must have been waiting. Had they seen her that dawn, kissing her hand to the moon? Her skin crawled, but she spelt it out slowly. She had to make sense of the lapse between that horror-struck moment and coming to consciousness in the castle prison.

What could they have been waiting for, if not to catch her and Hadrian in the act? Whether the carnal act or more chaste worship of the Mother, it would make no difference to them. The riders had been sent to intercept Hadrian, who had already waved. Somehow, every person of power had known he would come to her that morning, except her, who had the true power.

She hadn't used her power. That knowledge tore at her stomach, twisting her heart. She'd painted sigils of protection on every humble house in Oxford, it seemed. She'd made sacred protective amulets for everyone but them. The very invincibility of their joy had betrayed them. She twisted abruptly in her chains, unable to face the thought directly. She had failed them.

Night after night, the moonlight returned to soften her exile. As it waned, it shifted northwards and its shine crept up her body. It counselled her in calmness. Her mind and body drifted apart as her flesh wasted. No-one from the coven came with food, or the money to buy it. Had they fled, or were they too being held in these stone walls? *Hadrian, where are you? Do you get food, my darling?* The chains chafed and cut into her wrists. She used the blood for glamour spells, to make her as withered and unappealing as a crone to the guards.

On the fourth day, one tossed her a hard lump of bread. 'Eat that, old woman. You won't escape the fire by dying here.' That night, she saw the crescent moon and its thin thread of light fell on her face. The next night, it was dark and the sacred blood of her womb dripped through her clothes, onto the stinking straw. The church and chapel bells set up their cacophony of ringing and through the peals she heard the scrape of a metal key. In the absolute black of the new moon, she could not even see the shape of a person entering, but she heard the footsteps come towards her. The guards didn't bring water at this hour. She closed her eyes in despair. Oh, my Mother, she cried out in her heart, have you forsaken me? Matted, stinking, and chained on the stone floor, was she now to be mounted like an animal by the guard, violated at her sacrosanct time?

A lamp flared. She turned her face away from it. A choked sob broke the silence, then an urgent whisper.

'My angel, my bright one, what have they done to you?' Hadrian was kneeling by her side.

It is a vision. I've eaten so little, my mind is wandering. She gazed in feeble wonder at him, her eyes dull and confused.

'My love.' His tears were splashing against her face. A soft, damp cloth smoothed over her brow and face. Tender arms held her up to sip from a steaming cup, and she tasted her own recipes for healing. She lay, too weak to speak, while he wept and tended her. Lovingly, he washed her from the bowl and dried her arms and legs. He painted balm on the torn skin of her wrists, held the cup to her lips every few minutes, and wiped away the dried blood between her thighs. He spread a soft blanket beneath her. Her skin felt impossibly clean against the fine material. With shaking fingers, he tore new bread into little morsels that she could swallow, and fed her like a bird.

'Tomorrow you will be tried for witchcraft.' His words broke with grief. 'I will no longer be tried. My father – oh, my darling,' he blurted out, 'he won't help you, he won't, I'll do everything I can, whatever worth my name still has.' He tugged vainly at the chains fastened into the wall. 'If I could only carry you away.'

She watched him peacefully, barely comprehending what he said. It was enough to see him and feel his gentle hands. She tried to speak, and no sound came out. With another sip of the brew, she managed a few words. 'I love you.'

She fell asleep then, with his arms cradling her. She dreamt of being kissed in the blue light of dawn, and woke alone.

* * *

She only saw him once more. He wasn't at the trial, which was cursory in any case. He is being held by his father, she told herself, or fighting my case somewhere where it will make a difference. In the court, after all, there was nothing to be said. Her accusation was her condemnation. Women whose children she had rescued from death spoke up against her uncanny knowledge of medicine. Men whom she had helped against the injustice of the court said she had used her evil wiles on them. She lived alone. She never entered the church. She had once healed the wing of a sparrow, brought to her by little crying children.

She looked straight into the prosecution's eyes as he proclaimed her sins, and shuddered at what she saw there. The eyes of hell looked back at her, aflame with avarice and vicious lust. She blinked, and saw only a cruel man's cold blue eyes.

'Mother, grant me sight,' she murmured beneath her breath, lowering her eyes to her lap. When she raised them again, she saw a man being torn and devoured by a hungry beast. Its skin dripped with the putrefaction of a dozen untreated diseases. Its arms and legs were skeletal as a famine victim, while its stomach was bloated and rolled with fat. Claws of iron squeezed the man's heart, as his lifeblood dripped down to the floor. His eyeballs dangled loose on his cheeks, so that the beast's burning eyes could peer through his sockets.

'It is the Devil's minion!' she screeched in horror, whirling around to the judge. What she saw there made her scream hysterically, until her weakened body flopped into unconsciousness. After that, passing judgement was a mere formality.

She spent one more night in the cell and Hadrian did not come. *I have been tried by the Devil and my love has left me.* She lay awake all night, waiting for the scrape of the key that never came. The next day, tied to a pyre on Round Hill, she rested her eyes on him at last. On the far side of the river, he sat on horseback, flanked by his father's men. The fire ate into her legs and ran up her clothes, while her flesh bubbled and burnt, and yet it didn't hurt. Surely it should hurt, she thought, as the meat charred her bones and the fat dripped into the fire. All the time, her eyes never left him and he stared straight at her, unwavering.

9 **Chokmah**

'But we were going to do a divination!' exclaimed Henrietta. 'It's Seed Moon – it's such a perfect time for starting things . . .' Her voice trailed off helplessly. 'Don't you want to know what to do, to get Adrian back?'

Sarah's eyes glistened, even as her face hardened. The past month had been even more painful than Adrian's abrupt, inexplicable departure from her life. Her jaw tightened as she spoke in clipped tones. 'So that he can betray me a third time? Hen, it seems very clear that he's repeating past patterns. I told you what I saw. What I – went through. He sat and watched me!' Her voice rose towards hysteria. 'He sat on his horse and watched me burn!' She gripped the phone tighter, staring at herself in the spotted mirror above the table. He had tended her lovingly, as well – as lovingly as he had held her the night before he left. On the other end of the line, Henrietta was silent. Sarah struggled for control of her voice, so that she could speak again without crying. When she did, she sounded weary and dry. 'I don't have any reason to think it's a spell, anymore. So I think it's time I just concentrated on my own life for a bit.'

She stared at the pages, the lines of text dancing in front of her unfocused eyes. The ruby amulet nestled between her breasts under her blouse. In this particular trial, the principle evidence was from a respected member of the parish who said the witch had attempted to seduce him with evil enchantments. Her bruises and cuts were evidence of his virtuous struggle against her. Moreover, she had been seen licking the wounds – drinking her own blood. Saliva, thought Sarah. Antiseptic. Oh, you poor girl, if only you had been a witch. Smoothing her face with her hands, she gazed up at the library's painted ceiling in despair. Reliable, contemporaneous manuscript evidence of the Old Religion simply didn't exist. The best she could find were the accounts of the witch trials, which she could hardly stomach, the *Malleus Malifecarum*, and a handful of others in which the seeds of truth were distorted almost beyond recognition. She had to find some academic evidence of what she knew, before it could form part of her thesis. Without that, all the apparent embedding of specific secrets dissolved into the usual hodgepodge of mediaeval superstitions. The pattern was there, hidden in even the most sacred texts, but without a cogent explanation of the Old Religion, she could prove nothing. None of the forces shaping her life had any empirical proof. If only she had a supervisor she could ask. It was a quarter to five. Sod it, she thought, packing up her things. Dr Piedmont might not like the direction of her thesis much, but he was her supervisor, and she was damn well entitled to ask him. She could make it to his office before five, if she hurried.

As she raised her hand to knock, she heard voices inside and hesitated. She didn't want to barge in, demanding occult sources, in front of anyone. In that pause, she recognised the arrogant drawl of her supervisor, raised in anger, and then – she could swear the other was Clara's clipped bray, rising and falling in an anxious whine. Hadn't Jo said something about Clara and Dr Piedmont, when he'd warned her and Adrian to leave Oxford? And if Clara were there, Adrian might be alone. He might speak to her. Trembling, she lowered her hand.

The need to look at his face again was overpowering, if only to say goodbye. Whatever he'd done to her, she had loved him in that lifetime and in this one. Quietly, she backed away from the door. His room was so near – back down the stairs, along the corridor, up the next flight, back along the corridor, the one at the end, unmistakable. She hurried, her heart beating so violently that she thought she might be sick. Her spirit sang with joy and terror. It was enough just to see him, the light on his skin, the smoothness of his face. Even if he turned away from her in disgust, she would be with him, and hear his voice. He would be at his desk, working in the sunlight, turn to face the door. Her shaking hand rapped on the door. Her pulse raced as she waited for the priceless treasure of his voice saying, 'Come in.'

The silence lengthened. Tentatively, her hand clasped the doorknob and turned it. It opened slowly. The room was curtained, and empty. The shelves, walls, and open cupboard were bare. She shut the door behind her and sat down on the bed. Her hand brushed the mattress gently. He had slept here. She began to cry, softly.

As her tears eased, she heard arguing voices again, raised but muted through the wall. She lifted her head slowly, thinking again of the route she had taken from Dr Piedmont's room. It must be next door, just through the wall. Padding quietly, she took the glass toothbrush holder from the basin and held it against the wall. The words were indistinguishable, but without doubt it was their voices. She held her ear pressed into the glass, listening intently. Only because her head was held sideways did she see the doorframe behind the cupboard. Carefully, she set the glass down without letting it chink against the porcelain. With a rasp of wood against nylon, she dragged the cupboard slowly forwards over the carpet. She knelt, her eye to the keyhole

– all was dark, except for a tiny chink of light. She held one eye closed, peering, until she made it out to be a keyhole, about a metre away. Her movements were slow and deliberate as she tried the door handle, found it yielded, turned off her mobile phone, and slipped through the smallest gap she could into the black chamber beyond. She released the door catch cautiously, terrified of even the slightest click. The darkness was absolute, except for the tiny chink of light from the next room. Her hands drifted slowly through the air, as if weaving a spell.

'I don't know what to do anymore,' shrieked Clara from the next room. Sarah felt shelves, and something soft on them – towels? Smoother, rougher fabric was surely sheets. She drew a handful of towels slowly out, laid them on the floor, and knelt down with her eye to the keyhole.

On the far side of the room was Dr Piedmont's desk. He sat behind it, his face a sneer. Her vision was blocked momentarily as Clara stormed from side to side of the room.

'You said it would be simple,' she snapped accusingly. 'You said he'd come back, and that would be that.'

Sarah shuddered, wondering if Clara had seen the flicker of rage passing across the young professor's face. Dr Piedmont did not like being told off.

'And isn't he back?' he replied, dispassionately.

'Yes – yes – but I didn't expect all this, this – the weird rituals, the, the … I want out, I'm not even interested in him anymore, I only did it to please you!'

'To please me,' murmured Dr Piedmont. 'You expect to please me with your complete ineptitude, your inability to carry out even the simplest spells?'

'I did everything right, I swear.' The girl sounded wildly panicked. 'Everything exactly like you told me. But I tell you, it's not working properly.'

'How exactly is it not working? He is still with you and has made no attempt to contact Sarah, am I right?'

'Yes.' Clara sat down heavily in the armchair by the desk. It looked a comfortable, even cosy, chair, but Sarah knew from experience how discomfiting it was to sit in, and what a disadvantage it put the other girl in. Now, at least, her profile was clear. The usually immaculate make-up was smudged around her eyes, and she tugged awkwardly at the lace sleeve of her blouse. 'But it's like he's drugged or something . . .'

'Surely to be expected, when that's almost precisely what we're doing?' said the doctor sharply. 'Whether you keep someone under with an enchantment or a chemical, they're not exactly behaving naturally, are they?'

'No – I suppose not – but it's like he's in some other world, or something. As if the real Adrian has just gone – somewhere else. It's like he's not drugged, he's just left. He goes into a trance, for hours at a time, sometimes. And then . . .' She paused nervously, fidgeting. Dr Piedmont allowed the silence to draw out, uninterrupted. Sarah's heart was hammering so loudly in her ears that she drew back from the door, fearful that they could hear it. Her whole body shook violently.

'He's started bleeding,' came Clara's voice in a plaintive squeak.

'What?' bellowed Dr Piedmont. 'When?'

Sarah rocked to and fro in the darkness, her arms clutched tightly around her chest. She couldn't look at them again. She would fling open the door, beat it down if it were locked, stab them through the heart with the splintered wood. An it harm none, do as ye will, she repeated in her head. Harm none.

'About a month ago. It was a Monday, I remember, because I'd been to the Union.'

'This was the Monday of the full moon, then? A time I specifically told you not to leave him alone?' The deadly calm of Dr Piedmont's voice sent cold chills down Sarah's spine.

'I had to go – I'm on the committee! It was only for an hour or two – and when I came back, he was bleeding.'

'Where?' From his flat tone of voice, it sounded as if he already knew.

'The little doll of him – the poppet – with the nails around it – between him and, and her, the picture of her – all the places the nails were pointed. I checked. On his palms, his forearms, his thighs, his belly.'

'How curious. It shouldn't be possible, you know.' The anger appeared to have vanished, and he considered the question like an academic curiosity. 'The pain before it reaches that point should be so severe, to withstand that enough to actually cause bleeding! He must be stronger than we thought,' he mused. 'He was alone?'

'Yes. I locked the doors before I left.'

Sarah closed her eyes. He was being kept prisoner, while she chatted about astrology with Henrietta and Sarah. He bled, to reach her, while she did nothing. He, at least, had tended her wounds in the prison. Reluctantly, she leant forward to look through the keyhole again.

'And when I came back, he didn't even look up at me, he just kept talking to himself, like he was completely mad, staring into thin air, and the blood was running down his clothes, I could see the pain on his face, and this insane look in his eyes – it was horrible.' She started to cry, smearing mascara delicately onto the pale pink lace at her wrists.

'You have been doing everything else exactly as I said? Lacing his drinks with the potion I gave you? He's been drinking my sperm from that whorish little cunt of yours?' Clara was nodding frantically.

Dr Piedmont rose to his feet gracefully, moving from behind his desk. 'They must not meet. The dinner was a mistake, I admit that. I thought if she saw you two together, it would speed matters up. But they shouldn't meet. They must not know their strength. If he can do that alone, then if they're together, who knows? I shall have to discuss this with the Master, of course. In the meantime...' His sudden slap jerked Clara's face around, so that her horrified eyes seemed to stare straight into Sarah's. The girl cringed, whimpering, her hand raised to her cheek. He tugged it away and smacked her face again, viciously. 'That's for disobeying me.'

'I'm sorry,' she wailed, 'I love you, I'll do whatever you say.'

'You'd better,' he growled. 'This is getting out of hand.' Curling his hand around her head, he lifted her to her feet by a handful of her hair. 'Right now, we have business to attend to.' With his free hand, he swept the desk clear and forced her over it. With the belt from his trousers, he fastened her hands behind her back.

'Ouch,' she wailed, 'You're hurting me.'

'You deserve a lot worse,' he said coldly, 'and you'll get some of it before we're through.'

Sarah watched in horror as he set up the ritual, a twisted perversion of the opening of the circle. At six corners around the desk, he lit black candles, intoning the incantation in an unfamiliar language. She wanted to slip out of the linen cupboard and run for all she was worth, but forced herself to stay. If she knew what they were doing, she would have more chance of breaking it. As he cast his misshapen circle, she silently cast a circle of protection around herself. He disappeared from view, and reappeared naked. His body was hard and lean. As he leant over Clara, she saw he was wearing a black leather mask, covering his face and the upper part of his head. He pulled the girl to the ground.

'Suck,' he ordered curtly, splaying his legs.

Her hands twisted behind her back, she bobbed her head to reach the tip of his hardening cock. Her pointed tongue dabbed at it, manipulating it between her lips. He reached down to push her blouse off her shoulders and hauled her breasts out of the expensive bra. 'Massage it with your tongue,' he said hoarsely. The girl's cheeks contracted around the fleshy pole, slurping a little as she obeyed. It was swelling to fierce proportions. He began to move his hips, forcing the thick rod deeper into her mouth. She gagged, struggling to swallow it, rising higher on her knees to get the angle right.

'This is all you're good for, you little slag,' he muttered. 'Take it deeper.' He held her head still as he forced himself further into her mouth, groaning with pleasure. Lazily, he fucked her mouth, his enormous length disappearing down her throat.

Eventually, he pulled away. His erection dripped with her saliva.

'On your feet.'

Awkwardly, she clambered up.

'Bend over the desk.'

He lifted her skirts and pulled her panties down to her ankles, kicking her feet apart. Her shapely bottom parted just enough to reveal the slender crack of her pussy. He brought his hand down hard on her cheek. 'Bend over properly.'

She wriggled further down on the desk as he smacked her. His cock throbbed with each mewing wail that escaped her throat. Abruptly, he pushed two fingers inside her.

'Wet,' he said disgustedly. 'You actually like it, don't you?'

'Yes,' she panted.

He spanked her harder. 'You're mine,' he growled. 'You'll do whatever I say. You do not,' his words were punctuated with slaps, 'push off from your duties on silly little errands of your own. I want to make sure you remember this.'

He turned away from her, and reappeared in Sarah's vision holding a fat dildo. With the heel of his hand, he rammed it deep inside the squealing girl. 'You don't deserve my cock in this hole,' he said, thrusting the dildo in and out as he rubbed himself. Her bottom was bouncing up and down as the rubber penetrated her. 'But if I want to try and undo some of the damage you've done, I'll have to give it to you. So this,' he whisked the phallus out, 'will have to go somewhere else.' He began to twist it into her anus, ignoring her howls of dismay and pain. When it was lodged half-way, he stepped between her legs and guided his club between the folds of her cleft. His buttocks clenched as he pushed in.

'Now,' he said, stooping over her with his hands resting on the desk. 'It's halfway up your arse, and I'm halfway in your cunt. Every time I force more of myself into you, my belly will push it further into you. You'll be nice and crammed, and you'll squeal for me like the little tart you are. Understand?'

He seemed to take her whimper for assent. 'Ahh...' he leant back, his hands resting on her hips. 'You're a silly little girl, but your body won't disappoint me. Now, repeat the mantra for me.'

Her voice strangled, she said a few syllables in the same strange language he had used earlier. 'From now until I spill my semen into you, that's the only thing I want to hear you say.' He began to move back and forth, wedging himself into her by small increments, groaning with pleasure at the disproportion between his own hefty tool and her narrow slit. His body was bowed over hers, ensuring that the hard stomach muscles of his belly forced the dildo in equally. His head tilted back as he pierced her, the weird words falling lustfully from his mouth. At last he managed to drive the final inch home and began battering against her body in earnest. The slapping sound of his thighs against her butt cheeks and the squelch of his penetration mingled with the sound of their gasps. He drilled faster and harder into her, driven on by her yelps of pain. His bottom flew back and forth like a piston, speeding up until he spasmed, bellowing out the ritual words in tandem with Clara's screams.

He stood still for a minute, and pulled out.

'Turn over.' She obeyed, her face flushed and streaked with mascara tears. He hoisted her legs up onto the desk, her arms trapped beneath her. 'Lie like that, or it'll all run out.'

He closed the circle, blew out the candles, and dressed. Retrieving his belt from around her wrists, he fastened it around his waist. 'I'm off to hall for dinner. Make sure Adrian drinks that tonight.'

He left the room. Sarah watched as Clara massaged the life between her wrists and, with difficulty, extracted the dildo from her anus. She sat down heavily on the chair, looking around her forlornly. For a moment, Sarah felt sorry for her, then she thought again of Adrian bleeding (his precious skin, his priceless body) and her heart hardened. Clara was wiping her face clean in a small hand-mirror and reapplying her make-up.

You've only got what you deserved, Sarah thought with hatred, and then realised she had echoed Dr Piedmont's words.

* * *

She followed Clara from a cautious distance, up St Aldate's, through the crowds on Cornmarket, and up St Giles. Almost unconsciously, she performed the invisibility spell she had used in the graveyard, ducking around pedestrians who didn't see her. The early evening was still bright with sun glittering on the new leaves. She could feel the trees welling up with sap and she called to them for strength as she hurried past. Clara turned down Little Clarendon, walking slowly, idling in front of shop windows. After some hesitation, she walked into the Duke of Cambridge. Nervously, Sarah followed, weaving the spell around her more tightly. The Duke was filling up for happy hour, and Sarah lurked quietly in the crowd while Clara necked cocktails and wittered to one acquaintance after another. She clearly didn't want to go home to her bleeding, enchanted, stolen, imprisoned lover. Sarah warded off the evil thoughts of hatred that came to her one after the other, and fought to keep her invisibility spell in place. By nine, she was weak and dizzy from the perpetual concentration, and Clara was drunkenly swaying back into the street. She headed into Jericho, leading Sarah to Adrian.

As she approached the steps of a small block of flats, Jo appeared at the top, under the dull electric light, gesturing frantically to Sarah. Clara, climbing the stairs, gave no indication that she saw him as he ran down towards her. For a vertiginous moment, Sarah saw him run through the girl, who gave a small shudder.

'Stop!' Jo was yelling. 'Sarah, stop – you'll kill him – stop, for the love of the Mother. Hide, here.' He tugged her into the acrid gloom under the stairs.

'He mustn't drink it,' whispered Sarah in panic. 'I have to stop him, Jo, he has to know.'

'Wait – wait.' His usually immaculate hair was tousled and his face twisted. 'I was going to come tonight, to tell you. It's stronger than you thought, there's a poppet.'

'I know, I know!' She wanted to shriek, but kept her voice muted. Above, she heard the rasp of a key sliding into the door. 'But he mustn't drink . . .'

'What, the potion? I know – I told him. She never sees me, she doesn't have a shred of power. I can spy all I like.'

'Not the potion – the, oh it's awful Jo, it's his sperm inside her, not his, I mean, Dr Piedmont's – he mustn't drink it from her!' She was falling over her words with urgency.

Jo's eyes darkened with anger. 'I'll tell him,' he said curtly. 'But you can't see him – the nails dig into him every time he thinks of you, and he carries on till he bleeds, but he'll lose too much blood – they'll pierce his vital organs. Sarah, my angel.' He wrapped his arms suddenly around her, holding her as tightly to him as he could. 'I'm with him always now,' he whispered into her hair. 'He isn't alone. This is what you must do.' His words sped up, precise and anxious. 'The curse will rebound on anyone who touches the nails, or tries to remove the poppet. If he sees you, he may run to you – the moment he touches you, they'll go right through him. You have to draw him out of the poppet, not the nails away – understand? Find whatever part of him is trapped there and rescue it. His spirit – can you recognise it?'

She nodded, her eyes burning.

'Get the coven, you'll need all the help you can get. Clara and Adrian are going to the Christ Church Ball on Beltane eve. That's a powerful night. It's a masked ball. Buy yourselves tickets, and disguise yourself completely, for your safety and Adrian's. Until then, prepare yourself. I must go and warn him. Go home as fast as you can, the house is safe. Take the bus if you still can't fly. I will stay with him, I swear it on my love for you.' He kissed her lips violently and disappeared up the stairs.

10 **Kesher**

Three feathered faces, brilliant with sequins and alive
with human eyes, floated above satin folds as Sarah,
Henrietta and Caitlyn moved through the quadrangle of
Christ Church – pale gold for Henrietta, silvery graphite
for Caitlyn, and midnight blue for Sarah. She had sewn
their dresses, embroidering sigils of protection and
power around the cuffs, breasts, and hems. For the last
three days, her two friends hadn't left her house.
Between the constant meditation of sewing, the shared
celebrations of sunset and sunrise, and the fierce hope
burning inside her, Sarah felt her powers rushing and
redoubling. The secret store of spells had opened again,
and she stitched her spells with the dreamy certainty of
one who had made these shapes many times before. She
let the visions float in front of her eyes, knowing now
they were memories: the wattle-and-daub houses on
which she had painted these, the swaddling-clothes into
which she had discreetly woven them, and the wooden
beams into which she had engraved them. She ate little
and worked tirelessly. Her own gown had lace rising
high up her neck and down her arms, and her mask
covered her face entirely. She bought a wig to hide her
hair and practised spells of glamour until she could keep
her eyes blue as summer skies with hardly any
concentration.

The stern, stone lines of the college had been transformed into a peacock masquerade of fabric and lights,
draped in operatic folds. They moved through Persian
and Oriental rooms, through a temporary Indian temple

with a snake charmer, from candle-studded darkness into blinding disco lights that caught up the swirls of dry-ice smoke. Cocktails with names like Subterranean Lake and Deception were tipped stickily from vats into glasses, and left lying about the tables. An operatic quartet were singing Puccini and Verdi in an Arabian tent, while deep bass beats shook the floorboards of a darkened room.

From behind the filigreed, feathered doll-face of her porcelain mask, Sarah's unnaturally blue eyes peered into shadowy corners and combed through crowds. The age-old dilemma of the lost presented itself: was it better to wait in one place, watching all that came and went with an eagle eye, or hunt from room to room, marquee to marquee, knowing that the other might be moving into the very place just vacated?

By eleven o'clock, she had still caught no glimpse of him. They were walking back through the quadrangle, around the statue of Mercury, when she stopped abruptly and clasped her friends closer.

'What if I don't find him?' she whispered. Before she could continue, someone stumbled into her from behind, knocking her off the precarious balance of her high heels. She was flung to the floor, her wig tumbling ahead of her, the porcelain mask shattering on the brick. She whirled around in shock to see Tim swaying from side to side.

'Shorry,' he muttered, his eyelids drooping heavily with drink. He blinked as she came into focus. 'Sarah?' he cried out, disbelievingly.

She scrambled to her knees, crouching down to gather up the broken pieces of her disguise. 'Keep quiet,' she hissed.

'Keep quiet, keep quiet' he snarled belligerently, jabbing a finger in the air. 'That's all you fucking do, you arrogant cocktease, think you're too good to even return a phone call!' His voice rose angrily. His attack was gathering a circle of onlookers.

'Tim, please, just keep quiet,' she pleaded, glancing around frantically. Caitlyn was struggling to undo her own mask – it wouldn't cover her whole face, but it would be better than nothing. She tried to force her hair hurriedly back under the wig, catching her fingers on fragments of porcelain.

'Keep quiet,' he mimicked again, nastily. He was clearly very drunk. 'You keep quiet, Sarah!' he yelled.

Her fingers still caught in her hair, she saw a trio standing on the stairs slowly turn at the sound of his yell. *Please, no*, she thought in anguish, her stomach flipping painfully.

Clara's mouth and eyes were perfect Os of shock. Dr Piedmont's face had contorted in anger, his nose pulled upwards, his jaw working as if he were fighting something. And Adrian stood between them, his eyes staring with the helpless plea of the drowning man, of the climber whose grip on the rescuer's hand is irrevocably slipping.

Others' eyes followed her stare as Dr Piedmont lurched down the steps. He was moving like an automaton, or a puppet fighting his strings. In the centre of Adrian's starched white dinner shirt, blood bloomed.

'Sarah,' rasped her supervisor. His voice sounded utterly unlike him. With no trace of urbanity, no slick sneering wit, he sounded finally young. She realised, as she had forgotten since first she met him, that he was probably about her own age. 'Sarah, help me,' he gasped. 'I've failed – he's going to kill me – you can protect me, you have power.'

She pulled back, appalled, as he staggered towards her. Her eyes flew from his approach to Adrian's sorrowful eyes and reddening shirt.

'I only wanted success,' he whimpered, 'Who cares

about one's soul, when there's success – you have to help me, I didn't know – Aah-aahrrr...' With a sudden shudder, his eyes changed back to their narrow selves. He flung himself towards her, his hand already pulling a knife from his coat.

'You will not rise again,' he shrieked, lunging, and then he was writhing and screaming in the solid, muscular arms of the bouncers. They were strong, trained men, but he was fighting his way free like a dervish.

'Cast it out,' said Henrietta in a voice shaken with revulsion. 'He's possessed. Cast it out, quickly.'

Her hands moving in once-familiar circles, Sarah began to murmur the arcane syllables to release him. Whatever held him was immensely powerful – she felt as if she were trying to push a house over.

'Help,' she croaked, and felt her friends' arms encircle her waist, their voices falling into rhythm with hers. The sounds were so soft that even those standing next to them could not have heard, and yet to Sarah's ears they reverberated across the quadrangle. Her face drew out and tensed as she pushed her consciousness harder into that pure thought: get out of him. Cool waters of energy were flowing up into her from Henrietta, soft breezes from Caitlyn eased her. She let herself channel their force so that they flung themselves towards Dr Piedmont as tidal waves and gales. Suddenly, something snapped, Dr Piedmont sagged in the bouncer's arms, and she reeled. Standing next to him was a silver-haired old man, his mouth curling in a grin of absolute malice. She had last seen him in gardens of St Mary's Church, accepting the Devil's toast and smiling at his unwitting followers.

'Run!' she squealed to Caitlyn and Henrietta, and without waiting to see if they followed she tore off, kicking her heels away, making for the southern gates that led to the meadows.

'You're running away,' panted Caitlyn behind her. 'Sarah, why?'

'Running to,' Sarah called back hoarsely. In that moment, looking into the Devil's eyes, she had known she couldn't beat him within the stone walls and corridors. Too much of what had passed here, over the centuries, was his doing. The violence and hatred, the petty prejudices that destroyed lives and hopes, the haggling and arrogance, the ruination of pure lovely knowledge into battles of ego, all this had soaked into the rocks that had been torn from the Mother's womb. She needed the trees around her, the rich sandy soil under her feet – that was where her strength came from.

Halfway down the avenue of trees she stopped mid-flight, and spun around. Caitlyn and Henrietta hurtled to a halt just past her. The Devil stood there, barely a few metres away, calm and unruffled, as she'd known he would be.

'You can't run away from me, you know,' he murmured.

'I know.' She held out her arms behind her back, and felt the small, warm hands of her friends clasp hers.

'It would have been easier, you know, if you had just gone home with me when we last met. All the young man's suffering would have been avoided.'

'I have better advisers than you,' she replied coolly. Jo, she thought wildly, he must be here somewhere. Please let him be helping Adrian. She didn't have time for this, she could feel the nails sliding into Adrian as surely as into her own flesh.

'Sarah, who is he?' hissed Henrietta.

'An old friend,' the man replied genially, his eyes glittering with charm.

'The Devil,' answered Sarah curtly. 'Be ready.'

'You can't fight me.' He smiled. 'All you little mortals try. There's nothing on this earth, but me.'

Beyond him, she could see Adrian struggling through the lit porch way, supported by Jo. The front of his shirt was crimson and his face contorted with pain as he staggered towards her.

'You're killing him,' she said. Her words were matter-of-fact, but inside her she could feel the rage of the lioness rising. Her spirit darted out briefly and felt the twin heart fires of Caitlyn and Henrietta surging in unison, pouring energy into her. They love each other, she recognised distantly, as their smoky red ribbons twined together, linking up with her and offering their strength. Her mind ran along the pale grasses of the meadow, in places feathery and in places stiff and clumped where the cows had chewed it down. She felt her spirit sink deeper to feel the tree roots beneath her clutching at the soil, forcing the packed earth aside in their insatiable thirst. Deeper it ran, into the bedrock and the immense mantle, like a single particle of light scurrying through the magnificent weight and pressures of that compacted colossus. Help me, her soul screamed, as she fought her way deeper, to where jewels were molten and rocks burned without melting. *We haven't finished!* She was nothing but a spark now, and yet her determination blazed fiercer still and she could see again the light for which she had waited so long, finally entering the thin little layer of soft soil, floating deeper, hunting blindly for her. That time, that huge presence had sheltered her from the pressures, allowed her a tiny space, all she needed, in which to watch and wait. Help me! she screamed silently once more, and felt the leviathan head turning slowly to her, heavy with life and love that cared nothing for the millennia it took to shift a continent, but cared about the sparkle of a single, pale blade of grass in the sunlight. She knew, also, that she was exactly as important as that blade of grass, which is to say, priceless, and exquisitely brief. The immense presence glowed warmer, and a single feeling resounded in her. *Yes.*

Abruptly, she was above the surface again, imbuing her body with the furnace-heat of that furious, determined spark. As her arms rose, the gargantuan power flowed upwards into them, a borrowed force that could tear down heaven and hell by simply outlasting them, that had existed long before them and would continue after.

She saw the Devil again, with her own eyes and with the Mother's, no longer as the most powerful and ancient of evils to confront humanity but as an upstart. She had laboured for centuries to protect Adrian's spark, waited for it, found it, defended it, nestled it against the spark of herself, held it safe while the tides rolled across the earth and the planets spun. She had swayed with their gravitational pull, waiting, while trees extended and retracted, while the surface heated and cooled, until the best of all possible moments to release it back into the world. Only then, with that light glowing in a new tiny body somewhere, could she let herself drift back to the surface, and take her carefully-chosen place in things. And now this despicable nothing had torn a shred from her beloved light, and its light was fading.

Her mouth opened in a roar, and the words that rolled like lava from her tongue, the Mother's words and her own, were 'Leave my child alone!'

The sound rolled outwards from her, in concentric waves across the meadows, out onto the river, up the avenue, rebounding off the tall college walls and crashing back across them. Her body shone with radiance, her human eyes could hardly withstand the brilliance of Adrian. He stood upright, beyond the Devil, no longer needing support as the silver core of him coalesced into a whole once more and his luminous eyes met hers. A net of light spun itself between them, a spider's web, a canopy, of pure silver. Spears of power passed between them, from eyes to eyes, forehead to forehead, breast to breast, groin to groin, each a lance through the crumbling edifice of evil between them. As the old man's shape drifted into dust, the flaming giants rose up from them at last, again, reached out, and held each other close.

The black grass slowly turned to deep olive green. Behind taupe-coloured clouds, pieces of sky blanched, until the sparse golden lights of Magdalen's windows appeared to dim. The water rippled smoky blue and black as the punt glided between the fields and meadows. From dark silhouettes against the sky and deep black shadows, the trees began to reclaim their dimensions, little spears were touched with green and turned back to leaves. The branches reached out over Sarah and Adrian, forming a canopy above their close embrace. Far above, the sky had melted from hard black into Prussian blue, and now, slowly infused with light, softened into violet. The clouds dissolved into a fine spray of light pink. The white beaks of coots shone as they paddled across the water, dancing around the territory of the ducks who shepherded their tiny fluffy ducklings from beneath the bushes. Beyond the tower of Magdalen, over the fields, gold scorched the treetops, turned them to copper, and burnt the dissipating clouds to violent peach and lilac. Caitlyn brought the punt to a gentle halt by the wall of the Botanic garden, where the flat lawn was already regaining its daytime brilliance and tranquillity. With murmured blessings, Henrietta scattered crumbs widely for the water birds around them. Her arm passed through Jo, sitting alongside her, who smiled wryly at the two lovers. The crowds jammed from edge to edge of the bridge and stretching up the High Street were hushed as the choir began to sing. The clear voices rose through the sky, welcoming the sun with the Hymnus Eucharisticus. Sarah sang along softly in Latin, turning the words to a hymn to the Mother.

Caitlyn sat cross-legged on the wood, pulled a handful of trailing ivy onto her lap, and began to weave the glossy-leafed vines into crowns. Henrietta twisted open a flask, and poured a libation into the river and then filled glasses for all five. Sarah handed Jo his.

'Made with my own hands,' she said gently, and he sipped.

'Elderflower,' murmured Adrian, holding his own hot tea close to his face so that the steam drifted across his face. 'Nettle, burdock root, mullein...' He frowned in concentration, as he took a small sip. 'And rose hip.' He turned his face to Sarah, shining with love through his exhaustion. 'I can taste and smell again,' he whispered. 'I know the plants again. It was awful – the fog in my mind – like a landscape of mist...'

As he drank, she gently removed the hospital's bandages from his chest and thighs. 'Mother-medicine will do better for these,' she said, smearing her own ointment onto the cuts. The tea-tree oil would seal them almost instantly, while the olbas and eucalyptus cleaned and cleansed. The police had attributed Adrian's wounds to Dr Piedmont's knife, which was now in their custody. Its owner had been carried to an ambulance while they were giving their statements in the flickering red-and-blue of the police van. She had seen from the deathly black of his aura that it was already too late – the old man had claimed his payment, and all the doctors could do now was to establish what natural form that had taken.

Now, in the quiet of the remade day, they could return to the true tasks of the witch: healing, and celebration.

Caitlyn and Henrietta tucked the last flowers into the wreaths, the crowd on the bridge surged and broke into babble and music, and the water splashed as revellers in ball gowns and dinner jackets evaded the police to leap into the water. The punt glided away from the bridge again, guided by Caitlyn's steady hand. The long metal pole plunged deep into the river, pushed firmly against its muddy bed, and trailed behind them like a rudder. Crowns of ivy and almond flowers sat on their heads as they moved away from the hubbub, down the Cherwell, into the quiet seclusion of the river's left fork. The risen sun was already warm on their arms.

At the edge of the wood, they found the stump of a fallen tree to be their altar, and slipped their clothes off for the ritual cleansing. The water running between their bodies transmitted their passion as surely as it would transmit electricity, and they climbed back out weak with love.

'We consecrate this circle of power to the Ancient Gods,' said Sarah and Adrian in unison. 'Here may they manifest and bless their children.'

They turned to the east, where the sun stood above the trees, and raised their wands. 'This is a time that is not a time, in a place that is not a place, on a day that is not a day. We stand on the threshold between the worlds, before the veil of the Mysteries. May the Ancient Ones help and protect us on our journey.'

They trembled as their bare arms brushed. Together, they set the elements onto the altar, asking blessings on the water, earth, fire, and air within them. Around the icons of the Goddess and her lover-son, the Horned One, they placed the water chalice, the small dish of salt, and the incense burner bright with hot coals.

'Great Mother, bless these creatures of water to your service. May we always remember the cauldron waters of rebirth. Great Mother, bless these creatures of earth to your service. May we always remember the blessed earth, its many forms and beings.'

Adrian held the chalice of water and salt up to the sky, and carried it widdershins around the circle, sprinkling the mixture on the ground, before returning it to the altar.

'Great Mother, we give you honour!'

'Great Father, bless these creatures of fire to your service,' they continued. 'May we always remember the sacred fire that dances within the form of every creation. Great Father, bless these creatures of air to your service. May we always listen to the spirit winds that bring us the voices of the Ancient Ones.'

Sarah sprinkled ambergris onto the charcoal, and raised the burner high above her. Her breasts rose high in the sunlight as she held it aloft. She walked doesil around the circle, letting the smoke drift upwards to the skies, and replaced the burner at the centre.

'Great Father, we give you honour!'

Facing the sun once more, they lit the yellow candle and held up their hands in greeting.

'We call upon you, powers of air, to witness this rite and to guard this circle.'

Caitlyn, whose sun sign was fixed air, sat cross-legged in that quarter as they put the candle facing her on the altar.

To the south, they lit the red candle.

'We call upon you, powers of fire, to witness this rite and to guard this circle.'

Sarah, mutable fire, sat as Adrian put her candle on the altar and turned his back on the sun to light the blue candle.

'We call upon you, powers of water, to witness this rite and to guard this circle.'

Henrietta, the gentle child of Pisces, sat down in his shadow.

Finally, he lit his own green candle in the northern quarter.

'We call upon you, powers of earth, to witness this rite and to guard this circle.'

Instead of sitting, he returned to the altar and lifted his face to the warm rays that fell on it, his arms outstretched towards that source of gorgeous heat.

Jo, pure spirit, having no elements left to him, sat in the centre by the altar, at Adrian's feet.

'This circle is bound, with power all around. Between the worlds we stand, with protection at hand.'

Only Sarah could see how Adrian's hands touched Jo's head in blessing as his arms sank back down. He returned to his quarter opposite hers, and for a while they all sat in silence. She watched him with lovelorn eyes that still could not believe his presence. The tree stump hid most of his body, but his bare torso and shoulders glowed pale gold in the leaf-flecked sunlight. Above his head, the verdant crown rested gently on his hair. Their eyes stroked each other's bodies as tangibly as hands, fraught with longing. Warm tendrils of love, barely visible to their astral eyes in the bright morning, flowed between them, catching Jo in their loving net. From east to west, Caitlyn to Henrietta, the same sparkling lines ran back and forth like a glittering heat mirage.

The ritual was a simple offering of thanksgiving: there was little more to ask. Sarah cut the apple in half, and carved the five-sided star within it that symbolised the five elements.

'Great Goddess, Lady of the Summerlands, Mother to us all. We welcome you to this place of power and offer thanks to you for what you have given us. We are priest and priestesses of your path and we see with your eyes. You guide us in the lessons we must learn.'

She cupped three kernels of corn in her hands.

'As the Maiden is ripe with potential, so are our lives. As the Mother gives birth, so do our thoughts. As the Crone nourishes life, so do we nourish ours.'

She saw Jo's wince at those words, even as he closed his eyes and carefully blanked his expression. A flickering glance at Adrian confirmed that he, too, had seen that moment of pain. *He has done so much for us.* They didn't need words, their thoughts echoed in unison. A look of tenderness. *He loves me, he loves you.* A slight crinkle around their eyes of sadness and reluctance. *Yes? Yes.*

When the circle was closed, Caitlyn and Henrietta wandered deeper into the woods, hand in hand, their eyes glowing at each other with Beltane fire. Sarah's skin yearned for Adrian, but their unspoken agreement kept them apart. She drew spirals in the soil, in the soft fertile mulch of last year's leaves, sheltered from the sun by this year's fine new greenery.

Adrian was the first to speak.

'You kept me alive.'

Jo nodded, his eyes on Sarah's slowly twirling fingertip.

'Without you . . .' began Sarah, and found she couldn't continue. She could feel the self-effacing grief emanating from him, and it caught in her throat.

'It has eased the tedium of the last two hundred years, at any rate,' said Jo, his voice strained and artificially light. His eyes darted over Sarah's body and turned back to the ground. 'I'm tired,' he added casually. 'The dying always want to cling on, they never want to go, but they do. Do you know why?' He met their eyes briefly, his head moving from one to the other. 'There's nothing here for them. Unending tedium and a jealousy of the living that could poison one's soul. You've given me life.' His eyes rested on Sarah. 'That repays whatever I have done for you. But you are still alive, and I am not

– I must withdraw, gracefully, as I tried to do before. But the thought of those empty unrelenting streets ...' His voice petered out in anguish.

'There's no need for you to go,' said Adrian fiercely. 'We'll do anything for you ...'

'And when you die? No. I must go. But perhaps there is something you can do for me, if you can bear it.'

On the night of the next new moon, there were only eight and a half hours between sunset and sunrise, and the darkest point between them fell at ten to one in the morning. It was three o'clock, however, before the streets had emptied of the shouts and shiny clothes of the clubbers. Sarah and Adrian emerged from the shadows of the copper beech. With the sharp edge of the spade, they cut through the turf and lifted the squares of grass to one side, to reveal the blacker square of earth beneath it. Later, they would be able to replace the squares, and tangle the grass back together with their fingers. Working fast and neatly from either side of the hole, they began to lift the earth onto a tarpaulin. Neither spoke. From time to time, Sarah turned her wet face back to the shadows of the copper beech, but if she was crying she did so silently, and it didn't interrupt her digging.

'It was just a question of five minutes,' Jo had said in the sunlit grove. 'Such a little space of time. My friend was due to arrive five minutes before my father, and both were as punctual as the sun itself. The consumption had had me in its grip for months already, but then I could feel myself slipping, I knew I would not see them alive.'

The gritty rasping sound of the metal spades against the earth changed to a small, hollow sound, like that of a pebble hitting wood. Sarah shook violently, as if she had been struck. Her head turned again to the tree, where another shadow was just discernible next to the darkness of the tree trunk.

'Jo,' she mouthed silently, her face crumpled with grief.

'I had some knowledge from my researches,' he had told them. 'As well as the manuscripts, I had spoken to a few of the wisewomen that yet remained. I knew what could be done with willpower and words. All I needed was a few minutes, to instruct my friend – he was a natural sensitive, and I was certain he would hear me. My father could not be allowed to find it. I was too weak to write, my papers were out of my reach, but I could still will, and I could just manage to speak. So I set my soul to guard my masterpiece, the research that had sapped all my time and energy, and cost me my life. Just until it was delivered, and then I could fade.'

Sarah was on her hands and knees inside the grave now, hidden in the black earth, while Adrian kept watch. With her palms, she scooped the soil aside as gently as if she were washing a child's face. Her fingers slipped through the empty eye sockets and she withdrew them hastily. Her hands pushed through the packed earth covering the skull's dome. Her heart hammered like footsteps on the path.

'I can't hold the spell,' she whispered. 'Take it.'

She felt the force of concentration slipping from her as Adrian took over the invisibility spell to surround them. Blinded by the dark, she could feel the shape of the skull, the familiar line of the jaw she had kissed and the high slope of the forehead, the cerebellum. The sound of rain on the pavement was only her tears falling on the bare bone. She was kneeling either side of the skeleton, in the gap between the ribs and the pelvic bone. She must not hurt, she must not harm, she must not crack or splinter the fragile frame.

I knelt over you like this in joy, and all the time you

*lay here, cold, in the mud. My darling, will you not come
over just once, let me look on your living face?*

She knew he would not. He had said so, when he had
made his request. 'The only thing that stops me asking,'
he had said, 'is shame – fear – I can't bear to look at
your face if you see what I am, even if you know, once
you see ... How can you remember any of the love I
gave you, or the joy, after that?'

Her digging hands found their way beneath the skull
at last.

In the glade, she had taken his hand in her own and
held it to her cheek, and then clasped her palms around
his face. 'I swear by the Mother I will remember you
like this,' she had said, 'whatever else I may see.'

With skin warmed by the sun under her hands, the
light dancing through the leaves, and the sound of the
river, the promise had been easy to make.

'My father arrived first,' he had continued. 'He was a
religious man. He found my manuscript and read it –
not much, but enough. I watched him rage and curse at
Oxford, my friends, and me. I was hurling candles, pens,
whatever I could lift, at him when he approached the
fire. Even so, I thought he would thrust it in, but he
didn't. I never knew why. Perhaps he retained some
superstitions after all, despite the church's teaching –
the wisewomen said burning a letter was a way of
sending it, on the spiritual realm. So he didn't burn it.
He did ensure that it wouldn't be found, and that our
name would not be tarnished by association with witchcraft and occult practices.'

Sarah's fingertips felt a thick, waxy package. As
gently as she could, she eased it out from beneath the
skull, supporting the head like an invalid's, lying it back
down on the pillow of soil.

She held it close to her chest, and put her fingers on
the bare skull in benediction.

'I swear by my soul I will deliver this to the Bodleian library, and your work will be read at last. Entrust it to my care, and end your vigil, my darling.'

Warmth and softness were beneath her fingertips for a moment. She could see nothing in the impenetrable dark, as she ran her hands over the smooth skin of his face, his hair brushing her knuckles. By the time her hands reached his chin, it was naked bone once more.

They sat together at the kitchen table while the white light of an occluded dawn crept into the air. Sarah cried with her head bowed, her hands on the table under Adrian's. Occasionally, she spoke, her sentences truncated as the banal words snapped under the weight of meaning. 'It's like someone's died, but . . .' or 'Every full moon . . .' or 'It's because of him . . .'

In between, she drank the herbal teas Adrian made her, smoked an occasional cigarette, and stared out into the garden with glossy, unseeing eyes.

'I'd only just learnt to see . . .' She began another unfinished statement.

'I know,' said Adrian softly, as he had each time before. 'I know.'

'You know I love you, don't you?'

'Sarah – Sarah. I know.' Volumes of unspoken words filled the silence. 'Grieve, my darling. Look at me.'

She raised her chin and saw his face, too, was wet.

'For two months he has been a guardian angel in my pain, doing everything he could to lose you to me. He kept me sane, he never left my side, for two months, darling.'

She nodded, and touched the parcel with her hand. Grave soil clung to cracks in the old beeswax.

'I'll say I found it in the cellar,' she said unsteadily, rehearsing. They had already agreed this. 'It'll be the property of the landlord, I think, but they'll want it – if he won't give it, or sell it, they'll surely get permission to photograph the pages.'

'Open it.'

She slit the wax with her fingernails. It gave easily, coming apart in two shells. The cloth inside was soft and still bright, protected from the light and air all these years. Moving with the methodical care she always gave manuscripts, she scrubbed and dried her hands before unwrapping it slowly. The pages were crisp and heavy, made of linen, unbound. *Approximately A3, recto of – how many leaves? Numbered in ink in the bottom right-hand corner of the recto. Copperplate text in brown ink.* The phrases emerged in her head without her being aware of having thought them. The handwriting was familiar. She had had love notes from the same hand.

'On the three realms: being a theological disputation on the nature of heaven, hell, and Earth, and an historic and theological account of the Old Religion of the British Isles from manuscript and folkloric sources, by Jonathan Montjoie of Balliol College. 21 June 1811.'

She lay the first page on its front, to one side, and began to read. After a while, Adrian put the kettle on again. Later, he made them brunch. At noon, she came into the garden where he was working at the flower beds. She sat in the middle of the lawn, hugging her knees, watching him. Her grief had evaporated. It might return, later, but for now she felt absolute peace. He crouched next to her, touching her shoulder tenderly with a plant-stained hand.

'Back with the living?' he asked gently.

She nodded. 'It's going to make my thesis,' she said. Her voice's steadiness surprised her. 'It may even make my career. It's the missing piece. I'll deliver it for him all right – I'll deliver it to the world.'

His hand was warm on her shoulder, his bare chest shining with sweat in the sun. The smell of the plants greening in the heat and the overturned soil filled her nostrils. Agreeing not to bring any pain to Jo they could avoid, they hadn't done more than kiss each other since their reunion, almost a fortnight ago. He sat opposite her, holding her hands. His eyes were flecked with so many colours that she could hardly count or name them. His hair was messier than ever, with little leaves tangled in it. Were they the same eyes she had seen in her visions, she wondered, or was it just that she saw the same soul shining out of them?

'There's so much I haven't told you,' she said. 'You've been through so much, I was afraid . . .'

'I'm better now.'

The black eyelashes fringing his eyes dropped swiftly and lifted again. She could dive into his eyes, a tiny swimmer, and float in that sea of colour forever.

'You know the visions I had with you, before?' she said. 'Well, I had more – the tarot cards kept saying dream, dream, and there were more.' She began to tell the stories of Round Hill. After a few sentences, he could keep quiet no longer. His eyes were wild and shining.

'I was there, my love – I remember. I had them too. It was my only escape, falling into a trance, dreaming of you in a place where the nails couldn't get me. I saw it all darling. We were together, in the past and in the visions. Oh, love!'

He hauled her close to him, hugging her tightly. 'I saw you die,' he said into her hair. 'They had their swords out, behind and in front of me, so I would be run through if I tried to rescue you. All I could think of was everything you taught me, all the herbs and spells, but you never taught me to take someone else's pain, but I tried, the fire ate my skin beneath my clothes. I didn't dare move a muscle, and I watched you burn. But I tried.'

She closed her eyes, resting in his arms. The last splinter of doubt eased. 'You managed. I didn't feel a thing. It didn't hurt. I thought you had betrayed me. Both times, I thought that. Both times, you were taking the pain, and I didn't know.'

'Come bathe with me,' he whispered. 'I want to hold you in my arms clean and new again.'

He pegged a white tablecloth to the cherry trees to make a canopy for them, and spread a soft blanket beneath it. As always, he found his way unerringly around the house. Around him, the grass was littered with the small pink blossoms. She stood in the doorway watching him, still wet from the bath. The khoikhoi wrapped around her clung to her damp skin.

'Come here, my queen,' he said.

Timidly, she walked forwards, and he handed her into the open-sided tent.

'How are we so shy, now?' she said wonderingly.

He smiled, and began to unpeel the khoikhoi. 'Let the breeze dry us.'

They lay on the blanket side by side, naked, and let their fingertips relearn each other's contours. Their eyes soaked up each other's, the way mother and infant gaze for tireless hours. His fingers combed her hair and floated over her spine. For hours, they lay like that, moving hardly more than the flowers in the breeze. The birds grew bolder, and began to hop about the beds where Adrian had overturned the earth. Their chirruping mixed with the hum of heat. The shadow of the tent stretched slowly forwards as the sun slid across the sky.

'I know you again,' she said. His eyes said he understood. His mouth moved towards hers. Her spine moulded as she pressed her face closer. The softness of his lips opened to her, and their bodies clasped together as firmly as their mouths.

Their smooth, air-dried skin brushed together as they tangled limbs, her soft warmth against his firm strength. She held him cradled in her arms and was wrapped in his as lovingly, their tongues exploring and retreating. They had become one again long before their shifting movements brought the tip of his shaft sliding into her, sticking fast in the slick, narrow entrance. A violent jolt of bliss seized her. They groaned into each other's mouths as they ground closer, thigh to thigh and chest to chest, rolling this way and that, not willing to separate one square inch of skin, struggling together to push deeper. He grasped her buttocks, clutching her, as she rocked against his heavy staff. The smell of their skin perfumed the air like the ambergris she had sprinkled on the coals. She was licking the taste of it from his neck and shoulders, maddened with pleasure. His length wedged deeper with each rock and thrust of her hips, sinking succulently into her sheath.

'See . . .' he groaned, and she did. They were lying on the bed of her little shack in the fading pink and purple light of a summer evening, the ceiling covered with new greenery, their bodies slippery with sweat as he rode hard into her. They were in the river, secluded behind the drapery of a weeping willow, his back against the river bank, his bottom and her knees pressing into the soft mud as she bucked on him. In the blackberry forest on Port Meadow, in the middle of winter, she stood against a tree with her skirts raised, his trousers unlaced at the front, their bodies joined in such heat that the snow around them melted. He covered her with flowers at the spring solstice and the perfume of the blossoms rose in the air, crushed between their bodies. They painted each other's bodies with blackberries in the autumn and licked at the purple stains, until their mouths succumbed to temptation and drank each other's ripe juices. He joined her as the Horned One under the full moon, and made the Goddess herself scream with ecstasy and the stars shudder with orgasmic bliss. Kneeling on the ploughed fields, she held his hot trembling rod in her hands, playing it in her fists under the bright March sky until his seed blessed the newly planted crops. He was leaning over her shoulder in her shack, while she spelt out a Latin text, and his heart contracted with adoration. She watched him brew the tea that would ease the colic of his tailor's child, and her eyes swam with tears of love. They saw each other's eyes in candlelight, sunlight, cloud light, moonlight, and starlight. A thousand times he sank into her, shuddering, a thousand times the brilliant points of light at the heart of them each oscillated with the frenzied violence of love, spiralling around each other in infinity. Through her eyes, he saw the indomitable spark of her soul descend into the earth and fight the laws of life and death for the right to be with him again, saw her pleading with the Gaia, saw her watching and waiting. Through his eyes, she saw him lying on his bed, his skin raw with burns, clenching his jaw against the pain. She saw him with new-grown skin which was too thin, pink, and far too tender, hearing the death of his father from the lips of the men who had crossed their swords around him while his beloved burnt. They were his servants, now. She saw him walking in the moonlight, unable to sleep for the nightmares. She saw him turning away from the pretty girls who pressed their charms on the new heir. She saw him selling the family estates, signing and sealing the documents with the same blank indifference that marked everything he did, since that day at Round Hill. Alone, day after day, he sat and painted. She saw that he, too, was waiting for his spark to descend into the embrace of the earth. So many little lights were falling into the gloom, like a snowstorm by moonlight, and no two alike. So many cycles passed, the years wheeling as the earth spun and wheeled around the sun, as the shifting planets moved their influence back and forth, but at last she saw him – or *it* saw *it*, with the flash of instant recognition. Their warm, living bodies bucked and shuddered with life on the lawn, drenched each other with it, screamed it aloud to the sky, clutched at it, flaunted it to the world, and all the while two tiny glowing dots of pure being remained absolutely still, in breathless contemplation of each other.

A fortnight later, a letter arrived. Adrian brought it out to her on the lawn, where she sat under the canopy reviewing her transcription of Jo's thesis. The original was already with the Bodleian, who had eagerly agreed to care for it until its ownership was settled. He watched her for a while, smiling as she scribbled in the margins of her notes and arranged papers in piles around her, weighed down by stones.

He gave her the envelope, and a kiss that rapidly threatened to dislodge all the careful piles. Flushed and giggling, she looked at the back, and her face sobered instantly.

'It's from my landlord,' she said, slitting it open quickly. She held the paper so they could read together.

Dear Ms Kirkson,

I gather that you now know who, and what, you are. Forgive me for having kept my own knowledge to myself – I am sure you understand that this is something you needed to discover for yourself.

The house in which you are living has always only been held in trust by me, as it was by my ancestors. Although that trust could not be legally binding, for reasons which will soon become clear, it is nevertheless one which we have always intended to honour, and regard as a spiritual bond much more serious than mere signed papers. In 1536, it was left to my many-times-great grandfather by a friend of his, Sir Hadrian Morgan, with one binding condition – that when its rightful owner reappeared, it should pass to that person.

He left behind many of his paintings, all of which you will find in Mother's room, covered over with whitewash – a liberty that I hope you will excuse, as it can be easily removed without damage to the original paintings beneath. The largest of these is a portrait that you may find startling, bearing as it does a striking resemblance to yourself. This portrait is the sole proof of the rightful owner.

The same friend bequeathed much other land to our family, so you need not fear my being left in penury. I am only glad that I found you before age overcame me. My mother's spirit stayed to guard the house – perhaps you know that already? I am sure she will withdraw now that the matter is settled, it has been wearying for her.

In short, the house is yours, and was always meant to be. I have already instructed my solicitor regarding both the transfer and the repayment of your rent. He will contact you shortly.

Welcome home, my dear. I hope you will be very happy.

Blessed be.

Visit the Black Lace website at
www.black-lace-books.com

LOOK OUT FOR THE ALL-NEW BLACK LACE BOOKS – AVAILABLE NOW!

All books priced £7.99 in the UK. Please note publication dates apply to the UK only. For other territories, please contact your retailer.

LEARNING TO LOVE IT
Alison Tyler
ISBN 978 0 352 33535 7

Art historian Lissa and doctor Colin meet at the Frankfurt Book Fair, where they are both promoting their latest books. At the fair, and then through Europe, the two lovers embark on an exploration of their sexual fantasies, playing intense games of bondage, spanking and dressing up. Lissa loves humiliation, and Colin is just the man to provide her with the pleasure she craves. Unbeknown to Lissa, their meeting was not accidental, but planned ahead by a mysterious patron of the erotic arts.

Coming in August 2007

THE BLUE GUIDE
Carrie Williams
ISBN 978 0 352 34131 0

Cocktails, room service, spa treatments: Alicia Shaw is a girl who just can't say no to the little perks of being a private tour guide in London. Whether it's the Hollywood producer with whom she romps in the private screening room of one of London's most luxurious hotels, or the Australian pilot whose exhibitionist fantasies reach a new height on the London Eye, Alicia finds that flirtation – and more – is part of the territory.

But when internationally renowned flamenco dancer and heart-throb Paco Manchega, and his lovely young wife Carlotta, take her on as their guide, Alicia begins to wonder if she has bitten off more than she can chew. As the couple unleash curious appetites in Alicia, taking her to places more darkly beautiful than she has ever known, she begins to suspect she is being used as the pawn in some strange marital game.

DIVINE TORMENT
Janine Ashbless
ISBN 978 0 352 33719 1

In the ancient temple city of Mulhanabin, the voluptuous Malia Shai awaits her destiny. Millions of people worship her, believing her to be a goddess incarnate. She is, however, very human and consumed by erotic passions that have no outlet. Into this sacred city comes General Veraine – the rugged gladiatorial leader of the occupying army. Intimate contact between Veraine and Malia Shai is forbidden by every law of their hostile peoples. But she is the only thing he wants – and he will risk everything to have her.

Coming in September 2007

TEMPLAR PRIZE
Deanna Ashford
ISBN 978 0 352 34137 2

At last free of a disastrous forced marriage, Edwina de Moreville accompanies Princess Berengaria and her betrothed, Richard the Lionheart on a quest to the Holy Land to recapture Jerusalem from the Saracens. Edwina has happily been reunited with her first and only love, Stephen the Comte de Chalais, one of Richard's most loyal knights but, although their passion for each other is as strong as ever, the path before them will be far from easy.

After surviving a terrible storm at sea, Edwina and the princess fall into the hands of the cruel, debauched Emperor of Cyprus, Isaac Comenius. He has even more frightening plans for Edwina but, with Stephen's help, she and the princess escape. However, Stephen has an enemy he is unaware of, Guy de Lusignan, the King of Jerusalem, who also desires Edwina.

When they reach the besieged city of Acre, their situation becomes more perilous. Guy lures Stephen away from the Christian lines and, with the help of a group of renegade Knights Templar, has him imprisoned in their fortress. When Edwina tries to pursue Stephen, she is captured and enslaved by a Saracen nobleman who desires her for his harem. In the end only one man can help them escape their destiny, the great Saracen leader Saladin. But he also is in danger from the strange sect of assassins, the Hashshashin.

HOTBED
Portia Da Costa
ISBN 978 0 352 33614 9

Pride comes before a fall . . . but what if that descent becomes the wildest ride of your life? Two sisters – Natalie and Patti – become rivals when they challenge each other's daring on a dark, downward spiral where nobody is quite who or what they seem, and where transgressing sexual boundaries is the norm.

Black Lace Booklist

Information is correct at time of printing. To avoid disappointment, check availability before ordering. Go to www.black-lace-books.com. All books are priced £7.99 unless another price is given.

BLACK LACE BOOKS WITH A CONTEMPORARY SETTING

☐ ALWAYS THE BRIDEGROOM Tesni Morgan — ISBN 978 0 352 33855 6 £6.99
☐ THE ANGELS' SHARE Maya Hess — ISBN 978 0 352 34043 6
☐ ARIA APPASSIONATA Julie Hastings — ISBN 978 0 352 33056 7 £6.99
☐ ASKING FOR TROUBLE Kristina Lloyd — ISBN 978 0 352 33362 9
☐ BLACK LIPSTICK KISSES Monica Belle — ISBN 978 0 352 33885 3 £6.99
☐ BONDED Fleur Reynolds — ISBN 978 0 352 33192 2 £6.99
☐ THE BOSS Monica Belle — ISBN 978 0 352 34088 7
☐ BOUND IN BLUE Monica Belle — ISBN 978 0 352 34012 2
☐ CAMPAIGN HEAT Gabrielle Marcola — ISBN 978 0 352 33941 6
☐ CAT SCRATCH FEVER Sophie Mouette — ISBN 978 0 352 34021 4
☐ CIRCUS EXCITE Nikki Magennis — ISBN 978 0 352 34033 7
☐ CLUB CRÈME Primula Bond — ISBN 978 0 352 33907 2 £6.99
☐ COMING ROUND THE MOUNTAIN Tabitha Flyte — ISBN 978 0 352 33873 0 £6.99
☐ CONFESSIONAL Judith Roycroft — ISBN 978 0 352 33421 3
☐ CONTINUUM Portia Da Costa — ISBN 978 0 352 33120 5
☐ COOKING UP A STORM Emma Holly — ISBN 978 0 352 34114 3
☐ DANGEROUS CONSEQUENCES Pamela Rochford — ISBN 978 0 352 33185 4
☐ DARK DESIGNS Madelynne Ellis — ISBN 978 0 352 34075 7
☐ THE DEVIL INSIDE Portia Da Costa — ISBN 978 0 352 32993 6
☐ EDEN'S FLESH Robyn Russell — ISBN 978 0 352 33923 2 £6.99
☐ ENTERTAINING MR STONE Portia Da Costa — ISBN 978 0 352 34029 0
☐ EQUAL OPPORTUNITIES Mathilde Madden — ISBN 978 0 352 34070 2
☐ FEMININE WILES Karina Moore — ISBN 978 0 352 33874 7
☐ FIRE AND ICE Laura Hamilton — ISBN 978 0 352 33486 2
☐ GOING DEEP Kimberly Dean — ISBN 978 0 352 33876 1 £6.99
☐ GOING TOO FAR Laura Hamilton — ISBN 978 0 352 33657 6 £6.99

☐ GONE WILD Maria Eppie   ISBN 978 0 352 33670 5
☐ IN PURSUIT OF ANNA Natasha Rostova   ISBN 978 0 352 34060 3
☐ IN THE FLESH Emma Holly   ISBN 978 0 352 34117 4
☐ LEARNING TO LOVE IT Alison Tyler   ISBN 978 0 352 33535 7
☐ MAD ABOUT THE BOY Mathilde Madden   ISBN 978 0 352 34001 6
☐ MAKE YOU A MAN Anna Clare   ISBN 978 0 352 34006 1
☐ MAN HUNT Cathleen Ross   ISBN 978 0 352 33583 8
☐ THE MASTER OF SHILDEN Lucinda Carrington   ISBN 978 0 352 33140 3
☐ MÉNAGE Emma Holly   ISBN 978 0 352 34118 1
☐ MIXED DOUBLES Zoe le Verdier   ISBN 978 0 352 33312 4   £6.99
☐ MIXED SIGNALS Anna Clare   ISBN 978 0 352 33889 1   £6.99
☐ MS BEHAVIOUR Mini Lee   ISBN 978 0 352 33962 1
☐ PACKING HEAT Karina Moore   ISBN 978 0 352 33356 8   £6.99
☐ PAGAN HEAT Monica Belle   ISBN 978 0 352 33974 4
☐ PASSION OF ISIS Madelynne Ellis   ISBN 978 0 352 33993 5
☐ PEEP SHOW Mathilde Madden   ISBN 978 0 352 33924 9
☐ THE POWER GAME Carrera Devonshire   ISBN 978 0 352 33990 4
☐ THE PRIVATE UNDOING OF A PUBLIC SERVANT   ISBN 978 0 352 34066 5
       Leonie Martel
☐ RELEASE ME Suki Cunningham   ISBN 978 0 352 33671 2   £6.99
☐ RUDE AWAKENING Pamela Kyle   ISBN 978 0 352 33036 9
☐ SAUCE FOR THE GOOSE Mary Rose Maxwell   ISBN 978 0 352 33492 3
☐ SLAVE TO SUCCESS Kimberley Raines   ISBN 978 0 352 33687 3   £6.99
☐ SLEAZY RIDER Karen S. Smith   ISBN 978 0 352 33964 5
☐ STELLA DOES HOLLYWOOD Stella Black   ISBN 978 0 352 33588 3
☐ THE STRANGER Portia Da Costa   ISBN 978 0 352 33211 0
☐ SUITE SEVENTEEN Portia Da Costa   ISBN 978 0 352 34109 9
☐ SUMMER FEVER Anna Ricci   ISBN 978 0 352 33625 5   £6.99
☐ SWITCHING HANDS Alaine Hood   ISBN 978 0 352 33896 9   £6.99
☐ SYMPHONY X Jasmine Stone   ISBN 978 0 352 33629 3   £6.99
☐ TONGUE IN CHEEK Tabitha Flyte   ISBN 978 0 352 33484 8
☐ THE TOP OF HER GAME Emma Holly   ISBN 978 0 352 34116 7
☐ TWO WEEKS IN TANGIER Annabel Lee   ISBN 978 0 352 33599 9   £6.99
☐ UNNATURAL SELECTION Alaine Hood   ISBN 978 0 352 33963 8
☐ VELVET GLOVE Emma Holly   ISBN 978 0 352 34115 0
☐ VILLAGE OF SECRETS Mercedes Kelly   ISBN 978 0 352 33344 5

☐ WILD BY NATURE Monica Belle	ISBN 978 0 352 33915 7	£6.99
☐ WILD CARD Madeline Moore	ISBN 978 0 352 34038 2	
☐ WING OF MADNESS Mae Nixon	ISBN 978 0 352 34099 3	

BLACK LACE BOOKS WITH AN HISTORICAL SETTING

☐ THE AMULET Lisette Allen	ISBN 978 0 352 33019 2	£6.99
☐ THE BARBARIAN GEISHA Charlotte Royal	ISBN 978 0 352 33267 7	
☐ BARBARIAN PRIZE Deanna Ashford	ISBN 978 0 352 34017 7	
☐ DANCE OF OBSESSION Olivia Christie	ISBN 978 0 352 33101 4	
☐ DARKER THAN LOVE Kristina Lloyd	ISBN 978 0 352 33279 0	
☐ ELENA'S DESTINY Lisette Allen	ISBN 978 0 352 33218 9	
☐ FRENCH MANNERS Olivia Christie	ISBN 978 0 352 33214 1	
☐ LORD WRAXALL'S FANCY Anna Lieff Saxby	ISBN 978 0 352 33080 2	
☐ NICOLE'S REVENGE Lisette Allen	ISBN 978 0 352 32984 4	
☐ THE SENSES BEJEWELLED Cleo Cordell	ISBN 978 0 352 32904 2	£6.99
☐ THE SOCIETY OF SIN Sian Lacey Taylder	ISBN 978 0 352 34080 1	
☐ UNDRESSING THE DEVIL Angel Strand	ISBN 978 0 352 33938 6	
☐ WHITE ROSE ENSNARED Juliet Hastings	ISBN 978 0 352 33052 9	£6.99

BLACK LACE BOOKS WITH A PARANORMAL THEME

☐ BRIGHT FIRE Maya Hess	ISBN 978 0 352 34104 4
☐ BURNING BRIGHT Janine Ashbless	ISBN 978 0 352 34085 6
☐ CRUEL ENCHANTMENT Janine Ashbless	ISBN 978 0 352 33483 1
☐ FLOOD Anna Clare	ISBN 978 0 352 34094 8
☐ GOTHIC BLUE Portia Da Costa	ISBN 978 0 352 33075 8
☐ THE PRIDE Edie Bingham	ISBN 978 0 352 33997 3
☐ THE TEN VISIONS Olivia Knight	ISBN 978 0 352 34119 8

BLACK LACE ANTHOLOGIES

☐ BLACK LACE QUICKIES 1 Various	ISBN 978 0 352 34126 6	£2.99
☐ BLACK LACE QUICKIES 2 Various	ISBN 978 0 352 34127 3	£2.99
☐ BLACK LACE QUICKIES 3 Various	ISBN 978 0 352 34128 0	£2.99
☐ BLACK LACE QUICKIES 4 Various	ISBN 978 0 352 34129 7	£2.99
☐ BLACK LACE QUICKIES 5 Various	ISBN 978 0 352 34130 3	£2.99
☐ MORE WICKED WORDS Various	ISBN 978 0 352 33487 9	£6.99
☐ WICKED WORDS 3 Various	ISBN 978 0 352 33522 7	£6.99

☐ WICKED WORDS 4 Various   ISBN 978 0 352 33603 3   £6.99

☐ WICKED WORDS 5 Various   ISBN 978 0 352 33642 2   £6.99

☐ WICKED WORDS 6 Various   ISBN 978 0 352 33690 3   £6.99

☐ WICKED WORDS 7 Various   ISBN 978 0 352 33743 6   £6.99

☐ WICKED WORDS 8 Various   ISBN 978 0 352 33787 0   £6.99

☐ WICKED WORDS 9 Various   ISBN 978 0 352 33860 0

☐ WICKED WORDS 10 Various   ISBN 978 0 352 33893 8

☐ THE BEST OF BLACK LACE 2 Various   ISBN 978 0 352 33718 4

☐ WICKED WORDS: SEX IN THE OFFICE Various   ISBN 978 0 352 33944 7

☐ WICKED WORDS: SEX AT THE SPORTS CLUB   ISBN 978 0 352 33991 1
    Various

☐ WICKED WORDS: SEX ON HOLIDAY Various   ISBN 978 0 352 33961 4

☐ WICKED WORDS: SEX IN UNIFORM Various   ISBN 978 0 352 34002 3

☐ WICKED WORDS: SEX IN THE KITCHEN Various   ISBN 978 0 352 34018 4

☐ WICKED WORDS: SEX ON THE MOVE Various   ISBN 978 0 352 34034 4

☐ WICKED WORDS: SEX AND MUSIC Various   ISBN 978 0 352 34061 0

☐ WICKED WORDS: SEX AND SHOPPING Various   ISBN 978 0 352 34076 4

☐ SEX IN PUBLIC Various   ISBN 978 0 352 34089 4

☐ SEX WITH STRANGERS Various   ISBN 978 0 352 34105 1

☐ PARANORMAL EROTICA Various   ISBN 978 0 352 34132 7

BLACK LACE NON-FICTION

☐ THE BLACK LACE BOOK OF WOMEN'S SEXUAL   ISBN 978 0 352 33793 1   £6.99
    FANTASIES Edited by Kerri Sharp

To find out the latest information about Black Lace titles, check out the website: www.black-lace-books.com or send for a booklist with complete synopses by writing to:

Black Lace Booklist, Virgin Books Ltd
Thames Wharf Studios
Rainville Road
London W6 9HA

Please include an SAE of decent size. Please note only British stamps are valid.

Our privacy policy
We will not disclose information you supply us to any other parties. We will not disclose any information which identifies you personally to any person without your express consent.

From time to time we may send out information about Black Lace books and special offers. Please tick here if you do <u>not</u> wish to receive Black Lace information.   ❏

Please send me the books I have ticked above.

Name ....

Address ....

....

....

....

Post Code ....

Send to: Virgin Books Cash Sales, Thames Wharf Studios, Rainville Road, London W6 9HA.

US customers: for prices and details of how to order books for delivery by mail, call 888-330-8477.

Please enclose a cheque or postal order, made payable to Virgin Books Ltd, to the value of the books you have ordered plus postage and packing costs as follows:

UK and BFPO – £1.00 for the first book, 50p for each subsequent book.

Overseas (including Republic of Ireland) – £2.00 for the first book, £1.00 for each subsequent book.

If you would prefer to pay by VISA, ACCESS/MASTERCARD, DINERS CLUB, AMEX or SWITCH, please write your card number and expiry date here:

....

Signature ....

Please allow up to 28 days for delivery.